23. 2. 2024.

The Gift

ALAN TITCHMARSH
The Gift

HODDER &
STOUGHTON

First published in Great Britain in 2022 by Hodder & Stoughton
An Hachette UK company

1

Copyright © Alan Titchmarsh 2022

The right of Alan Titchmarsh to be identified as the Author of the
Work has been asserted by him in accordance with the Copyright,
Designs and Patents Act 1988.

A CIP catalogue record for this title is available from the British Library

Hardback ISBN 9781473659063
Trade Paperback ISBN 9781473659070
eBook ISBN 9781473659087

Typeset in Sabon MT by Palimpsest Book Production Limited,
Falkirk, Stirlingshire

Printed and bound in Great Britain by Clays Ltd, Elcograf S.p.A.

Hodder & Stoughton policy is to use papers that are natural,
renewable and recyclable products and made from wood grown in sustainable
forests. The logging and manufacturing processes are expected to conform
to the environmental regulations of the country of origin.

Hodder & Stoughton Ltd
Carmelite House
50 Victoria Embankment
London EC4Y 0DZ

www.hodder.co.uk

For
Polly and Camilla,
with love

gift (noun) a thing given to someone willingly without payment

gifted (adjective) having exceptional talent or natural ability

The New Oxford English Dictionary

AUTHOR'S NOTE

The King's Touch

'The King's Evil', they called it in the Middle Ages. We know it today as scrofula, a form of tuberculosis, which occurs outside the lungs, attacking the lymph nodes in the neck and causing considerable pain and disfigurement. Scientific name: cervical tuberculosis lymphadenitis. Nowadays a doctor will prescribe antibiotics; in the Middle Ages the sufferer would have been advised to avail themselves of 'The King's Touch'.

First adopted in England by Edward the Confessor and in France by Philip I, those who found themselves infected by the King's Evil believed that their best chance of a cure was to be touched by the sovereign.

Edward the Confessor was probably the most effective royal dispenser of the King's Touch, not least because after the laying on of hands he would order that the patient be maintained at royal expense until they were cured. The improved diet and living conditions might have had a bearing on the matter, though the Divine Right of Kings – authority coming in a direct line from God – was perceived as the prime cause of a return to health.

The popularity of the Royal Touch presented certain logistical problems. How could one man – the King – possibly lay his hands upon all those who wished to be cured? During the thirteenth century a solution was found in the form of a coin, which had itself been touched by the King, being given to those who suffered from his eponymous complaint.

And yet the 'touching' of individuals continued until the reign of Queen Anne, often in great numbers and with considerable ceremony. Louis XIV of France is reputed to have touched 1,600 people one Easter Sunday, and while exiled in the Netherlands in 1650, Charles II of England was so besieged by sufferers that would-be patients were trampled to death in the rush to benefit from his curative powers.

From the time of Henry VII, whose own 'surgeries' were more modest in scale – between 1530 and 1532 he touched a total of fifty-nine people – the coin itself was of considerable value. Introduced in 1465, but not used as a cure for the King's Evil until Henry's reign, it was of pure gold and depicted the Archangel Michael defeating the devil in the form of a dragon. This regal talisman, pierced to take a ribbon, would be hung around the neck of the patient.

We shake our heads and smile indulgently at the ignorance of our forebears, for they were easily led: their scientific knowledge was primitive, their medical rationale in the early stages of development.

Today few of us would be convinced of the value of . . . what? Alchemy? Wishful thinking? Blind faith? And yet, even now, there are those whose talents defy a rational explanation, whose sensitivities are better developed than those who have spent their lives enslaved by technology. These are individuals whose raw aptitudes have been nursed by their own, often unique, environment and set of circumstances.

For every hundred charlatans, there may well be one genuinely gifted individual whose ability to heal defies all rational explanation. Such a gift is not easy to come to terms with. It imbues the possessor with feelings of responsibility, anxiety and fear, for it is a power every bit as much beyond their own comprehension as that of others. And if they themselves do not understand it, how can they believe in it, or trust in its durability? Might it, one day, simply disappear and leave them open to even more accusations of dishonesty and fraud?

This is the story of one possessor of 'the gift'. His name is Adam Gabriel, which is rather fitting, for the name of the shiny coin that once hung around the necks of the sick had a divine ring to it. It was known as a Golden Angel.

THE BOY

1

THE GOLDEN ANGEL

Traversing in its upper length a region of grand hills
amid noble scars of terraced limestone, and in its lower
a rich storied vale, the entire course of the river is full of
a rare charm, a charm which in a variety of scenic
beauty, historic interest and old-world life, is not
surpassed by any river-valley in the kingdom.

Harry Speight, *Upper Wharfedale*, 1900

It was generally agreed, from the day he was born, that Mrs
Gabriel's lad was a bit of a looker. Not that many folk had the
opportunity of passing comment, favourable or otherwise.
Langstroth Farmhouse – a long, low building of smoke-darkened
millstone grit, which seemed to crouch beneath its surrounding
crags, was off the beaten track as far as hikers were concerned,
and not easily reached even by those determined locals who had
business there. These rare visits – most of them for the benefit
of the ewes and lambs that were thicker on the ground in this
part of the dale than humans – were confined to moments of
ovine need: the supply of extra feed, or veterinary care, and

very occasionally some provision that Bethany Gabriel had omitted to store in advance of the foul weather that made the moorland track too perilous to risk even in a rackety old Land Rover.

This particular part of Upper Wharfedale was seldom referred to at length in the guidebooks, being neither on the way to the tourist honeypots of Hawes in Wensleydale and Reeth in Swaledale nor the increasingly chi-chi Richmond with its Georgian theatre and growing number of upmarket shops. Situated in the upper reaches of Langstrothdale – turn left at Buckden, carry on through Yockenthwaite – it was actually on the way to nowhere, and that was why the Gabriels had fallen in love with it. Sparsely populated and regarded by even the most generous-spirited of geographers as harsh country from which any kind of living had to be wrested, it seemed to suit their needs . . . and their dreams.

Bethany Cross had been twenty-five and Luke Gabriel ten years her senior when she had first set eyes on him at Kilnsey Show, he parading his prize tup and she a novice shepherdess watching in awe as this fair-haired god (in her eyes) led his charge around the parade ring. He looked slightly uncomfortable in his clean white coat, his tie askew, but she liked the way his pale blue eyes sparkled when someone made him laugh. She did not suspect for a minute that he had even noticed her, leaning on the enclosure fence enveloped in an old duffel coat, her feet thrust into a pair of mud-encrusted wellies. (Those women who had turned up in floral-print dresses and sling-backs were cursing their own folly on the soft ground and rough grass freshly laundered by heavy overnight rain.) But that was Bethany – practicality and comfort before show and high fashion.

Not that she was without style, for it was that which caught

Luke Gabriel's eye, distracting him from the job in hand. A prize tup, strong of shoulder and broad of beam, demands unflinching concentration when it is being paraded in front of the agricultural cognoscenti. There was a moment when the beast decided to head for the fells and a spot of mischief, but it was only a moment. A muscular pull on the halter brought him back to the matter in hand, but not before Luke had registered the presence of 'the girl in the duffel coat' – his description of her when looking around the animal pens and casually (lest anyone should assume he was too keen) enquiring as to her whereabouts and identity.

They finally met up by the heavy horses. She was standing, hands thrust deep into coat pockets, her lustrous dark hair tied back in a ponytail, watching as a stable lad groomed the feathers of a statuesque inky-black Clydesdale, whose coat glistened in the strengthening afternoon sun.

'Handsome beast,' he said, at her shoulder.

'Yes,' she said. And she thought: *You are*.

It was a whirlwind romance. He had never met such a lively and headstrong girl – well, woman – and she could not believe that such an Adonis, albeit ten years older than her, would give her a second look. Their common bond, which amused them, was sheep. Neither could articulate the reason, but both felt at home high in the Dales, she as a hired shepherdess, moving from place to place as the work took her, he a retired farmer's son who had been bequeathed a passion for the rugged landscape and a willingness to earn a living from it.

With a helping hand from his parents they bought the dilapidated Langstroth Farmhouse for far too much money and spent the first few years of their married life repairing the roof, replacing windows, fettling a smoky kitchen range and generally putting the rundown farmstead in good order. They also spent time building up a flock of Swaledale sheep and made a name for themselves as custodians of a highly regarded strain of the native Yorkshire breed.

They had been lucky to find the farmhouse. Most old barns and farmsteads in this part of the Dales were prettied up and rented out as holiday lets: certainly an alternative form of income for the landowner but not conducive to the raising of livestock. The upland pastures were in the main rented to tenant farmers, and Luke and Bethany were overjoyed to find a building that could be made habitable once more, along with fifty acres of their own and a further five hundred rented on which to graze their expanding flock. It was not exactly prairie farming, but neither of them would have wanted that. Hands-on shepherding and the ability to make a modest living suited them down to the stony ground.

It was five years before Adam was born. It is not unexpected that the arrival of children changes the life of any married couple. The arrival of Adam was to change theirs in a way that no one could have foreseen.

2

LANGSTROTH FARMHOUSE

Here are some picturesque cottages with old grey
walls and time-worn roofs covered with rich-tinted
moss, shaded by the spreading branches of fine trees,
remnants of a vast forest of oaks, which spread in
olden times far over the chase on either side. Upwards,
the country becomes more wild.

Edmund Bogg, *A Thousand Miles in Wharfedale*, 1892

From when he reached the age of four it was clear that Adam
was no ordinary child. More than one pushy parent has claimed
their offspring is a remarkable prodigy – startlingly good with
numbers or articulate beyond their years. Mrs Mozart was
particularly impressed with Wolfgang's musical prowess but,
then, so was everybody else. In none of these areas did Adam
evince any unusual talent. His was more of an aptitude, an
attitude towards the land and a relationship with nature and,
in particular, animals. At first, Luke and Bethany thought that
such a temperament must be present in any country child. Adam
was, after all, being brought up among the hills and dales, where

sheep and occasionally cattle, rabbits and badgers were part of everyday life. Since babyhood, carried on Bethany's back as she clambered over the pastures and fells in all weathers, his eyes had lit up on spotting anything that moved: the sight of the beck below the farmhouse in full spate, or a flock of sheep careering down the pasture in front of Finn, the Border collie with the wall-eye. His rosy cheeks would shine, his mouth break into a wide grin, accompanied by a contented gurgle that turned into an infectious giggle.

At the age of five he was already proving useful to his parents, helping Bethany and the increasingly savvy Finn to round up sheep for shearing or for market, standing behind his father on the 'Little Grey Fergie' that delivered winter feed to the flocks higher up on the moorside, his hands around his father's neck, his little feet thrust into red wellies. A hand-knitted bobble hat was pulled down over his fair curly hair to prevent the cold from biting at his ears.

Summer days were the best of all, for the sun turned the lower pastures of Langstrothdale into emerald velvet, studded with glinting buttercups. Into the gin-clear beck, on its way to becoming the youthful River Wharfe, Adam would plunge a willow wand, to the end of which his mother had fastened a wire hoop and the foot from an old pair of tights to act as a net. Then he would fish for bullheads, minnows and the elusive catfish, plopping them into a jam-jar and watching them swim in circles before gently tipping them back into the rippling water. On other days he would sit on the sun-warmed riverbank sucking at a stem of cocksfoot grass while his father cast a fly to tempt brown trout and grayling. Adam's skill at removing the hook from the fish's mouth was evident from the age of three, and he would hum softly to himself as he deftly extracted the barb and carried the grayling back to the river, or slid a plump, glistening trout into his father's creel before taking it home for supper.

Luke would smile at the little lad, whose rolling gait, under the weight of the fish-filled wicker basket, gave him the appearance of an old man staggering home after one too many in the local hostelry. In winter, muffled up in a miniature version of his mother's duffel coat, woolly gloves attached to each other by a short length of baler-twine that ran up his sleeves and across his shoulders, he seldom complained of the wet or the bitter cold but – after the fashion of a dog or a cat – stood by the farmhouse door waiting to be let out, whatever the weather.

It was Adam who persuaded his parents to let Finn sleep in the house, the dog's home having been hitherto a homemade kennel just inside the long, low hay barn after the habit of all Dales' farmers. Working dogs, however kindly they were regarded, lived outside, not in the house. But Adam's baleful gaze, as Finn was banished for the night, along with his eyes, blue as sapphires and brimming with tears, got the better of his parents' finer feelings. After one of these all-too-rare outbursts of emotion, Finn was allowed a basket not far from the comforting kitchen range. He would spend the rest of his nights indoors.

As if he recognised his good fortune, Finn slept quietly and seldom stirred until Luke or Bethany put on their coat to venture outdoors, at which point he would move swiftly to the farmhouse door and sit silently with his eyes fixed firmly on the iron sneck. When the door was open barely six inches, he would slide through it as sinuously as a snake and await the bidding of his master and mistress. And Adam.

In the early part of those long winter evenings, Adam would

lie on the rag rug in front of the coal-black cast-iron range, the glow of the logs casting an amber light on his cheeks – rosy from the day's exertions – and cradle Finn's head, stroking it with his plump little hand.

It was after a few weeks of this new canine regime that Bethany asked Luke if he had noticed the change that had occurred in Finn.

'What? You mean being indoors? He's quieter than he's ever been, I'll say that for him. Probably doesn't want to push his luck in case we turn him out again.'

Bethany smiled. 'No. Not just that. I mean his eye.'

'What about it?'

'The wall-eye. Have you noticed that it's not as pronounced as it was? The white seems to be getting smaller.'

Luke shrugged from behind his copy of *Farmers Weekly*. 'Can't say as I've looked really.'

'Maybe I'm imagining it,' said Bethany. 'But I'm sure it's getting better.'

Luke lowered the magazine and smiled. 'Probably just contentment. I mean, look at them.'

Bethany turned her gaze towards the kitchen range where Adam and Finn were, as usual, entwined with one another on the rug, the boy stroking the side of the dog's head and humming quietly to himself. 'Perhaps it happens with age. Maybe it's a natural phenomenon.'

'Well, I've not known it happen before,' said Luke, 'not after four years, anyway.' He picked up his magazine and flipped through the pages, muttering absently, 'It never happened to Dad's terrier, Smudger. He had a wall-eye from birth to death, but he was still a bloody good ratter.'

'Luke!' Bethany admonished him for his language.

Her husband looked up again and grinned, nodding in the direction of Adam and the dog. 'Sorry. But I don't think he heard. Too busy in that little world of his own.'

'Talking of which . . . Come on, little one. Time you were in bed. What do the hands on the clock say?'

Adam turned towards his mother, seeming to come out of whatever reverie had been occupying his five-year-old mind. He slid out from under the dog and walked across to the long-case clock that stood in the corner of the farmhouse kitchen. It had originally belonged to Luke's father and was fully five times taller than the little boy who gazed up at its friendly face. The painted moon at the top of the dial smiled back at him, and the deep, slow tick . . . tock . . . tick . . . tock that dictated the rhythm of life inside the house brought him back to earth. 'The little hand is on seven and the big hand is on three.'

'Which means?' asked Bethany, with a smile in her voice.

Adam cast his eyes downwards. 'Bedtime.' He sighed and walked over to his father, reaching up and kissing his cheek.

'Night-night, Daddy.'

'Night-night, son,' said the father, without looking up from his magazine.

Mother and son walked towards the white-painted plank door in the corner of the kitchen. Bethany lifted the latch and the two began the climb upstairs. 'One, two, three, four, five . . .'

Their voices grew fainter, but Luke could still hear their muffled conversation as Bethany prepared the child for bed. He laid down the magazine, lifted his aching body from the chair and walked over to the fire. Reaching into the wicker basket at one side of the range he pulled out a couple of dry logs and lobbed them into the grate. A shower of sparks, and the dying embers soon became leaping flames, highlighting the form of the sleeping Finn in his now customary place on the hearthrug. Luke knelt down beside the dog and stroked his head. 'What a life you lead, eh?' He eased back the dog's eyelid and looked at the once almost entirely white wall-eye. Funny, really. Bethany was right. It had been much more pronounced when they'd got him. But now it seemed only half the size he remembered.

He stood up and admonished himself for not having noticed before. They had bought Finn a year after Adam was born. Any good shepherd worthy of the name would know every aspect of his dog, be alert to any changes in his health or demeanour. But the changing appearance of the wall-eye had escaped him. Perhaps because he had not thought to look for it.

He shook his head and frowned. Next time he saw the vet he would ask him if that sort of thing happened often. If so, would the dog have better eyesight than before? 'Funny,' he murmured to himself.

It never occurred to him that Adam might have been in any way responsible for the change. Why would it? That sort of thing only happened in fairy tales.

3

VILLAGE SCHOOL

Doris Carr and the children of Malham Tarn School,
where she taught from 1930 to 1942. Miss Carr at first
stayed there during weekdays, then walked home each
night to Lee Gate on Malham Moor until her father
provided her with a pony.

Marie Hartley & Joan Ingilby, *A Dales Album*, 1991

They had been there before to take a look and to familiarise
themselves with things before the fateful day when Adam would
go to school. Kettlewell Primary was a small stone-built village
school with around twenty-five pupils divided into two classes.
It was a half-hour drive from the farmhouse down the rough
track and the narrow roads, snaking between dry-stone walls,
crossing and re-crossing the river. Luke and Bethany were relieved
that – after taking Adam there in the Land Rover for the first
week – their boy would be picked up by minibus at the end of
the farm track each morning, and delivered back there at the
end of the school day.

The school's mission statement had chimed with their own

outlook on life: 'Our vision is to create a curriculum that encourages children to discover, explore and create. We want to help each child flourish into a caring, confident and resilient young person who has a love of learning.'

Like any parents, they worried about how he would fit in: he was an only child, unused to the daily company of children his own age. They had made efforts to integrate him (the word, which they hated, made the process sound impersonal – the very opposite of what it was meant to be) but, although he mixed with other children when Bethany took him to a play-group in the nearest village, he remained most comfortable on his own at the farm.

Their first parents' evening, six weeks after Adam had started school, helped to ease their anxiety.

'He's a delightful child,' confirmed Mrs Lambert, his form teacher. She nodded at them and motioned them to sit in the corner of the empty classroom, surrounded by paintings of horses and ponies, sheep and cows.

'Not too quiet?' asked Bethany, a note of concern clearly identifiable in her voice. Luke's neck was reddening under the collar and tie he wished he hadn't worn. The tweed jacket, too, was contributing to his unease in the warm classroom. He hoped he didn't look as uncomfortable as he felt.

Mrs Lambert laughed. 'There's nothing wrong with being quiet! Believe me, I wish I had a few more who were.' Then, seeing the look on Bethany's face, and noting the discomfiture of her husband, 'Well, thoughtful, perhaps. I do like a bit of spirit, but I like a capacity for concentration, too. Adam has plenty of the latter. He seems to take it all in, and when I ask questions he sometimes has the answers, sometimes doesn't. Pretty much like all the others. And at playtime he's not standing on his own in the corner. He was at first – that's understandable, bearing in mind his upbringing high in the dale – but now he joins in with their games. You really have no need to worry.'

Luke slackened his tie and Bethany heaved a sigh of relief. 'We were just concerned that he should fit in. He spends so much time alone on the farm – I mean, on his own with us, rather than with other children.'

'Oh, that's the case on all the hill farms, Mrs Gabriel. I'm well used to their individual quirks and their ability to be self-reliant. I've come to admire it. I can't imagine teaching in an inner city again, which I did in my twenties.'

'Gosh, what a change!' offered Bethany.

Mrs Lambert smiled. 'I was fired with a missionary zeal in my younger days. I wanted to make a real difference, especially to those I felt had had a raw deal, those to whom life had dealt a poor hand. I battled away for the best part of ten years until my father told me I had done enough. He knew I loved the countryside – the Dales in particular. He was a classic quiet Yorkshireman.' Here she glanced at Luke. 'He said to me one day, "You know, country children deserve a good education from a dedicated teacher every bit as much as those who live in the city."' Mrs Lambert smiled again at the memory. 'I've never forgotten. He was right, of course. And I realised I'd done my bit by then. I imagine he thought that if I carried on for much longer in the middle of Bradford I'd just burn myself out.'

'So you came here?' asked Bethany.

'Yes. And that was twenty years ago. I've not regretted it. This is a special place, filled with special people. Some are a bit odd', she raised an eyebrow, 'but aren't we all? Individual, perhaps. Which is why I especially warm to Adam. He's an individual and this school prides itself on bringing out the best in every child – making the most of his or her capabilities and aptitudes, rather than believing that one size fits all and placing academic achievement above all else.' She turned to Luke, who had been attentive but silent through the conversation so far. 'I should think that's what you would want, isn't it, Mr Gabriel?'

Startled to be addressed directly, Luke coloured. 'Yes – yes, of course.'

'Please take your tie off, Mr Gabriel. You must be roasting. These classrooms are heated for children who have less in the way of natural insulation than their parents, not to mention less tweed!'

Luke was grateful for the concession. He slipped the tie into the pocket of his jacket, then leant forward on his chair. 'So you think he'll be all right, our Adam?'

'I'm sure he will. I've been watching him carefully. One of the best things about a village school is that our classes are small. I have only fifteen children in my care, which means that I can get to know each of them well and see what needs addressing, what their strengths and weaknesses are.'

'Mmm.' Luke's brow furrowed.

'Adam does have weaknesses – he's not very keen on sums, but he sticks at it and eventually masters them, and his writing is . . . not the neatest.'

'Like his father's,' murmured Bethany. Then, conscious of having unintentionally slighted her husband in front of their son's teacher, she turned to Luke. 'Sorry. I mean . . .'

'Not my strong point,' agreed Luke. He held up a large, calloused hand, ingrained with the oil that even Swarfega struggled to banish. 'Used to fettling sheep and tractors rather than wielding a pen.'

Mrs Lambert continued: 'What he loves are our "Forest School" sessions when we're out in the dale – in the woods or down by the river. He seems to come into his own there. Suddenly, instead of being just one of the crowd, he takes the lead. Not in a bossy way, you understand. He just has a natural affinity with nature and the other children are aware of that and respect it.'

'But don't they all have that up here?' asked Luke, genuinely surprised.

'No. Oh, they're all familiar with their surroundings, but . . . How can I put it? Adam is really at one with the countryside. He not only knows the names of the birds and the wild flowers—'

'Oh, that's me, I'm afraid,' confessed Bethany. 'I've been talking to him about nature here in Langstrothdale ever since he was born, even when he couldn't understand the words. We used to press the different wild flowers between newspaper put underneath the rug in the sitting room and then stick them into an album and write their names alongside them. You know, horehound and evergreen alkanet. He liked the sound of them as much as anything.'

'Well, it's paid off. But, as I was saying, he not only knows their names but . . . Have you ever read any of Laurie Lee's books, Mrs Gabriel?'

'Just the one – *Cider with Rosie*.'

'Do you remember what Laurie says about his mother? That the plants and flowers used to turn towards her almost as though she were another sun?'

Bethany laughed. 'Yes, I do!'

'I have a feeling that Adam is a bit like that. It will be interesting to see how he develops. But for now, rest assured, he's doing just fine.' Mrs Lambert rose to her feet, indicating that the interview was at an end.

'Thank you so much,' said Bethany, a note of relief in her voice.

'It was my pleasure. Oh, and as far as the school nativity play goes, do you think Adam would be comfortable playing a shepherd?'

4

SOLO

Only children believe they're capable of everything.
They're trusting and fearless . . .

Paulo Coelho, *Aleph*, 2011

'Nice to know we needn't worry,' said Luke, as he eased into bed beside her.

Bethany did not look up from her book. 'Yes,' she said absently.

'What are you reading?'

Obligingly, she folded the book so that he could see the jacket and the title. Luke leant forward and read out loud: '*The Enchanted Places* by Christopher Milne.' He frowned. 'Should I know him?'

'You probably do as Christopher Robin.'

'The one who "went down with Alice"?'

'Yes.'

Luke lapsed into silence. Bethany hoped that the interview was completed and that she could get on with her bedtime reading. Her hopes were short-lived.

'I didn't know he'd written anything himself. Didn't his dad write *The Wind in the Willows*?'

Bethany sighed impatiently. 'No. That was Kenneth Grahame. Christopher Milne's dad wrote *Winnie-the-Pooh*, and *When We Were Very Young* and *Now We Are Six* and—'

'Oh. I never read *Winnie-the-Pooh*. Beatrix Potter was more my thing. *Peter Rabbit* and *Jemima Puddleduck*. My dad said you knew where you were with a duck and a rabbit. *Winnie-the-Pooh* always seemed a bit . . . well . . . wet.'

Bethany raised an eyebrow, made to reply but thought better of it and went back to her book.

Her husband persisted, 'Why are you reading this one?'

Bethany sighed again, more heavily this time. Luke was clearly in a chatty mood, and she was attempting to immerse herself in the childhood of Christopher Robin. 'Because he was an only child.'

'And?'

'Adam is an only child.'

'Yes. But—'

Bethany gave up and closed the book. 'Christopher Milne really suffered as a grown-up. Everybody knowing he was Christopher Robin, and all the baggage that came with it.'

'What sort of baggage?'

'Well, apart from "going down with Alice", there was stuff about Christopher Robin saying his prayers and drawings of him as a boy wearing baggy bloomers and hauling Pooh around everywhere. He became famous all over the world.'

'Scarred for life, was he?'

'I think he was a bit.'

'What happened to him? Sticky end?'

'No. He opened a bookshop in Dartmouth.' Bethany glanced at the photograph of the bespectacled author on the back flap of the jacket. 'But he seems a bit chippy. Well . . . quite bitter,

24

really. It certainly affected him as an adult. All that fame and adulation as a boy.'

Luke flopped back onto his pillow. 'You're thinking that Adam will go the same way? Resentful of being an only child?'

'I hope not.'

'But he's not in the public eye. Nobody's selling poems about him or drawings of him hauling a teddy bear around, are they?'

'No, but . . . Oh, I just worry that he'll miss out. Being on his own. Not having a brother or a sister.'

Luke stretched out his arm and tucked a stray wisp of hair behind Bethany's ear. 'You're not worrying again, are you?'

'A bit.'

He stroked her forearm with the back of his hand. 'You really shouldn't. It doesn't matter, you know.'

'It's just—'

'One of those things,' cut in Luke. 'Just one of those things.'

'But it's my fault.'

Luke propped himself up and cupped his hand beneath her chin, turning her head to look at him. 'We've been here before.'

'Too often?'

'Often enough to know that it doesn't do any good, doesn't get us anywhere.'

'But it is my—'

'No. I'm not having this.' A hint of steeliness had crept into Luke's voice. 'It's not right that you blame yourself for us not having any more children.'

'But the doctor said—'

'The doctor said you were lucky to survive the first and that it would be unwise to have any more. That's just the way it is.'

In the silence that followed Bethany's eyes filled with tears. 'But you'd like—'

'I'd like a wife who doesn't beat herself up about it. Who doesn't take the weight of the world on her shoulders, or who thinks I'm unhappy because we've only got one child.'

'And aren't you?'

Luke shook his head emphatically. 'No! Not at all. You heard what Mrs Lambert said. Adam is a happy country boy. We've always thought he was and now she's confirmed it.'

'But he has to be so self-reliant.'

'Is that such a bad thing?'

'No, but . . .'

Luke turned to face her square on. 'He has two parents who think the world of him. He lives in a magical place that he loves, and now we know he's getting on all right at school. Where's the problem? Nobody's forcing him into the public eye, or publishing drawings of him dragging a teddy-bear around. He's not shy and retiring and he's not loud and attention-seeking. It strikes me he's about as balanced as he could be.'

Bethany sighed resignedly. 'I know. We're very lucky. It's just that every now and again, when I see other families . . .'

'The grass is pretty green up here in the dale, you know.'

She rested her head on Luke's chest. 'It's not that I'm unhappy. Just wistful sometimes. Wondering . . .'

'Well, stop wondering and be grateful for what we've got. We've got a lovely little lad and so far he seems as happy as a sand-boy.'

'He does, doesn't he?' Bethany spoke as though to reassure herself. Then she asked, 'Do you think he'll stay on the farm? Would you want him to?'

'I want him to do whatever *he* wants to do.'

'You say that, but you'd be a bit disappointed if he didn't want to, wouldn't you?'

Luke thought for a moment, his eyes focused on the middle distance. 'I suppose I'd be a bit surprised because he seems so happy here . . . so comfortable.'

'But if he didn't want to stay, you wouldn't force him? I mean, you wouldn't put any pressure on him to carry it on?'

Luke looked hurt at the suggestion. 'Of course not. I've seen enough families ripped apart by parents who expect their children to fulfil their dreams. The parents' dreams, I mean. Especially when it comes to farming. It can only end in misery . . . or even tragedy.'

Bethany was surprised at the anger that seemed to have crept into Luke's voice. 'Tragedy?' she asked.

Luke nodded. 'The Fletchers. Over the moor towards Hawes. Old man Fletcher had three sons and none of them wanted to take on the farm – having seen what it had done to their father. It had made him a slave to a particular way of life.'

Bethany did not frame a question, but it became clear from her expression that she was unaware of the Fletcher story.

'Ted Fletcher ran the family flock on Wether Fell Side for years, as his father had done before him. He took it for granted that at least one of his lads would want to continue. His Swaledales had one of the best reputations in North Yorkshire. Ted's lambs always got the best prices at the auction mart in Hawes. The envy of the county they were.'

There was a faraway look in Luke's eye, that of a sheep farmer mentally appraising another's flock. Bethany had seen it before, whenever they attended Kilnsey Show or their Land Rover was held up on the road by a stray ewe determined to throw herself under their wheels. 'And none of the boys took it on?'

Luke shook his head, his jaw set and his eyes staring at some invisible remembered scenario. 'The eldest went into engineering

– somewhere in Leeds – and the middle lad became a teacher, up in . . . Darlington, I think.'

'What about the youngest?'

'His last hope?'

Bethany nodded, her expression betraying her fears.

Luke shook his head. 'They thought he'd be the one to carry on. He said he would, and for a while it looked as though all was going well, but after three bleak winters he decided he'd had enough and went down to London to study law.' Luke paused, as if marshalling his thoughts. He went on in a soft voice, seemingly devoid of emotion. 'Ted and his wife carried on for another year, but the next winter was bitterly cold. Houses were cut off by snowfall and the becks froze solid. It just went on and on for weeks on end. Then one day Ted went off in his Landy over the moor. His wife saw him go and thought he was off to find any sheep that had been cut off by snowdrifts. By the time it got dark and he hadn't come back she called the Swaledale mountain rescue team.' Luke stopped. Despite the evenness of his tone the memory was clearly painful.

Bethany was reluctant to break the silence, but her eyes asked the question.

Luke smiled, which ran counter to the words that followed. 'They found his body in a gully with a twelve-bore shotgun by his side.' He turned to Bethany and she could see the mixture of anger and despair in his eyes. 'I'm not going there. It's not worth it.'

'Did you know him well?'

'Dad did. It hit him hard. He didn't show much emotion, my dad, but I remember him taking me on one side – I suppose I was about eighteen at the time – and telling me that nothing was worth a life, not the dale, not the sheep, not anything. The important thing about families, he said, was to realise that they were all different, and that every member of your family was different from you. They might be *of* you, but they're not the same as you, and if you make the mistake of trying to mould them in your own image it can only end in disaster.'

Bethany squeezed Luke's hand. 'But you *did* follow in your dad's footsteps. You *did* become a sheep farmer.'

Luke's tone changed as he made to brighten the atmosphere. 'Lack of imagination. Couldn't think of anything else.'

A cynical frown crossed Bethany's face. 'Really?'

'No. I'd always wanted to be up here. Knew this was where I was meant to be, what I was meant to do. I think Dad just wanted to let me know there was no way he'd force me to do it, and that if I wanted to do something completely different it was all right by him.'

'*Would* it have been, do you think?'

Luke laughed softly. 'Oh, I think he would have been heartbroken, but he wanted to let me know that he knew he had no right to expect me to take on the flock. It was his way of giving me a let out if I wanted to leave, even if by then he must have known I was willing to carry on. I suppose he just wanted to be absolutely certain that he was doing the right thing as a parent.'

'What about your mum?'

'She kept her peace. Never really entered into it. I think she wanted it to come from my dad – the admission, I mean – but I always knew she thought any child should be allowed to find its own way. They might have been hill farmers born and bred but they were surprisingly open-minded when it came to careers. I've always been grateful for that.'

Bethany put aside the book she had been cradling throughout

the conversation, placing it on top of the growing pile on her bedside table.

Luke changed the subject. 'That heap's going to topple if you don't thin it out. Why do you keep them all there?'

'Because my sheep-farmer husband has never got round to putting up the bookshelf I've been asking for in the corner of the front parlour. Short of stacking them up the stairs I have nowhere else to keep them.'

'Oh. Yes. Right. Well, I'd better get on with it, then.'

'If you would. In the meantime I'll just have to get used to being surrounded by books and sheep.' She put out her bedside light and turned on her side. 'I've just had a thought . . .' she murmured.

Luke switched off his own bedside light, eased himself alongside her and kissed the back of her neck. 'What's that?'

'What part is Adam playing in the school nativity?'

'I know,' he replied, a note of resignation in his voice. 'A shepherd.'

'And who illustrated *Winnie-the-Pooh*?'

'Walt Disney?'

Bethany dug him in the ribs with her elbow. 'Philistine.'

'Ow! Who, then?'

'E. H. Shepard.'

Luke chuckled and held her closer. 'It seems you just can't get away from sheep and shepherds, can you?'

5

WHILE SHEPHERDS WATCHED

We pictured the meek mild creatures where
They dwelt in their strawy pen,
Nor did it occur to one of us there
To doubt they were kneeling then.

Thomas Hardy, 'The Oxen', 1915

The December day had been bitterly cold. 'Too cold for snow,' muttered Luke to his farmhand, Jack Knaggs, as they brought down the sheep from higher ground into the folds nearer the farmhouse. Jack's reply had been typically curmudgeonly, yet not without its own inarguable logic: 'It snows in t'Arctic, dunt it? An' it's bloody cold theer.'

Luke had heard the pronouncement countless times over the years, but it still made him smile. Jack had worked with Luke's father for as long as either of them could remember. Then, when Andrew Gabriel had retired as a tenant farmer on the moors above Hubberholme, Jack considered that his own employable days were numbered. Who would employ a man in his fifties when they could just as easily choose a twenty- or thirty-year-old with a longer working life in front of them?

A widower now, Jack lived in the smallest imaginable terrace cottage – two up, two down – in Yockenthwaite, a couple of miles downstream from Langstroth Farmhouse. After about a month of going for his copy of the *Yorkshire Post,* and walking a neighbour's dog down by the river, it was clear that such sedentary pursuits would not be conducive to a happy retirement.

''S mekkin' me maungy. It'll not be long afore I'm carted off to t' loony bin.'

So, when Luke and Bethany bought their own farm they took pity on a man who was clearly not relishing his days of inactivity and who still had plenty of muscle and an aptitude for hard graft that would be useful to the young couple and their expanding flock. The fact that the nearest 'loony bin' had long since been converted into smart apartments meant that Jack's prediction was unlikely to translate into reality, but they were happy to play a part in preserving his sanity.

Jack Knaggs had been a fixture in Langstrothdale and on Luke's father's farm since Luke was a child. His bandy legs and rolling gait, along with the short shepherd's crook, seldom out of his right hand, and the flat cap always tilted heavily over his left ear, had meant he was easy to spot from a distance by everyone in the village. 'All reet then Jack?' they'd shout across the lane or the field, even schoolchildren who should have been taught better manners.

'None so bad, considerin',' was his unvarying reply.

He'd turn up for work each day – regardless of the weather – in a pair of black wellies, which Bethany was sure were at least two sizes too big for him (she couldn't bear to think about the state of the socks encased within them), a pair of dark blue bib-and-brace overalls and an old pinstripe suit jacket, tied round the middle with orange baler twine, all topped off with the flat cap, whose peak was darkened from years of contact with Brylcreem. (Not that his hair was on regular view: he had a newer, smarter cap for 'best'.) Only in the middle of winter would he condescend to top off his sartorial arrangement with an old donkey jacket, but never a pair of gloves. 'I'm not *that* soft.'

'Time you were off,' said Luke, looking at the colour of the lowering sky – as heavy as an army blanket and a deeper shade of grey. 'I think you're right. Snow tonight.'

'Reet. I'll be on me way, then.' Out of habit, Jack touched the peak of his cap, picked up his crook and ambled off down the track whistling softly under his breath.

Snowfall in the Dales was not as great a rarity as it had become in southern England, where some children of Adam's age had yet to experience its purifying and silencing effect on the landscape. That said, even on higher ground its arrival seemed less predictable than when Luke was a nipper. Christmas nowadays in Langstrothdale could be mild and damp – the busy corners of the cart track a quagmire just waiting to catch out the unwary – or the earth trapped within the icy grip of frost, no one could guess which. In Luke's childhood, being snow-bound for weeks on end was a common occurrence between the months of November and March. Even if snow was not forthcoming, the ground could remain hard as iron for a month or more, offering little sustenance to livestock and placing an even greater burden on the shepherd and the cowman.

'In the bleak midwinter, frosty wind made moan; Earth stood hard as iron, water like a stone,' they sang at Christmas in

Hubberholme church – words with which Luke Gabriel felt a great affinity. He'd always meant to read up about Christina Rossetti, who had written them, but somehow he'd never got round to it. Bethany would know about her. She was the reader in the family – a trait she seemed to be passing on to their son. Luke was proud of that.

As he walked past the barn, Luke could see feathers of frost beginning to make their way across the water in the old horse trough. Tomorrow Adam would have fun stamping on the puddles between the ruts on the track to crack the ice. He glanced upwards. The clouds were thicker now, dense and darkening, as though heavy with snow. He shivered involuntarily and went indoors. With any luck, the weather would hold off until the evening's entertainment had finished.

The school nativity play, performed in a hall decorated with festive paper cut-outs and packed with expectant parents, grandparents and general hangers-on, was a highlight of the village year. Mrs Lambert and her colleague, the well-meaning but often disorganised Mr Latimer – tall, angular with horn-rimmed spectacles – would make sure that every child was involved, even when it meant that some had to divert their modest theatrical ambitions into playing the third palm tree or the fourth tadpole. (No one would have dreamt of questioning the presence of tadpoles during December in Judaea. In this part of the Yorkshire Dales tadpoles were resident in every moorland tarn and, along with generosity of spirit, they played an important part in scholastic Yuletide traditions.)

Along with Mary (red hair, face liberally dusted with freckles) and Joseph (an uncomfortable-looking eight-year-old, whose right hand shared duties between holding the donkey – originally a fluffy dog on wheels but now equipped with long cardboard ears – and pushing his glasses back up his nose) came a bevy of angels selected for the blondeness of their hair rather than uniformity of height. The taller ones, the cherubim and seraphim, supervised the lowlier angels and archangels with a well-placed wing (made of chicken wire and real chicken feathers by Mrs Postlethwaite, the local poultry farmer) or, in desperate circumstances, with a deft kick on the shins, should the more junior members of the cast find the contents of their nostrils more engaging than the Christmas story.

The events unfolded at a brisk pace – interspersed with the obligatory carols – during which, thanks to a dodgy wheel, the 'donkey' fell over twice. Mercifully, Mary, who was famed for her skills at the local gymkhana, had had the presence of mind to ride side-saddle and avoid being deposited in the hay (donated by Luke), but Joseph became increasingly nervous as events progressed. It would later become evident why.

Little credence was given to the time-line when it came to the birth of Our Saviour: the entire company, from the ox and the ass to the more exalted dramatis personae, had assembled at the stable before the parents of the baby Jesus had arrived at the inn – it's difficult to keep twenty-five children under the age of eleven silent in the wings as events unfold chronologically. Not that there were any wings – except those on the angels, which (as one cynic remarked) would have looked more authentic had Mrs Postlethwaite's flock been composed of Light Sussex, rather than the orange-feathered Buff Orpingtons. Their fiery tints aligned the heavenly host more with Hell than Heaven.

The Three Kings in their glorious gold- and silver-paper crowns, each trailing a robe recognisable as one of the old village-hall curtains, made their way with pomp and ceremony to the stable, constructed from cunningly reconfigured wooden pallets, as Mr Latimer played 'The Arrival of the Queen of Sheba' on the upright piano. Reverently (with an occasional glance at the audience to try to spot their mums and dads), they deposited their gold (a plastic dome of Ferrero-Rocher chocolates), frankincense (an empty bottle of Chanel N°5, courtesy of Rita, the barmaid at the King's Head) and myrrh (a packet of Wrigley's: someone had told the boy playing Balthazar that myrrh was a kind of gum, and he would not be diverted from his own view of authenticity).

Then came the moment that Bethany and Luke had anticipated with some degree of apprehension. The arrival of the shepherds. Even though Adam was inexperienced in the ways of the theatre, no one who knew him would have expected anything less than a conscientious approach to the job in hand. With every bit as much dignity as that of king or cherubim, he marched solemnly to the side of the manger, tea-towel on head, toy woolly lamb under arm, and leant on his walking stick, just as he had seen Jack Knaggs lean on his crook when surveying the family flock. He beamed across at Luke and Bethany, who squeezed each other's hand with a mixture of pride and relief.

After three verses of 'While Shepherds Watched' Joseph, having deposited Mary and the lopsided donkey on one side of the stage, walked towards the door of the inn, stage left, and knocked.

Barely had his knuckles left the timber than a surly-looking innkeeper appeared, stepping sideways from behind the door (Mr Latimer had forgotten to ask the local carpenter to make it functional and equip it with hinges). Jakey Learoyd was the son of the local electrician and not renowned for his sunny disposition. 'Yes?' he enquired gruffly.

Joseph cleared his throat and declared, 'I am Joseph and this is m-m-y wife M-m-mary. We have travelled far. M-m-may we have a room in your inn?'

The innkeeper did not hesitate. 'No,' he said, and dodged back behind the door. At this, Joseph looked nonplussed. He glanced to right and left before knocking again. This time the innkeeper took a few seconds to appear, his face contorted with a deep frown.

'I am Joseph and this is my wife M-m-mary. We have travelled far and she is expecting a baby. Have you got room for us in your inn?'

The innkeeper was once more unequivocal in his reply. 'No. I 'aven't.'

He added a sigh to the mix, and once more dodged back behind the door.

Having so far tried – relatively unsuccessfully – to pretend that this was all part of the story, Joseph now evinced signs of unease, bordering on fear. His lower lip began to tremble and he glanced at Mary, as if pleading for moral support. She nodded towards the inn door, encouraging her spouse to have another attempt at finding accommodation.

Joseph pushed up his glasses and knocked. The innkeeper hove into view, with something of a swagger. 'Yes? What is it now?' he asked, looking at his fingernails and adding, 'I haven't got all night, you know.'

At this the audience laughed uproariously, which gave rise to a smirk on the innkeeper's face but did nothing to restore the confidence of Joseph, who realised that the innkeeper was now going dramatically off-piste. He made one last-ditch attempt to get the story back on track. Dragging an unwilling Mary with him towards the door of the inn, he explained, 'I am Joseph

37

and this is my wife M-mary. She is going to have a baby very soon. It is very important that we find accomm- . . . that we find accomm- . . . that we have somewhere to sleep. If you have no room in the inn, please m-m-may we sleep in your stable?'

'No. Yer can't,' came the emphatic reply.

Joseph's voice cracked with desperation and emotion. 'But why not?'

'Because I wanted to be bloody Joseph.'

The rest of the performance passed in a blur, as Mrs Lambert did her best to marshal a confused cast into some sort of order around the manger, and Mr Latimer launched into one verse of 'Away in a Manger' before giving up on such a gentle carol, which barely covered the sound of chattering children and resorted instead to thumping out a fierce rendition of 'Hark the Herald Angels Sing'.

The assembled cherubim and seraphim sang lustily, along with parents, friends and family. A little later, over mince pies and cups of tea (and the odd bottle of smuggled-in Timothy Taylor's bitter), everyone agreed that it was the best nativity play the village had ever seen, even if the story varied slightly from the authorised version.

Funnily enough, Adam didn't seem to have noticed anything out of the ordinary, but then he was new to performing, and there were greater things on his mind. As they left the building, a small cage containing the school's pet hamster was cradled under his arm: his to look after for the duration of the holidays. He could not have been happier. Added to which, it was beginning to snow.

6

ABIDING IN THE FIELDS

When icicles hang by the wall,
And Dick the shepherd blows his nail,
And Tom bears logs into the hall,
And milk comes frozen home in pail . . .

William Shakespeare, *Love's Labour's Lost*, 1595

The snow fell . . . and the snow continued falling . . . until, by Christmas Eve, the track to Langstroth Farmhouse was impassable. A deafening silence fell upon the dale. Every crest of every fell lay like some fallen giant cloaked in a pure white shroud, the only movement that of a brave hare, leaping across the crisp crust in search of a crumb.

Adam got out of bed and crossed the room as the weak morning light crept under the curtains of his tiny window. Looking out across the pristine landscape, he scratched at the frosted corners of the panes with a finger. The cold and the sharp tang that seemed to emanate from it stung his nostrils. At the age of five he had no need of explanations, he just gazed in wonder at the overnight transformation, the purity and whiteness of the view, then ran excitedly downstairs, not caring to put on a dressing-gown or slippers, despite the chilly morning air. Central heating would not come to Langstroth Farmhouse for a few years yet: sweaters, scarves and a roaring kitchen range provided the family with all the warmth it needed – along with a morning bowl of honey-speckled porridge.

Bethany turned as she heard the staircase door open. Adam ran towards her, beaming. 'It's snowing! It's snowing!'

His mother laughed. 'It is! I don't think we'll be going anywhere today.'

'But outside? I can go outside?'

'Of course you can, once you've got some breakfast inside you. Now go up and get dressed – a thick sweater, mind – and I'll have your porridge ready for you when you come down.'

'Where's Daddy?'

'He's out feeding the sheep. They can't get at the grass under all this snow, so he's out with the tractor giving them some hay. And some pellets.'

'Is Jack coming?'

'Not today, I shouldn't think. He won't be able to get up here, will he? The snow is nearly as deep as you are tall – especially on the sides of the track where it's been drifting.'

Adam looked puzzled. 'What's drifting?'

Bethany turned down the gas on the Calor stove and stirred the porridge to stop it sticking. 'It's when the wind blows the snow up against a hedge or a wall and it piles up really thickly. Sometimes you can't even see the dry-stone walls because the snow has drifted so deep and so high.'

'Wowsers!'

Bethany laughed. 'Where did you learn that?'

'What?'

'Wowsers!'

'At school.'

'Of course you did.' (Then, to herself, *Along with a lot of other things I shouldn't wonder.*) 'Now go and get dressed – quickly before you freeze!'

Adam ran to the door at the bottom of the stairs. 'Is Finn out with Daddy?'

'He is. And if you're careful you can go out with them, too, so long as you don't wander off. We don't want you disappearing under the snow, do we?'

Muffled up to the nines, Adam went out, his mother with him. They followed the tractor tracks up the hillside and came upon Luke throwing down hay to coax the last remaining ewes towards the farmhouse and the inner folds where they were less likely to be buried in snow or where, at the very least, an eye could be kept on them. Luke had grown up with one particular pearl of wisdom, probably coined by Jack Knaggs in particularly mordant mood. 'Remember,' he had said to the young Luke, 'sheep just want to die.'

Luke had long since learnt the veracity of this observation. If a sheep can see a way of shuffling off its mortal coil it will invariably go for it – on the road running out in front of a car, getting through a fence that's meant to stop it falling over a cliff. It makes no difference to a sheep: the quickest and easiest way to leave this earth is always the best option. It mattered not that, way back, Luke's father had endeavoured to convince him that, in reality, sheep were very intelligent animals. That may, indeed, be so but by their actions they had an unfailing knack of persuading others to come round to Jack's point of view.

Adam needed no invitation or instruction when it came to

helping his father. He was used to getting stuck into the job in hand, be it feeding livestock or repairing a tractor's three-point linkage. Small though his frame might be, he pulled at the bales on the back box of the tractor, sent them tumbling onto the snowy ground, cut the baler twine with his dad's penknife (his mother had long ceased to worry – Adam knew exactly what he should and should not do with the sharp blade) and kicked out the hay to make it more accessible for the sheep.

Bleating and shouldering each other out of the way, the last of the Swaledale ewes jostled down the hillside as Bethany, Luke and Finn kept them in as tidy a flock as possible, Finn rounding up any determined strays with a well-placed nip at the heels.

They had been out for an hour or more and were approaching the gateway to the inner fold. 'Good job, Finn,' shouted Luke, as the dog brought into line a particularly stroppy ewe that had been giving him the eye.

'I could do with a mug of tea,' said Bethany. 'Adam?' Leaning on her crook, she turned to him and was surprised to see him walking away up the hillside.

'Adam! What are you doing? Come on! Time for a hot chocolate.' But the boy paid no attention. It was not like him. He had a mind of his own, yes, but when called he generally came, unless there was some obvious temptation that sidetracked him. Here there was none, just a pure white, featureless hillside under threat of further snowfall. The wind was whistling gently over the nearby wall, lifting a skein of snow and sending it skittering across the dale.

'Adam! Come back!' Bethany turned to Luke. 'You go on down. I'll round him up and follow on. What he thinks he's doing I don't know.'

By the time Bethany reached him, Adam was standing quite

still, up to his knees in snow and staring at the top of a dry-stone wall just visible above the crest of a deep drift.

'What are you doing, poppet? Come on, we need to go down before the snow gets heavier.'

It had begun to fall again – great goose-feathers tumbling from the dense welter of cloud, settling on eyelashes and reducing visibility by the minute.

'Sheep,' said Adam.

'Yes. We've got them all. Good job done. Come on, before we get snowed in up here.'

'Sheep,' repeated Adam. He pointed at the wall.

'What do you mean?' asked Bethany.

'Under the snow. A sheep.'

'Where?' Bethany walked forward towards the deep drift where Adam was pointing, pushing her crook into the snow, to keep her footing as much as to search for whatever Adam thought was there. All was silent. There was no sign of life. And then her crook struck something. She pushed it in again and then, with a flurry, like a monster rising from the deep, a lone ewe bounded out of the snowdrift. In a cascade of icy white powder she launched herself down the hillside in the tracks of her companions, bleating wildly.

Bethany stood open-mouthed. 'How did you know she was there?' she asked.

Adam shrugged.

'You, young man, deserve the best hot chocolate this side of the dale. Well done! Your dad will be *so* pleased!'

It was late in the afternoon of Christmas Eve when they finally closed the door of the farmhouse and flopped into chairs around the kitchen range and its welcoming log fire. Three large stockings hung from the mantelpiece and their once-frozen cheeks glowed from the longed-for heat.

'That's the best Christmas present I'm likely to get this year,' said Luke to his son, pouring himself a glass of Black Sheep ale.

'You don't know that!' said Bethany, with mock indignation. 'You don't know what Father Christmas will bring you.'

'He's brought me a good young shepherd, anyway,' confirmed Luke, ruffling the hair of the boy who sat at his feet in the fireside's glow.

The three were silent for a while, Luke wondering how on earth his son could have known the whereabouts of the errant ewe, and Bethany content in the knowledge that all was 'safely gathered in, ere the winter storms begin'. Yet even she was infused with a mixture of wonder and apprehension at the child's apparent sixth sense. She shook her head, as if to clear it of preoccupations.

'Anyway,' she said, 'it's time for supper. And then it's off to bed with you, little man. An early night.'

'Ohhhhh!' Adam wailed.

'Christmas Day tomorrow, and Father Christmas won't come if you're not asleep, will he?'

'How will he get through the snow?'

'Oh, snow doesn't stop the reindeer. Not *his* reindeer, anyway.'

Adam frowned. 'They don't really fly, do they? *Real* reindeer, I mean?'

Bethany glanced across at Luke, looking for reassurance.

Luke came to the rescue. 'Not *real* reindeer, no. But Father Christmas has special reindeer. How else can he get round all the houses in one night?'

Adam frowned. 'Mmm. I don't know.'

'Perhaps it's magic,' offered Bethany.

'I don't think I believe in magic.'

'You don't?'

Adam shook his head.

'How did you find that ewe today, then?'

'I'm not sure.'

Bethany went on: 'There was no sign of her. She was completely covered up with snow and she wasn't making a sound. Nobody else knew she was there. But you did. What made you go back up the hill? And what led you to that particular bit of wall where she was buried?'

Adam looked thoughtful for a moment. Then he said, 'Magic?'

7

THE LITTLE MIRACLE

Where there is great love there are always miracles.

Willa Cather,
Death Comes for the Archbishop, 1927

With the new year came the thaw. The icicles on the eaves of the farmhouse dripped with meltwater day after day, and the snow sneaked back up the hillside to the safety of loftier ground where the chilly breezes of January would preserve it far longer than they would lower down in the valley. Until the next blizzard, at least.

Adam had enjoyed his Christmas holiday from school, helping his mum and dad – Jack, too, since the snow had receded enough to allow the old man to make his way back up the farm track to work.

Now that Adam was five, Jack had discovered the boy was quite useful – fetching this or that, and even helping with mucking out the barn just across from the farmhouse where injured or sickly ewes were tended. When he was a toddler he'd got in Jack's way, asking questions the whole time. That he still did, but with intelligence greater than his years would suggest, along with an ability to reason that had been absent earlier in his childhood.

Luke joked to Bethany that Adam was clearly destined to spend his life looking after lame ducks, since he was drawn like a magnet towards any animal showing signs of sickness or infirmity. He would speak softly to frail ewes or lambs and stroke them, as much as they would allow, until they began to recover. Subsequently they often followed him around the farmyard until, tiring of their company – his aim, apparently, having been accomplished – he would shoo them off to join the rest of the flock. His concern for them seemed to be practical, rather than sentimental, and Luke approved of that. It didn't do for farmers to become too attached to their livestock, bearing in mind the ultimate fate of sheep and lambs, pigs and cattle.

'I know we don't want to force him, but do you think he *will* be a farmer when he grows up?' Bethany asked Luke one evening, as they sat by the fire, long after Adam had gone to bed.

'The way things are at the moment I don't see him becoming anything else,' Luke replied. 'He does seem at his happiest with animals. He's never been afraid of them and he does seem to have . . .' He paused, ordering his thoughts.

'What?'

'A gift, I suppose. A natural aptitude when it comes to livestock.'

'Isn't that just through watching you?'

'A bit. But not entirely. It's like Mrs Lambert said, you can't teach a child to be good with animals. It has to come from inside.'

'Innate, you mean?'

'If you want to be posh about it, yes,' he teased.

'A kind of instinct, then.'

'Yes. Without that he'd just be going through the motions and his heart wouldn't be in it, but he's totally at ease with animals and they seem to respond to him.'

'Early days, though,' cautioned Bethany. 'He might turn out to be a wizard with computers.'

Luke frowned. 'Well, he's shown no sign of a fascination with them yet. If he did I should think you'd be grateful, wouldn't you? He could help you with the accounts.'

'The way our internet functions up here I should think he'd give it very short shrift. Did you see how long it took me to get online when I was ordering Christmas presents?'

'Well, I could tell from your language – and you tell me off for talking like that in front of Adam.'

'He was in bed! There was no chance of him hearing.'

'Thank God! "Wowsers" is about the extent of his swearing at the moment and that'll do for a while. I've noticed that Jack's moderated his language now that Adam's around him more.'

'Well, I'm glad of that,' said Bethany. 'Though I suspect it's all in there somewhere, being processed.'

Luke agreed. 'It'll probably come out at the most inappropriate moment. Like during next year's nativity play.'

Bethany chuckled. 'Poor Mrs Learoyd. I bet she wishes her boy *had* played Joseph, rather than the innkeeper.'

'Yes, but the evening wouldn't have been nearly so entertaining if he had, would it? It's Harry Broughton I feel sorry for – the lad who played Joseph. I mean, why would you give a lad with a stammer a leading role? Unkind, I call it.'

'No. Not at all. They thought it would give him confidence. I thought he did really well until . . . Well, it's a shame he didn't get much of a chance to shine. His mum said he wouldn't speak the following day. Just sat in his room playing video games. I bet he'll never want to go on the stage again.'

'I don't think *I*'d want to go on the stage again if the Learoyd lad had said that to me. In front of all those people.'

Bethany laughed. 'You? On stage? You blush when we sit in the audience at a village hall meeting, never mind having to speak.'

'Well, some folk are gifted that way. Others have different talents.'

'I'm still trying to discover yours!' She grinned.

'Hoy, you!' He got up and walked over to her, then knelt down at her feet and kissed her.

'Luke Gabriel, what are you thinking?'

Luke shrugged. 'The boy's in bed, fast asleep. It's cold and dark outside, the day's work is done. What do you *think* I'm thinking?' He chuckled. 'And who's blushing now?'

The start of the school term was upon them. Bethany had prepared a cooked breakfast for Luke and Adam – 'Something more substantial than porridge to set you up for the new term.'

She loved watching the two of them sitting at the kitchen table – her boys tucking into a meal she had prepared. There was something primitive about it. Bethany had never seen herself as a mother figure, not when she was in her teenage years, anyway. Back then she had thought she would travel, see the world, be beholden to no one, but after one extended trip 'looking for herself' in India and Thailand, it had gradually dawned on her that she was here in the Yorkshire Dales all along. Well, her heart was anyway, and now – with Luke and Adam – her soul, too. She cradled her mug of steaming tea and thought how lucky she was.

'So have you got everything you need?' she asked Adam. 'School bag, gym kit, reading record, diary?'

Adam nodded, his mouth full of sausage.

'Aren't we forgetting something?' asked Luke, gesturing towards the windowsill at the other end of the kitchen.

Adam swallowed his mouthful. 'Does he *have* to go back? Can't he stay for just a few more days?'

The hamster had been a great hit with Adam over the school holidays. He would watch it in the early evening, running round and round in its wheel, then take it out and make small obstacle courses for it with cereal packets and the cardboard tubes from kitchen and loo rolls. The hamster slept for most of the day, so it did not occur to him on this particular morning that it was unusually silent. He finished his breakfast and asked to leave the table, then went to the small cage and lifted it down from the shelf. 'Shall I wake him up?' he asked.

'I suppose we'd better see if he's all right before he goes back to school,' agreed Bethany. She had heard several cases of hamsters not surviving the holidays, and of anxious parents making emergency visits to pet shops to enquire if they had in stock a hamster that might pass as a doppelgänger of the corpse they carefully unwrapped from the toilet tissue cradled in their hand.

Adam opened the door of the cage and felt inside the cocoon of cotton wool and shavings that passed as home for the school hamster. Carefully he withdrew the dormant ball of fur, stroking it gently in the hope of waking the slumbering rodent. But it steadfastly refused to stir.

A look of anxiety crossed Bethany's face. 'Oh dear!' she said. 'Do you think we've lost him?'

'He was all right yesterday,' offered Adam, his voice beginning to tremble. Luke came over to where they were standing. 'These things happen, Adam. You know that hamsters don't live long. Three years is a good innings, they say. It's not your fault.'

Adam lifted up the motionless coiled body and laid it in his father's outstretched hand. Luke could feel the creature was stone cold and rigid. 'How long has this one been at the school?'

Adam shook his head.

'A couple of years, I think,' offered Bethany.

'Well, then . . .' said Luke.

Adam looked up at his father and a tear rolled down his cheek. 'Can I hold him for a bit?'

'Of course you can. Go and sit down by the fire. You don't need to leave for school just yet.'

Bethany glanced at Luke, who winced.

Adam was used to death on the farm, be it a sickly ewe or a still-born lamb – but the hamster was different. It had been his responsibility, and he had become fond of it during the Christmas holidays, had built up some kind of vague rapport with the tiny creature.

'I'll call the school and say we might be a bit late in,' said Bethany. 'Give him time to get himself together.'

Luke was by the door, putting on his coat. 'I've the vet coming in half an hour to see to that ewe in the barn. Perhaps he can have a chat with Adam, explain it's not his fault the hamster died.'

Bethany nodded. 'I'll get on with things here, leave him on his own for a bit until he's sorted himself out. He'll be all right in a while, I'm sure.' She smiled sympathetically. 'He was fond of that little thing.'

'Mmm. Always a problem when you get too close to them,' admitted Luke.

'Yes, but he's only five . . .'

'I know.' He kissed Bethany's cheek and made to go. 'I'll be up at Twenty Acres until the vet arrives. I'll get down to the barn as soon as I see his Range Rover coming up the track.' He looked across at Adam and murmured, 'Poor little bugger.'

'Adam or the hamster?'

'Both.'

Having examined the troubled ewe, Martin Hebblethwaite, the local vet, was pretty sure of his diagnosis. It looked like a straightforward case of mineral deficiency, but he'd send off a blood sample just to be sure. It was easily enough remedied with feed supplements, he assured Luke, and the ewe would probably make a full recovery. Best to give the supplement to all the flock, to make sure that the rest remained healthy through the winter, ahead of the lambing season.

'Before you go,' asked Luke, 'can you just have a word with our little lad?'

Martin tilted his head to one side. 'About?'

'The school hamster.'

'Ah! Perished, has it?'

''Fraid so.'

The vet smiled knowingly. 'It's more common than you'd believe. I know school hamsters have a death wish but I do wish they wouldn't always choose the holidays to pop their clogs. Come on, then.'

They made their way towards the farmhouse in time to see Bethany and Adam coming out of the kitchen door. The boy held his cupped hands in front of him as he walked towards the two men. Both were about to offer their commiserations when they saw the smile on Adam's face.

'Look, Dad! He's alive!'

Luke put his hands on his hips. 'How did that happen?'

'Magic!' said Adam.

The vet beamed and turned to Luke. 'The magic of heat.'

'Sorry?'

'Adam, have you been holding the hamster since you found him?'

Adam nodded.

'So you've kept him warm for how long?'

Bethany butted in: 'About an hour, I suppose. I just left Adam sitting beside the fire. You know, letting him get over it.' Looking at the handsome young vet, she could feel the colour rising in her cheeks.

Martin Hebblethwaite was in his thirties, tousled of hair, rugged of frame and muffled up in his customary Aran sweater and cords with a woolly scarf wound around his neck. His rugged charms had set many a young female heart fluttering in Upper Wharfedale, but so far he had resisted being pinned down. Bethany's spirits always lifted at the prospect of his arrival, about which Luke would tease her mercilessly.

'That's the secret, then,' confirmed the vet.

'What secret?' asked Bethany, trying to look composed.

'Hamsters can go into hibernation mode when they get cold. Their bodies shut down and they really do look as if they're dead. Sometimes the condition lasts for days – even a week or more. But keep them warm and they'll wake up. We kept one going for four years once – thanks to Mum's Aga. Whenever it looked as though it had hopped the twig we put it at the back of the stove and warmed it up a bit. It was right as ninepence after that.'

'Not magic, then?' asked Luke.

'Well, a kind of magic,' confirmed Martin. 'And if Adam hadn't worked *his* magic the hamster might well have slipped into what you might call "permanent hibernation".'

Adam beamed up at the vet. 'Will he be all right now?'

'As long as you keep him warm. Your hands are doing the trick. If I were you I'd get him back to school as soon as you can.' Then, once more directing the advice to Bethany and Luke, 'Let someone else have the worry!'

'Oh, there is one more thing,' added Luke. 'You know Finn's eye?'

'The wall-eye? Has it been giving him trouble?'

'No. Quite the reverse. It seems to be getting better. The white area I mean. It seems to be reducing in size.'

'Really? That's not usual. A wall-eye normally stays like that for the animal's life.'

'Well, he sits with his head in Adam's lap every evening by the fire, with the boy stroking him, and . . .' Luke hesitated, as if he were embarrassed to go on.

'You think that might have had some effect?'

Luke shrugged. 'I don't know. Something's changed, because it's certainly better than it was.'

'Well, who knows?' said the vet. 'Stranger things have happened.'

He shook Luke's hand, winked at Bethany and walked across the yard to his Range Rover. As he opened the door he turned to address Adam again. 'You keep working your magic on animals, Adam, and I'll have a job for you in a few years' time. How would you like that?'

The boy beamed back at him. 'Maybe.'

The vet paused momentarily, shook his head at the apparent non-sequitur, then climbed up into his Range Rover and with a brief wave, drove off down the farm track, still musing on the indefinable characteristics of the five-year-old he had just encountered. He would be curious to see how he got on in the world.

THE YOUTH

8

YOUNG TYKE

Say from whence
You owe this strange intelligence?

Macbeth, Act I, Scene III, William Shakespeare, 1606

There are many ways of bringing up a child. Some parents will push and cajole with a view to ensuring their offspring has 'a better start than we ever had'. Others are more sanguine and rear their progeny more after the fashion of animals – offering a nudge in the right direction here and gentle discouragement there, with a view to keeping their children out of danger yet allowing them to find their own way through the woods. Luke and Bethany Gabriel fell into the latter category.

The aspirations of the son of Yorkshire shepherds whose lives have been lived on a remote moor are, of necessity, realistic. It is, in the balance of probability, unlikely that such a child will have his sights set on a high-flying city career or a meteoric rise to pop stardom, not only because such opportunities seem so geographically distant but also because, while the North Yorkshire moors have an excellent track record when it comes to breeding sheep, that reputation is not duplicated in the nurturing of prime ministers, stockbrokers, clergy or film stars. There were rare exceptions to the rule – the Fletcher boys whose father had taken his own life were an uncomfortable example, but such occurrences were not the norm. In short, it was under-stood by all the locals that Adam Gabriel was a 'lovely lad', who would most likely follow his father and become a hill shepherd, continuing to breed Swaledale sheep and eventually taking over the family flock. Apparently he had a way with animals. Such was the extent of local wisdom. Nothing more. Dalesmen are not given to fanciful notions. They will invariably find a way to reconcile themselves to unusual events and happen-ings. Look hard enough and there will be a rational explanation for even the most mystical of events.

Despite the concerns Luke and Bethany had about not affording Adam other opportunities than that of hill farming, it seemed that the boy cherished no great desire to do anything else with his life. Luke would talk to his growing son about different avenues of work, not in a heavy-handed way but with the intention of demonstrating that other careers might be just as rewarding as rearing sheep, and a darned sight more comfort-able during the darker months of the year. To no avail. While his parents did not take his acceptance of the shepherding mantle for granted, it seemed that Adam did.

There were times when Bethany felt Luke might be going too far. 'Are you trying to discourage him from taking on the flock?' she asked one day, when they were clambering up the fell to retrieve half a dozen bloody-minded ewes. Adam was ahead of them, calling to Nip, his own Border collie, who was being groomed to take over from the ageing Finn.

'No. Not at all. I just want to make sure I'm not taking it

for granted that he will.' They stood for a while, watching the teenager working his dog and systematically rounding up the excitable sheep.

'Does he look unhappy?' asked Bethany.

'No,' admitted Luke.

'Then perhaps you're worrying too much.'

'It's just . . .'

'I know. But I think you've done enough to show him that you don't have unreasonable expectations. And you're no Ted Fletcher.'

Luke shuddered. 'No. Thank God.'

At that moment the half-dozen ewes capitulated in the face of the canine opposition and came tumbling down the fellside in front of Luke and Bethany, Nip and Adam in hot pursuit. He beamed as he passed his parents. 'Not doing bad, is he?' he asked, waving in the direction of his dog.

'Not bad at all. I think he's just about there now.'

'Good training, you see!' said Adam, looking back over his shoulder with a twinkle in his eye.

Bethany gazed admiringly at the lad, who was growing to look more and more like his father every day, with his mop of fair hair and clear blue eyes.

'Yes, all right. I can take the hint!' Luke shouted after him.

'See what I mean?' murmured Bethany, grinning. 'He's sixteen now. Knows his own mind. Doesn't need a father fretting over him.'

'Sixteen. Where did the years go?' asked Luke. Then, softly to himself, 'Buggered if I know.'

The years between boyhood and youth had been relatively uneventful, apart from the usual hiccups involved in raising a son. It had gradually become apparent that Adam's talents lay in the direction of practicality rather than academic achievements, and parents' evenings at secondary school – larger and more impersonal than Kettlewell Primary – were generally predicated on that fact. He was firmly in the middle rank when it came to classwork in English and maths, a little better with science, biology in particular, and somewhat lower in French, information technology and the performing arts, where his father's discomfort at standing up and speaking in public seemed to be mirrored in his son. When it came to practical tasks – the cultivation of a patch of ground for the school garden, or the construction of nest boxes and bird tables, or even stage scenery – he was in his element and possessed a degree of craftsmanship beyond his years.

What escaped nobody was Adam's affinity with livestock, whether sheep and cattle or the bird and insect life of the dale. Bethany had taken him along to occasional meetings of the Wharfedale Naturalists Society from the age of eight, where he surprised the more mature members of that organisation not only with his ability to identify the 'little brown jobs' that flitted from tree to hedgerow, but also the ease with which he related to all forms of wildlife and – it seemed – the ease with which they related to him. Perhaps such thoughts were fanciful, but if that were the case, they were espoused by more than one member of that august body of natural historians.

Alas, the same ease of communication did not evince itself in the classroom. Where once the little boy of five or six had been an object of fascination for his peers, the teenager could all too easily become an object of teasing and, in moments of typical adolescent unkindness, ridicule.

Nicknamed 'Angel' by his classmates, Adam did his best to

rise above the taunts and the gibes. But it was not always easy. His lack of interest in all things digital did not help.

If anything, he blamed himself. He just felt so different from everybody else, their priorities at variance with his own. Why could he not take pleasure in a small screen? Why did he not care two hoots for Instagram, Twitter and texting, but was far more interested in the different hoots of the tawny owl and the barn owl, and the contrasting tweets of the reed and the sedge warbler? Was he, as Jakey Learoyd, the erstwhile innkeeper in the primary-school nativity play, regularly reminded him, a 'weirdo'? Certainly the isolation of Langstrothdale had bred within him self-reliance, but did that mean he was unsociable? Antisocial? He hoped not. He enjoyed the society of those who accepted him for what he was and allowed him to be himself without being judgemental.

He was at heart a confirmed country boy, happiest on the land and in the landscape, although his senior school – just a stone's throw from the village of Grassington – could hardly be described as 'urban'. He found life in the classroom frustrating, a waste of time compared with what he could be achieving outdoors, helping his father with the livestock, rebuilding dry-stone walls, fettling a three-point linkage and getting to know even more about the wildlife that populated that part of the dale, from the otters, the dippers and the king-fishers down by the river to the curlews of the moorland and the rare sightings of a merlin, which made his heart sing. He did not know why. That was just the way it was. There seemed a kind of purity in those forms of life, though it was beyond Adam to articulate the reasons for his deep-seated affinity with the natural world. He didn't let it bother him, except when the classroom taunts became prolonged. Then, on returning home to the farmhouse, he would sit up in his room, on the pretext of doing his homework, gritting his teeth as the tears coursed down his cheeks and he reproached himself for not having a thicker skin.

Beyond him though it was to understand the complexity of his own personality, he realised early on that his innate characteristics were a double-edged sword: the very sensitivity that made him so at ease with the natural world laid him wide open to the unkindness of his fellow pupils. If he was more resilient to their gibes, perhaps a part of him might also be less open to the feelings he had for animals, for the sheep and the dogs, the birds and the insects. His ability to connect with them, which sometimes seemed to show itself in an improvement to their health and wellbeing, he declined to question. It frightened him a little, and even his parents – otherwise so open and outgoing with him – did not mention this unusual manifestation of his talents, assuming that it equated to nothing more than a natural aptitude. It seemed to all three of them that such an apparent gift might have an evanescent quality, might even be imagined, and it best suited their equilibrium to leave its existence acknowledged but unspoken.

The river valley was Adam's place of solace. He would sit for hours, when homework and shepherding allowed, upon the water-worn pads of limestone on the riverbank. With luck he would catch sight of an otter surfacing and looking about, then submerging in a cluster of sparkling bubbles, or be thrilled by the flash of a kingfisher diving for minnows in the clear pools at the water's edge. Nip would lie at his feet, trained from an early age to be as still as his master.

While Luke and Bethany admitted to themselves that their child was 'unusual', his classmates used the more pejorative 'weird', an indication of their lack of understanding of Adam's differing priorities and aptitudes from their own.

He did his best to 'fit in' during break time, kicking a ball about with Jakey Learoyd and the rest. He was no great sportsman, but when it came to cross-country running he was regularly in the top three to return from the fellside – nimble footwork and the stamina of wiry youth stood him in good stead when it came to endurance.

Not all his classmates were unkind. Harry Broughton, the lad who had played Joseph in the Kettlewell nativity, was another sensitive soul who, when Adam was not bearing the brunt of the Learoyd cohort's barbs, was himself subjected to the standard taunts of the teenage bully. The two endeavoured to weather the storm, and it worried Adam that Harry took their goading even more to heart than he did.

'Don't let it get you down,' he urged Harry, as the lad stood silently in the corner of the playground during one lunch break, his eyes filling with tears that he was doing his best to staunch. 'They're just stupid.'

'Doesn't it g get to you?' asked Harry, softly, his jaw set tight lest the tears fell and he became the object of even more raillery.

'Yes. It does. But if we let them know it does they'll just keep on.'

'So what do I d-do?'

'Walk away. Just walk away.'

'Easy to say. Not really anywhere to g-go here,' said Harry, looking to left and right in the fenced-off area of the playground.

Adam noticed that he was rubbing his left shoulder with his right hand. 'What did they do?'

'Oh . . . shoved me into the wall over there. B-buggers!'

'Any reason?'

Harry shrugged. 'Jakey said I was in the w-way.'

Adam put his hand on Harry's injured shoulder to sympathise. The boy made to pull away. 'Don't! He'll only do it again for snitching on him.'

Adam left his hand where it was for a few moments. 'I don't think it's broken. Or dislocated or anything. Can you move it?'

Harry lifted his left arm and winced. 'Not m-much. It hurts like hell.'

Adam glanced over his shoulder, the better to locate Jakey Learoyd and his cronies. There were five of them, now over on the other side of the playground making the life of some other poor soul a misery. He turned back to Harry. 'He's not looking.' Then he put his hand on Harry's injured shoulder and seemed to concentrate as though he were trying to detect something.

'I think it might be b-broken.' said Harry, with a tremor in his voice.

Adam did not speak. He gazed into the middle distance, as though his mind were elsewhere.

It was something less than a minute, perhaps only half a minute, before Harry said, 'I think you can let go now. It feels different. Not so painful. Look, I can move it easily now. Probably just bruised.' He was unaware that he had got the sentence out without stammering. Neither would he have noticed that Adam seemed weary, as though drained of energy. But it was only lunchtime.

Harry felt slightly uneasy. There was nothing remotely threatening about Adam's behaviour. Neither did it have an uncomfortable degree of intimacy. It was simply an overwhelming sensation of kindness that took Harry by surprise, even though he was acquainted with what a few of his classmates would call Adam's knack of easing sprained joints. Some said he had had secret training sessions in sports therapy, though when it came to giving precise details of how this might have been vouchsafed to him when Adam hardly ever left the farm, no one could be sure. Still, it suited them to have a prosaic answer to what would otherwise be beyond their comprehension.

The conversation between Adam and Harry was interrupted by the bell signifying the commencement of afternoon lessons.

'Thanks,' said Harry, earnestly. 'Thanks for listening.'

Adam simply shook his head and turned away, walking slowly back to the classroom. Harry watched for a few moments as his friend retreated. He looked as though he had just returned from a cross-country run. Harry put his hand up to his shoulder once more. It felt warm, almost hot, but it didn't hurt nearly as much as it had done. Clearly it was just a bruise, and a slight one at that. But it was really nice of Adam to try to help him. His schoolboy physiotherapy must have done the trick. What was more, Harry felt a strange calm coming over him, a kind of invincibility. It was a novel feeling, but not one he felt, as yet, willing to test. He looked across the playground, hoping that Jakey Learoyd hadn't noticed.

9

Brother Wilfrid

The shepherd on his pasture walks
The first fair cowslip finds,
Whose tufted flowers, on slender stalks,
Keep nodding to the winds.

John Clare, April: *The Shepherd's Calendar*, 1827

When spring comes to the Yorkshire Dales the countryside is bathed in a diamond light. The 'early bite', the sudden rush of grass so important to hill farmers, means Nature helps with the feeding of flocks and the shepherd's load should be lightened. But it's lambing time: sleep is caught up on 'as and when', and the weather, every bit as much as good farming practice, dictates the likelihood of future feast or famine.

In Langstrothdale the lambing starts in earnest in early April when, with any luck, the earth and the air will have warmed up sufficiently to allow the ewes to give birth outdoors, with only the 'special cases' being brought under cover, or into the folds nearest the farmhouse. Here their progress can be more closely monitored and, if Luke, Bethany and Adam are lucky, disaster averted.

For Adam spring is a longed-for time of year, a season of renewal and reassurance that the meadows will bloom again and Nature will wake up from a long and often snowbound sleep.

The fields nearest the house glow with buttercups, the sides of the dry-stone walls are veiled with cow parsley, which the posh folk call Queen Anne's lace. The dandelions shine like twopenny suns while the flax-flower sky and cotton-wool clouds convince even the hardest cynic that winter is over and summer is just around the corner.

Through the sleepless nights and the frantic days of complicated deliveries, of too many singles and not enough twins, Adam would help with the lambing as much as he could, between school hours. Occasionally he would be allowed a week away from lessons to help, the head teacher knowing that, far from skiving, the lad would be working his socks off at the family business, whose very survival depended almost entirely on the success of one brief month in the shepherd's calendar.

Luke and Bethany would glance away now and again from their own labours and watch with justifiable pride as their lad delivered a breech-birthed lamb, or skinned a stillborn of its fleece to wrap around another and encourage the attention of a foster mother. It was hard not to smile at his dexterity and marvel at his apparent stamina. Even Jack Knaggs was impressed. He seldom admitted as much, but Bethany noticed that occasionally he would allow himself a surreptitious smile at Adam's unflappable approach to the daily deliveries.

Aware of the relentlessness of the lambing season, Luke and Bethany would make sure that Adam had time to catch his breath, to take time out with Nip, which almost always meant a walk down to the river's edge, perhaps with rod in hand to cast a fly and bring home supper. They worried less about Jack, since Jack did that – constantly chuntering under his breath about this and that, only the odd word intelligible to the Gabriel family, and not a syllable understood by anyone outside the county. It was the word in the village that his gentle grumbling was what kept him going, that and the fact that he would regularly park his body on a straw bale and drink strong, sweet tea from a pint pot, which seemed unfailingly to fuel his exertions. Between the four of them they managed well in most years, provided the weather was kind.

The end of lambing in the middle of May would herald the arrival of an annual visitor. Thoughtful as to timing – and not wishing to add to a family's burden when to do so would be to risk, at the very least, irritation and, at worst, lack of hospitality – Brother Wilfrid would appear.

They would hear him in the distance, singing as he approached the hollow in which nestled Langstroth Farmhouse. Usually it was a snippet of a favourite hymn, or a passage from a Handel oratorio. Today it was Stainer whose notes floated down on the air: 'Fling wide the gates for the Saviour waits to tread in his royal way . . .'

Bethany was at the kitchen sink and looked up, thinking at first that the radio had switched itself on. Then she turned towards the view and saw the figure in the black habit crossing the stream, crook in hand. Tall and angular with a shock of white hair, Brother Wilfrid continued with his song: 'He has come from above in his power and love . . .'

Bethany was outside the back door now and shouted a greeting. 'Brother Wilfrid! We wondered when you'd arrive. Welcome!'

'Mrs Gabriel! My annual pilgrimage. How are you? How are the lambs of God? Has it been a good year?'

'It has, thank you. More twins than usual – a really good result.'

'Oh, I'm so pleased! And how is Mr Gabriel?'

'He's well, thank you.'

'And Adam?'

'Well, too. And growing. You'll hardly recognise him. We missed you last year. Where were you?'

Brother Wilfrid flopped down upon the old stone bench alongside the farmstead and heaved a sigh. 'A busy year. I couldn't get away. Too much praying for the ills of the world, I'm afraid. But now we're seeing light at the end of the tunnel I have come once more unto the hills to give thanks. From the ills to the hills, eh?' He chuckled at his joke.

His voice had an Irish lilt, though the one thing that Luke and Bethany had discovered about Brother Wilfrid was that he was always vague about his background. He had begun arriving in Langstrothdale five or six years previously. He would suddenly turn up in the middle of May when lambing was coming to an end, asking for nothing more than a chat, a cup of tea and a sandwich. Sometimes, if the weather was bad, or he was particularly fatigued by his exertions – more frequent in recent years – he asked permission to sleep in the hayloft.

Bethany had offered him a bed in the house, but he was adamant that the hayloft would suit him fine. 'I wake up in the morning and my habit smells as sweet as the bedding on which Our Saviour lay. If it was good enough for him it is certainly good enough for me.'

Bethany had long since given up trying to persuade him otherwise, and that occasional overnight stay had turned into an annual custom. But only for the one night. He was quite determined that he should be on his way come the morning, withdrawing from the neat haversack upon his back a capacious waterproof cape in which he would swathe himself should the weather be inclement.

'Let me take your rucksack,' offered Bethany. 'The kettle is on.'

'Oh, bless you. I will not demur.' The monk propped his crook against the wall, slipped off his pack and handed it to Bethany, then took from his pocket a red and white spotted handkerchief and wiped his brow.

From inside the house Bethany enquired, 'Have you come far today?' knowing that that answer would, as always, be hazy.

'Just over the moor, over the dale, but my legs are not getting any younger.'

When Brother Wilfrid had first turned up on their doorstep those few years ago they had regarded him with some suspicion. A spate of thefts from farms around Litton and Buckden had made the community wary of strangers.

Who knew what ruse would be brought into play to 'case the joint', as Luke put it? (Bethany told him he watched too many old American movies.)

They were quickly put at their ease by Brother Wilfrid's manner and his ability to listen as well as to talk. When Brother Wilfrid listened – *really* listened – it was difficult not to take advantage of what, to all intents and purposes, was a confessional, a therapy session, though the thought of such a thing would have horrified Luke and Bethany should they have considered it such. If 'Brother Wilfrid', as he asked them to call him, were, indeed, 'casing the joint', Luke and Bethany had played into his hands by talking about themselves far more than they would to any normal stranger. When, after his departure, nothing went missing from the farm, they reproached themselves for having been suspicious of the monk's motives. And he was, after all, a man of God. Wasn't he? But where did he come from? North Yorkshire was not short of abbeys: Byland, Rievaulx, Fountains and Bolton Abbey had all been monastic communities, but most of them had ceased to function as such after Henry VIII's Dissolution of the Monasteries. The most likely location was Ampleforth Abbey, but whenever that holy place was mentioned Brother Wilfrid would look sad and shake his head. Luke and Bethany felt it best not to pry any further.

They would sit down each year after his departure and ask themselves why he came to see them each May. His timing never varied. Where had he been, and where was he going? Neither answer was ever forthcoming so they simply stopped enquiring and took the visit for what it was – a pleasant encounter and good company after weeks of hard days and sleep-deprived nights. With Brother Wilfrid they could let off steam in a way that would not seem appropriate with any of their farming neighbours, whose own travails were their preoccupation.

As the man of God leant back against the sun-warmed wall of the farmhouse, eagerly devouring his cheese and pickle sandwich, Adam and Nip could be heard coming up the track on the farm's new quad bike.

Bethany was standing at the kitchen door, tea towel in hand, grateful to be enjoying a slightly less frantic pace of life than of late. She had worried about the acquisition of the powerful four-wheeler, but Luke had explained how valuable such an all-terrain vehicle would be in getting to livestock that was unreachable by any other means than on foot – a slow, often uncomfortable and unproductive means of travel. And, anyway, they were about the last farmers in the dale to avail themselves of what was now considered a vital piece of equipment in this part of the world.

'Oh, goodness!' exclaimed Brother Wilfrid. 'A transport of delight!'

'Some would say,' murmured Bethany, 'they've both got legs . . .'

Adam parked the quad bike by the barn, then he and Nip jumped off it and walked towards the house. 'Hello, Brother Wilfrid,' said Adam, with genuine warmth in his voice.

'Master Gabriel!' The monk looked Adam up and down and shook his head. 'Though Mr would be more appropriate now, I suspect. I shall resist saying the obvious, but I'm most certainly thinking it.'

Adam grinned. 'It's the fresh air. Good for lambs and good for me.'

Brother Wilfrid drained his mug of tea and put it down on the bench beside him. 'You know, it's so good to hear from someone who's happy with their lot.'

'Most of the time,' admitted Adam. He cast a glance at his mother, before adding, 'All of the time while I'm here.'

Brother Wilfrid looked from one to the other, his expression clearly intent on eliciting further explanation.

Bethany addressed her son: 'Your sandwiches are on the table and there's a flask with them. Are you staying or going?'

'Going, I'm afraid.' He cast an apologetic look at the monk. 'But I'll be back for tea, Brother Wilfrid, and I'll see you then – if you're staying?'

A glance at Bethany confirmed the invitation. 'Of course you will. You get on. A busy time of year.' He watched as Adam took the sandwiches and the flask, climbed back onto the quad bike and called to Nip, who leapt onto his lap. They roared off up the track and out of sight, Adam's fair hair blowing above his head like a halo.

Brother Wilfrid turned to Bethany. 'He's grown into a grand young lad.'

'Yes. He has. But . . .'

'Problems?'

'Oh, not serious ones. I can never get over how easy he's been to bring up. It's just that he's not very happy at school. Wants to leave early – before his A levels. We're trying to discourage him.'

'Why?'

The question was so blunt that for a moment Bethany did not quite know how to answer. After a brief hesitation, she said, 'Well, he'll need exams to get on, won't he?'

'To get on in what?' asked the monk. His tone was gentle, not remotely critical.

'Well . . . life.'

Brother Wilfrid looked thoughtful, then asked, 'What does he plan on doing?'

'Oh, he's desperate to work here, eventually take on the farm.'

'I see. And how many A levels will you require of him?'

When it was put like that the absurdity of the situation hit home. Bethany sighed. 'I just don't want him to feel he's second best, and without qualifications he might . . .' Her voice dwindled into silence.

'How old is he now?'

'He's sixteen.'

'Is he *allowed* to leave school?'

'Well . . . technically, yes. His seventeenth birthday is at the end of August. They can't really stop him, but it will mean that he misses out on his A levels and will have to make do with his GCSEs. He just wants to learn about livestock management really.'

'Which he could do here on the farm presumably.'

Bethany could feel that this was an argument she showed no signs of winning.

Brother Wilfrid registered her discomfort. 'I know you must want the best for him, but since I've been coming here it's been quite clear to me that this is the life he loves. He's not lazy, is he?'

'No! Far from it. We have a job to make him slow down.'

'Is he useful?'

'Absolutely. He just gets on with things, often notices what needs doing before Luke or I do. It's just that I feel he should have some experience of the world before he settles down on his home turf. That's all.'

'Like you did.'

'Yes.' At that moment Bethany realised where the conversation was going. 'Oh, no . . . I don't mean . . .'

Brother Wilfrid continued, 'And when you went away travelling – forgive me, remind me where you went . . .'

'India, Thailand, Myanmar – Burma as was . . .'

'And here you are back in Wharfedale . . .' Bethany made to interrupt, but Brother Wilfrid continued, '. . . and it did you a world of good, opened your eyes to other cultures.'

'Yes.'

'Which for someone like you is invaluable. It informs the rest of your life, makes you appreciate what you've got here in the Dales.'

'Yes.'

'Which is exactly what Adam does already, without the need to travel.'

'Well, yes, but . . .' Bethany's resolve was withering in the face of what was, clearly, sound common sense.

Brother Wilfrid offered an olive branch. 'Forgive me. I'm not judging. Just pointing out that when it comes to travel and experience there are no rules. It's quite possible to live in one place and be a rounded, thoughtful, contented individual. Look at the philosopher Immanuel Kant. Never travelled more than a hundred miles from Königsberg. It's in Prussia. Or what was Prussia. Or Socrates. Never one for foreign holidays, Socrates. Yet I think you'll agree that they're both regarded as having been quite bright.'

Bethany was gazing at the luminous view of the sun-drenched dale – divided up by dry-stone walls and peppered with sycamore, oak, hawthorn and rowan. The Swaledale ewes – their main maternal duty accomplished – were grazing contentedly as their lambs frisked about them. It didn't always look quite so picturesque, but when the sun shone and the air was fresh and clear, it did, indeed, become a little piece of Heaven from which it was hard to tear oneself away. She was not at all sure who Immanuel Kant was, but she took Brother Wilfrid's point. If Kant had been born in Wharfedale she could have understood why he never felt the need to go away.

The monk's gentle voice seeped into her reverie. 'The most important thing in life, it seems to me, is to be allowed to follow your bliss. This is yours. It seems that it's destined to be Adam's, too. Is that something you need to discourage?'

Bethany turned towards him. It was as if a weight had been lifted. 'What a lovely expression. Perhaps you're right. Perhaps we should let Adam . . . follow his bliss.'

10

HOME TRUTHS

The traveller can get the greatest joy of travel even
without going to the mountains, by staying at home
and watching and going about the field
to watch a sailing cloud, or a dog, or a hedge,
or a lonely tree.

Lin Yutang, *The Importance of Living*, 1938

Since Brother Wilfrid's arrival at midday (he invariably appeared
at a time convenient for refreshments), they had each gone their
own way: Luke was in Skipton at the agricultural-supply
merchants, Adam and Nip checking on the far reaches of the
flock and Bethany, perforce, making arrangements to accom-
modate and feed their visitor. He might insist that the hay barn
would be sufficient to cater for his nocturnal needs, but at least
she could augment such modest comforts with a couple of
blankets.

Brother Wilfrid had climbed up Deepdale Gill to the waterfall where he sat and gave thanks for his good fortune. There
was something comforting to the occasional passer-by at the

sight of a monk in silent prayer by a waterfall, regardless of their own faith, or lack of it. Common to all was astonishment that anyone, regardless of the nature of their God, could traverse the Yorkshire Dales in a monk's habit and sandals, but Brother Wilfrid's feet had been hardened to it for the best part of forty years now, or so he would explain to those who enquired as to the discomfort felt in his pedal extremities.

To the Gabriels his yearly arrival had become a symbol of spring. It engendered hope and a sense of renewal. Both Bethany and Luke were believers – in some greater force than themselves at any rate. If you were to question them about their faith they would prevaricate, not wanting to be thought overly 'religious' or remotely evangelical. Luke would shrug and gesture to the hills and valleys around him as if to demonstrate some greater power than his own. Bethany would be more forthright in suggesting that it was something private. They had both been brought up to go to church – low church, that is. Luke's mother became uncomfortable if someone lit so much as a single candle in the House of the Lord, and as for incense – well, that didn't bear thinking about.

Luke and Bethany would go to Hubberholme church at Easter and Christmas, for the annual harvest festival, burials, marriages and christenings, and take Adam with them. They seldom, if ever, talked of their beliefs at home and Adam grew up absorbing any kind of faith he had by osmosis. The Gabriels' Christianity was that of quiet acceptance rather than demonstrative evangelism, but they loved the warmth and the welcoming atmosphere, the woodwork bearing the carved mice of 'Mousey' Thompson and the candles that hung in clusters from the rafters in the church of St Michael and All Angels, which seemed appropriate given their family name.

Brother Wilfrid had the good manners not to inflict his own beliefs on others, relying instead on his attitude and general demeanour to make clear to all and sundry the nature of his own faith. But what precisely was that faith? Benedictine? Franciscan? Cistercian? High Church? Low Church? Anglo-Catholic? Whenever the subject came up he was adept at swerving, subtly steering the conversation in a different direction. Talking about himself seemed anathema to him and the Gabriels were too polite to pin him down. It seemed best to accept him for what he was – a man whose company they enjoyed, who expressed a genuine interest in their lives, and who would leave them feeling all the better for seeing him, brief though his visit might be.

In between Luke's return from Skipton and sitting down for supper, Bethany had talked to him about Adam, about Brother Wilfrid's thoughts and the way in which her own opinion of the boy's future had been affected by what he said. As he changed out of his working clothes, showered and put on a clean shirt and a pair of chinos, Luke listened as Bethany explained that perhaps it would not be a totally irresponsible idea if Adam were allowed to leave school at the end of the summer term.

Her exposition of the facts complete, she sat on the bed and asked, 'What do you think?'

Luke turned to face her. She looked so beautiful sitting there in her blue and white floral frock – the first time she had put on a dress this year – her shiny dark hair freed from its customary ponytail and now brushing her shoulders. She could still make his heart miss a beat more than twenty years after they had married. 'If you want my honest opinion I think, in the end, that it's the only way he's going to be happy,' confirmed Luke. 'He's going through it at school at the moment, with Jakey Learoyd and his mates. He doesn't say anything, but Jack Knaggs reckons Jakey and his hangers-on are making the lives of one or two of their classmates a misery. Not that that's a good enough reason in itself to let him leave. I've tried hard enough over the years to let him see that there are other things in life he could do – not just shepherding. But he won't hear of it. I was going to have a word with you about it anyway. Trust Brother Wilfrid to beat me to it.'

Bethany got up from the bed, walked towards her husband and kissed him. 'Thank you. I didn't know what you'd say. How you'd take it.'

'I want Adam to be content in life. That's the most important thing. And he's content when he's here. Happiness doesn't last long. I'm not daft enough to think it does. But contentment can. Adam's seen enough foul weather to know how difficult this sort of life can be. The sun doesn't shine all the time, like it did today, but he knows that. My only worry is that he might be lonely. Where's he going to meet other people? If he does want to settle here and make this his life, is he going to be on his own?'

'I've thought about that. We just need to make sure he has a chance to get away from the place.'

'On holiday?'

'Well, yes, but more regularly than that.'

Luke said, 'We could encourage him to go to the Wharfedale Naturalists more often. And to join the Young Farmers' Club – plenty of girls there.'

Bethany looked him in the eye. 'You're assuming . . . It's just that . . . we don't know . . .'

'You mean . . .?' Luke's face betrayed his unease.

Bethany smiled. 'Yes. He's sixteen and we don't know—'

'Whether he likes girls or boys,' answered Luke.

'Or both.'

'It never occurred to me . . .'

'Well, you've been busy these last sixteen years, haven't you?'

Luke walked across to the window and looked out across the rolling hills. 'Yes, but . . .'

'Does it matter? As long as he's happy? Sorry, content. Or are you going to be a bloody-minded Yorkshire farmer and disown him?'

'Hey! Hang on! I haven't said anything!'

'No. But your expression, your tone of voice . . .'

Luke turned back from the window. 'I'm not my father's generation, you know.'

'Maybe not, but there are lingering prejudices, aren't there?'

Luke shook his head. 'Not to that extent, no. If Adam . . . well, if he . . .' He sighed heavily. 'If he falls in love, then, whoever it is, as long as they're . . .'

'Nice?'

'Yes.'

'Shall we leave it at that, then?' teased Bethany.

Luke forced a smile. 'I think we'd better, don't you?' He crossed to the bedroom door, but paused before opening it. 'So, are you going to tell him about leaving school or shall I?'

'Oh, I think it's definitely a father's job. Do you want to do it over supper?'

'Only if it comes up. I think I'd rather tell him when it's just us three.'

'Not in front of Brother Wilfrid?'

'I'll do it when it feels right, OK?'

Bethany grinned. 'Of course you will.'

'And when it comes to . . . the other,' said Luke, 'can we cross that bridge when we come to it?'

11

HEAVEN'S GATE

Oh thou, that dear and happy Isle
The garden of the world ere while,
Thou paradise of four seas,
Which Heaven planted us to please . . .

Andrew Marvell, *Upon Appleton House*, 1681

'So how long are you staying?' asked Luke of their guest.

'Well, if I may remain here just the one night, please?'

'Of course.' Luke smiled. 'In the barn?'

The cleric nodded eagerly.

They were sitting at the kitchen table eating supper. As she did every year, Bethany had treated the evening as a special occasion – a clean green and white gingham tablecloth was stretched over the circular scrubbed-pine table; she would sit opposite Luke, and Adam opposite Brother Wilfrid. A pot full of primroses stood in the centre, and there was Timothy Taylor's Landlord bitter, a jug of cider or a rich Rioja to go with the home-grown lamb. One advantage of being a sheep farmer was that there was always a joint of lamb in the freezer in case of fire, flood, famine, snowfall or unexpected guests.

The sunshine of the day was reflected in their faces, each of them sporting a gentle glow as the grey pallor of winter was banished from their cheeks – temporarily at least.

Adam had appeared a few minutes after the others had seated themselves at the table. 'Sorry I'm late,' he murmured.

'Well, at least you're clean,' replied his mother, as she brought dishes of vegetables to the table. 'Here we are: the first new potatoes of the year.'

Brother Wilfrid's eyes lit up. Luke and Bethany glanced at one another. One thing with which they always had difficulty was keeping a straight face at Brother Wilfrid's unashamed delight in food. He approached every meal as though it was the first time he had eaten in days. Every mouthful was savoured, every scrap cleaned from his plate. Second helpings were never declined. It was as if he was stocking up for the privation that lay ahead.

'Oh, my goodness!' he exclaimed. 'Have you grown these yourself?'

'Not up here,' explained Luke, pouring himself a glass of beer and nodding at Adam to indicate that tonight he, too, would be allowed to do likewise. 'Only a half, mind,' he added.

'No. I suppose not,' murmured Brother Wilfrid.

Bethany brought warmed plates to the table as Luke began to carve the large leg of lamb beside him. 'They're Jersey Royals,' she explained. 'The first always come from the Channel Islands. They've been in the greengrocer's in Skipton for a while now but they're so expensive when they first arrive that I usually wait a few weeks before we treat ourselves.'

'International Kidney,' said Adam, softly.

'I'm sorry?' said Brother Wilfrid.

Adam cleared his throat. 'International Kidney. That's the variety of potato they grow on Jersey. You can buy them anywhere that sells seed potatoes. It's just that because the weather's so mild in the Channel Islands they can plant them early and call them Jersey Royals.'

'Oh, I see. And how early would that be?'

'In November under glass, any time from January outside. We don't plant our early potatoes on the mainland until March so they're not harvested till June.'

'Adam, you are, as ever, a mine of information.'

Adam blushed and took a sip of the beer.

Luke made to cover his son's embarrassment. 'Adam's been after getting me to have a veg patch up here. We started last year – a sheltered bit of earth alongside the barn. It faces south, so it gets plenty of sun – and we've no shortage of muck . . . er, manure, but the ground warms up slowly this high in the dale, so we don't really get any seeds in until early May.'

'April in a good year,' cut in Adam.

Bethany made to clarify matters: 'Luke is, like most farmers, useless at gardening. But Adam persuaded him that home-grown veg would be a good idea.'

'It's not that I don't like it,' said Luke, defensively. 'It's just that I've enough to do with the sheep all day without having to come home and dig a veg patch.'

'And Adam hasn't?' quipped Bethany.

'Now I don't want to be responsible for a family argument,' Brother Wilfrid said. 'But good for you, Adam. If you enjoy it, you carry on. I shall certainly enjoy what's in front of me. Shall we say a brief prayer?' Without waiting for an answer he closed his eyes, put his hands together and intoned, 'Boiled and stewed, fried and roast, praise Father, Son and Holy Ghost. Amen.'

Immediately his brief grace ended he opened his eyes, lifted up his knife and fork and began to tuck in to the comprehensive arrangement of meat and vegetables that filled his willow-pattern plate.

There was a moment's pause from the other three before they, too, grasped their cutlery, unsure whether Brother Wilfrid's intonation was intended to be as funny as it sounded.

Bethany thought it best to move the conversation on. 'So what news today, Adam?'

'Not much. Couple of sickly lambs, but I brought them down to the barn and I think they're on the mend. I looked in on them before I came in.'

'And your dog?' enquired Brother Wilfrid. 'How's he doing? I forget his name.'

'Nip,' confirmed Adam. 'He's fine, thanks. Learning fast.'

'He was just a pup last time I was here. Now the older dog I do remember. Finn, isn't it?'

Adam nodded.

'He must be getting old now?'

'He's fifteen. Still working but Nip shares the load.'

'Do they get on?'

'They do now,' said Adam, glancing at his father.

'It was tricky at first,' said Luke. 'A bit like having two old tups competing with one another. But, well, Adam worked his magic—' He stopped short, not wanting to make too much of the situation.

Brother Wilfrid smiled knowingly. 'Yes. I remember. It's quite a gift.'

Bethany interrupted, even though she knew her enquiry would lead nowhere. 'But what about you, Brother Wilfrid? When did you set off? How long have you been travelling?'

'Oh, a few days. The weather's been lovely, which is a blessing.' He took up his pudding spoon to make the most of the gravy that formed a circular pool around his plate.

Bethany persisted in her quest for more information. 'And where are you going?'

Between slurps, the reply came: 'Oh, wherever the dale takes me. I have no timetable, no ultimate destination.' He paused. 'Apart from the ultimate destination, that is, and I hope that will be some time hence.'

The Gabriels had become used to Brother Wilfrid's deft prevarications. When one of them had broached the fact some years ago that he always wore the same habit, yet gave off an aroma of new-mown hay rather than rampant body odour, he smiled indulgently and promoted the virtues of laundering his clothing, along with his corporeal self, in moorland springs and then drying both upon sun-drenched banks of moss.

This evening their conversation gently dwindled to a standstill, with nothing more than pleasantries – Bethany embarrassed by her rather clumsy annual attempt to learn more about Brother Wilfrid and divert the attention from Adam, and Luke unable to think of any avenue of conversation other than the one he and Bethany had explored before supper. Rather than allowing the evening to end on a slightly uncomfortable note, he glanced at Bethany, then said to Adam, 'Your mum and I have been talking about the future.'

Adam looked fearful of what might follow.

'Provided you go to day-release classes to continue your training, and provided it doesn't mean you're stuck here and never get out, then your mum and I have decided you can leave school early.'

Adam's jaw dropped. 'Really?'

'Really.'

'Bloody hell!'

It was unnecessary for Bethany to apologise to Brother Wilfrid for her son's language, simply because the monk was laughing so much that the tears were coursing down his cheeks.

12

MOST JUSTLY DUE

As an apostolic pioneer, a monastic founder, a builder of
churches and patron of art, and as a person of remarkable fortitude and persistence, inspired by grandiose ideals
and imaginative vision, he deserves to be considered one
of the most important men of the Old English Church.

David Hugh Farmer, *St Wilfrid,*
The Oxford Dictionary of Saints, 1978

They walked to the top of Cush Gill, Adam leading the way
with Nip at his heel, followed by Brother Wilfrid carrying his
haversack, perspiring heavily and relying on his crook for
stability on this unseasonably warm spring morning. It was time
for the monk to resume his pilgrimage, wherever that might
lead.

Adam leapt onto a rock that offered a clear view of the valley,
and Brother Wilfrid sat below him, mopping his brow with his
Dick Whittington kerchief and attempting to get his breath
back. 'You're like a gazelle,' he said, as much to himself as to
his companion.

'Cross-country running,' replied Adam, by way of explanation.

'And youth,' added the cleric.

Adam grinned. 'Sorry. Just used to it, I suppose.'

'As am I, but perhaps at a more sedate pace.'

The boy came and sat next to him. 'Can I ask you a question?'

Brother Wilfrid tucked his kerchief into some distant recess in the folds of his habit. 'What sort of question?'

'Do you think I'm odd?' On receiving no immediate answer he continued, 'I mean for wanting to carry on living here. For working with animals. For being happy on the farm.'

Brother Wilfrid said softly, 'That's not really what's worrying you, is it?'

Adam was surprised. He should not have been. He knew by now that Brother Wilfrid had a way of getting to the heart of the matter with a frankness that could take the breath away.

He sought to prevaricate. Leaning down towards Nip and stroking the dog's neck to avoid eye contact, he asked, 'What do you mean?'

'Your gift. Is it worrying you?'

Adam turned to face his inquisitor. 'My gift?'

'Adam, I might come here only once a year – and last year I was absent, I know – but I've watched you since you were a small boy and I know what you're capable of. I've seen you with animals – dogs, sheep and the like. I've seen the effect you have on people by your presence.'

The boy made to brush off the compliment: 'Oh, I just . . . well . . .'

'Whatever you call it, and however you try to explain it to yourself, I'm sure it is as much a curse as a blessing.'

Adam looked at Brother Wilfrid with the expression of a

young boy who had been caught scrumping apples. 'How do you know?'

'I've spent many years caring for souls, my own and other people's. There are those who are kind and those who are cruel. Society today is very concerned with self. The sense of entitlement is quite breathtaking. "I want it so I should be able to have it." Many individuals seem unable or unwilling to accept the point of view of others as valid. If an opinion or a feeling is different from their own, it should not be tolerated, not given a voice. And then there are the enablers.'

'The enablers?'

'Those whose concern is less for themselves than for the good they can do for others. You are one of those.'

'You make me sound like a saint.'

Brother Wilfrid smiled. 'Perhaps you are in a way. And the saints have never had it easy. Torture figures largely in their lives – and in their deaths. And torture can be both physical and mental.'

'I just try to help. That's all.'

Brother Wilfrid apologised – to himself as much as to Adam. 'I'm sorry. It's just that I wouldn't want you to think that your talent was underestimated or unappreciated.'

'Is that what you think it is? A talent?'

'Most definitely. And talents can be a heavy burden as well as a benison. They engender expectations in others. And jealousy. When people encounter something they don't understand, something for which no rational explanation can be found, they employ some kind of safety mechanism. That mechanism can take many forms – refusal to take at face value what they see, suspicion, the attribution of ulterior motives to the possessor or perpetrator. Instead of accepting a set of circumstances beyond their comprehension and marvelling at them, they attempt to traduce them.'

Adam looked puzzled. 'Traduce them?'

'Undermine them, belittle them or, worse, exact some kind of punishment.'

'But I've done nothing wrong!'

'Quite the reverse. You have done wonderful things. But in this day and age, where science and technology offer explanations for everything, the things we don't understand frighten us. We try to explain them away, pretend they don't really exist. People will happily take a little piece of plastic out of their pocket, press a few buttons and speak to a friend on the other side of the world. They take such forms of "magic" for granted. They've become used to them. They may not understand how such things are possible but they don't feel threatened by them. But if someone possesses an unusual gift – an aptitude or an ability that defies what they consider to be rational or scientific explanation – they're at best suspicious and at worst frightened. And when they're frightened they act irrationally. They may even become violent. They want to find some explanation for the inexplicable or else to prove that such a thing is false.'

Adam spoke softly, Nip's head resting on his lap. 'Yes.'

Brother Wilfrid stared out across the dale. 'Hundreds of years of technology have caused us to lose touch with many of our natural aptitudes and instincts – the ability to nurture things, to grow things.' He swept his arm across the view of the sun-drenched landscape below them. 'To be good stewards of the earth. Words like "husbandry" have disappeared from our vocabulary. But such a responsibility for living things, such stewardship, is what makes this a better world. That's something you possess and which you use for the greater good.'

'But I'm just a boy with an interest in nature.'

'And a gift. Don't forget the gift.'

'I wish I could,' Adam murmured.

'Does it exhaust you, as well as worrying you?'

'Yes. When it happens I feel drained. As if I'd just done a long cross-country run.'

'And how often does it happen?'

'Not every day, not even every week. Perhaps half a dozen times a year. I don't plan to do it, it just happens.' He thought for a moment. 'Perhaps I should have been born hundreds of years ago when people were more in touch with nature.'

'Oh, don't imagine it was any easier then. You'd probably have been burnt at the stake.'

'I thought that was just witches – women?'

'Men suffered, too. The Salem witch hunts in the United States back in the sixteen hundreds were indiscriminate when it came to gender. I'm afraid society has always acted badly in the face of abilities beyond its comprehension.'

Adam looked at the monk enquiringly. 'So what can I do?'

'I wish I knew. I wish I could offer you an answer. I wish I could say that people will come to understand, but I'm not sure they ever will. What's important is that you should not feel in any way inferior to them. You might not feel gifted academically – which is why I think it's great that you're leaving school to work on the farm – but your individual gift is far and away more important than that. Academics are ten a penny – believe me, I was one of them – but your gift is rarer than hen's teeth. Cherish it and use it to good effect.'

'Even if it means being called a weirdo?'

'I fear so. But you don't have to be conspicuous. It's a part of you and, as such, it helps to make up your character. You can't deny it, but at the same time you don't need to be ostentatious in employing it.'

'You mean, be more choosy about where I use it?'

'A little. Though that will test your conscience.'

'How?'

'There will be times when you feel you need to help, but it will be difficult to keep such help "under the radar", so to speak.' Brother Wilfrid changed gear. 'But I was hoping to offer you some help and I fear that I have simply exacerbated the problem. I'm sorry if that's how it feels.'

'No. You haven't. Really you haven't.'

'What do your parents think?'

'They've seen what I can do – some of what I can do: healing Finn's wall-eye is one they tell me about – but they don't know about the other things. They'd only worry.'

Brother Wilfrid patted Adam on the shoulder. 'I believe they know more than you think. But they're probably as concerned as you are about the attitude of others. They'll be avoiding the subject in case it makes you uncomfortable. I'm sure they have your best interests at heart.'

Adam stood up. 'So I've just got to live with it.'

Brother Wilfrid gripped his crook and rose to his feet. 'But you're not alone. I share your burden as much as I can, and although that may seem small comfort, I hope it makes you feel less like a "weirdo", as you put it, and more like someone who has been especially blessed.'

Looking Brother Wilfrid in the eye, Adam said, 'I've not spoken about it before. Never. Not to anyone.'

'Well, you have now, and if it's any consolation, I'm honoured to know you and full of admiration.'

'Oh, I'm just me, nothing special.'

'And there, young Adam, I must respectfully disagree. You are incredibly special. You have the Touch, once reserved for kings and now the province of a young shepherd in the Yorkshire Dales. Use it well, and good luck.' He shook Adam's hand, turned and strode out across the moor, with a seemingly boundless supply of energy that had not been apparent before. It was as if his whole being had been renewed. As he disappeared from view across the undulating moorland, Adam heard him singing, 'Fling wide the gates for the Saviour waits to tread on his royal way . . .'

He called to Nip, turned to the valley and began the climb down towards the farmhouse.

13

FOURTH REMOVE

Nothing in his life
Became him like the leaving it:

William Shakespeare, *Macbeth*, Act II, Scene III, 1606

Luke and Bethany went to see the headmaster alone. They felt it best to beard the lion in his lair without their son. What if the head were unwilling to agree to Adam's wish to leave at the end of term? Could he prevent such a thing? *Would* he prevent such a thing?

They were asked by the school secretary to sit on two chairs in a corridor outside the headmaster's office. It was a modern school, rather than one of those ancient Victorian edifices of blackened stone outside and gloss-painted brick walls within. There were plenty of them in Yorkshire. This example had been built in the 1970s and as such was light and airy, yet showing the wear and tear to be expected after fifty years of daily bruising from around three hundred teenagers.

Bethany glanced sideways at Luke who was looking ahead as though in a trance. 'You all right?' she asked.

'Mmm?'

'Your neck's gone red.'

'My neck's always red,' muttered Luke. His palms were sweating. He'd left off the tie today but still wore thick corduroy trousers and a tweed jacket that, cut into handy-sized squares, could have kept Bethany in scouring pads for the rest of her life.

'Take off your jacket.'

'I can't. Not here. Not now.'

Their discussion was interrupted, first, by the ringing of an electric bell, which caused them temporarily to leave their seats, then by the opening of the door on their left.

'Mr and Mrs Gabriel? Come in, please.'

Seated in front of the headmaster, Bethany explained the reason for their visit. She kept glancing at Luke for support, but he seemed miles away, as if he wished he could be up on the moor with a flock of unruly sheep, rather than down in the valley with a flock of unruly children who were noisily flooding past the door of the head's office on their way to another classroom. The racket was such that, on occasion, Bethany had to raise her voice rather more than she would have liked. It made her sound angry, she thought, rather than considered.

The head listened patiently. James Addison was a mild-mannered man in his forties with a shock of dark hair and the beleaguered air of a juggler who was only just managing to keep all his plates spinning on a series of wobbly sticks, fearful that at any moment one might crash to the ground and shatter. As a result, Bethany felt as though she were adding even more to his load, to the extent that she considered abandoning the whole idea and their son to his fate. But no: she must do what they had agreed they would do and ask if Adam might finish his studies in a couple of months' time.

The worried expression on the face of the headmaster did not bode well. He repeatedly looked down at his desk and ran his hands through his thinning hair, as though in supplication, or else hoping that some shaft of divine inspiration might lift this heavy burden from his shoulders. As Bethany went on, feeling she had to justify their request more than amply, he slumped lower and lower until, having run out of further reasons (or were they just excuses for her son's lack of academic ability?), she sat back in her chair, silent.

The headmaster looked up, aware that the noise both outside and inside his office had abated. His facial muscles relaxed. He gave a weak smile. 'Well, if you're sure?' It was as if he was relieved that his workload would be relieved by one three-hundredth.

Pricked by guilt at having let his wife bear the burden of responsibility, a hitherto silent Luke stepped up to the plate. 'We are. We've thought about it a lot and we think it's the best thing for the lad. He's quite determined that he wants to farm and there are other reasons why . . .' Luke did not want to elaborate on more grounds for Adam's unhappiness at school, lest he be thought an over-protective father whose son was unable to stand up for himself. He was most certainly not in the former camp and his son would never forgive him if he implied the latter.

The headmaster offered what he hoped would be an olive branch. 'We are having one or two problems at the moment, and I think that Adam is one of the pupils who is feeling the consequences more than most. I hesitate to use the word "bullying", but I would assure you, Mr and Mrs Gabriel, that we will not condone or tolerate over-assertiveness or unwarranted aggression.'

Neither Bethany nor Luke felt able or willing to join in this line of conversation, not least because 'over-assertiveness' and 'unwarranted aggression' seemed to make light of what they knew was partly responsible for Adam's keenness to leave school. If Adam were to be allowed to take up an apprenticeship on the farm, all that would be behind him – and his family. It seemed churlish – unwise, even – to exacerbate matters by drawing things out at this late stage.

'No,' was as much as Luke was prepared to offer.

For a few moments all three were silent. Then Luke said, 'Well, if it's all settled,' and began to rise from his chair.

'There is one thing,' interjected the head.

Neither Luke nor Bethany spoke. They were fearful of this late intervention, even though Mr Addison appeared to have agreed to their request. What caveats was he about to put in place? Perhaps they should not have expected things to go quite so smoothly.

'Would it be possible to borrow a couple of lambs for our May bank-holiday celebration?'

Towards the end of the lunch break Adam was called to the headmaster's office. Not having seen his parents since they had left that morning, he was unsure of the outcome of their meeting. His heart beat loudly in his chest as he sat in the corridor on one of the chairs they had occupied, waiting for the green-painted door to open.

What if the headmaster had refused their request? Weak he might be, but Adam knew all too well that weak people often used stubbornness and intransigence as a form of defence.

A gaggle of half a dozen youths came down the corridor, talking loudly and jostling one another as they passed. A voice he recognised came from among them and Jakey Learoyd lurched forward threateningly.

'What yer done, Weirdo? In trouble are yer?' He grinned and turned to his acolytes. 'The Angel's fallen off his cloud! Got 'imself into bother.'

Adam did not rise to the bait. Instead he remained seated, gazing fixedly ahead, as Jakey kicked at the legs of the chair to unsettle him. Still he made no response.

Jakey continued as his classmates watched and sniggered. Adam felt the colour rising in his cheeks. The kicking became progressively more forceful, accompanied by mocking laughter from the pack of youths. After one particularly hefty kick, which threatened to unseat Adam, he leapt to his feet and thrust his face towards that of his tormentor. It was a big mistake. Jakey Learoyd launched his head at Adam's face and sent him reeling backwards, blood pouring from his nose.

'Try making that one better, Weirdo!' spat the youth.

At that precise moment the door of the headmaster's office opened, but with the practised speed of the accomplished combatant, Jakey Learoyd slipped into the centre of his cohorts and the entire group scuttled off, leaving their victim to manage the copious stream of blood as best he could and the headmaster gazing powerlessly after them.

'Come in,' he said, resignation in his voice.

Adam could barely see through watering eyes as the headmaster pushed a box of tissues towards him.

'Are you all right?' It was a pathetic comment from a man whom Adam had come heartily to dislike. If the head had been an uncompromising disciplinarian, he might have commanded respect as well as fear and loathing. As it was, his inability to maintain order, or to intervene when it most mattered, played into the hands of any group of bullies who cared to flout the rules.

James Addison was clearly uncomfortable, but adopted one of the most frequently used tactics in his modest armoury, that of ignoring what was going on around him in the hope that by so doing it would disappear. 'Your parents came to see me this morning . . .'

Adam nodded, as yet unsure of his ability to speak clearly since the nosebleed had yet to abate and the wad of tissues would make clarity of speech difficult, if not impossible. He could do nothing but listen and endeavour to staunch the flow.

At least the message was positive, even if the attitude of the man who delivered it lacked conviction. Realising that circumstances had conspired to preclude any contribution from Adam, the headmaster explained in his soft monotone that Adam might leave school at the end of term and that he wished him well. His message delivered, he got to his feet and moved to the door, opening it to allow his unfortunate pupil an unimpeded exit.

Six weeks later, Adam's schooldays came to an end and he was free. Any misgivings he might have had were assuaged by the words of Brother Wilfrid: 'Follow your bliss.' And bliss it most definitely was: to be free to live among the rolling Dales, among valleys and streams, to care for a flock of sheep and to face the future with a song in his heart and a crook in his hand. Some folk would laugh at the simplicity. What kind of ambition was that? What about travel? University? What about meeting people? What about girls? The first three were easily put from his mind, and when it came to the last two, well, there was plenty of time for that. Wasn't there?

14

THE GOOD SHEPHERD

Happiness depends on being free,
and freedom depends on being courageous.

Thucydides, *History of the Peloponnesian
War*, *c.*400 BC

Although Fred Pennock, the postman, visited Langstroth Farmhouse on his daily rounds, it was not every day that his services were needed. When he did turn up it would usually be to deliver some DEFRA missive with innumerable forms to be filled in, or a brochure that Luke had requested, or the usual bills and unsolicited circulars. What was rare was for him to deliver personal letters. Nobody wrote them any more, at least not to Bethany, to whom this handwritten envelope was addressed.

She was on her own when Fred arrived. 'Nice one for you, missus,' he said, as he strode from his red van and handed over a bundle of circulars held together with a pink elastic band. 'It's on the top.'

'Cup of tea, Fred?' asked Bethany, hoping that the postman would refuse since she had enough to be getting on with in advance of the mammoth shearing operation, now looming large in their lives.

'Not today, thanks. Too many calls. But thanks all the same.' And he was off. An untypically short visit for a man who liked to chew the fat about all and sundry and the various goings-on – imagined and actual – in the dale. As his van rumbled off down the track, Bethany slipped the letter from the bundle and turned it over, seeking some kind of clue as to the sender as she walked back into the house.

She glanced at the clock. At least she had a few minutes to make herself a cup of tea, and the brief respite from chores would eat up less time than would have been devoted to Fred and his 'Tales of the Dales'.

She boiled the kettle, put a teabag into a mug and sat at the table to read the letter. The rather nice envelope was, as Fred had indicated, addressed to her alone. Bethany took a kitchen knife and slid it neatly under the flap, withdrawing a single sheet of writing paper of comparable quality. There was no address at the top and, having looked again at the front of the envelope, no discernible postmark to indicate when the letter had been posted, or where.

She turned over the sheet of paper to look at the signature. It comprised a single initial. She turned it back and began to read the small, neatly formed handwriting.

My dear Bethany,

Feelings of guilt overwhelm me, not least because having enjoyed your generosity and hospitality for numerous years I have not, hitherto, ever written to say 'thank you'. I do so now in the hope of making some kind of reparation for my previous lack of good manners – implied but not intentional. You are always so welcoming and so accommodating and send me off with a spring in my step and renewed energy for the fray.

This time, in particular, I had the great good fortune to speak with your amazing son. It has been such a delight to watch him grow into a young man with his own mind and his own talents, and it is this which has spurred me into writing to you as his mother.

I can imagine that there are worries concerned with Adam's future because of his particular nature and his undeniable gift. Do not be troubled. Be grateful. He is, above all things, a gentle soul. Spirited, yes – thank the Lord – but at heart he is infused with a rare gentleness.

Gentleness rarely impresses those who encounter it. It is all too often perceived as weakness, feebleness or a lack of backbone. This may well be the case with some mortals who are regarded as being 'gentle': maiden aunts are a case in point – the ones who are not fero-cious. But true gentleness, born of a deeper well of feeling than mere apathy, is a facility to be respected in those who are possessed of it and who use it not to gain personal advantage but to better assimilate themselves into their surroundings, to make a difference by way of empathy and observation. In such circumstances it is also a powerful ally in dealing with animals, and people.

True gentleness is devoid of guile. It has its own laws of tolerance and reasoning, laws that may be subconscious but which are cherished and, though threatened, are tempered by fairness and justice. When it is a deep-seated part of a person's character, gentleness remains at the core of their being and governs their every action, until it is disturbed or abused. Then it can be replaced by uncontrollable anger or a degree of impetuosity that may put the possessor at great personal risk. Such occurrences are rare and, in most instances, frightening – for both the recipient and the perpetrator. But rest assured, I am quite certain that Adam will survive the travails of life, which he is sure to encounter on the way.

Oh dear. This letter was meant not only to thank but to reassure the mother of a gifted child, rather than to alarm her. That it should not do. I am sure I have not told you anything you do not know, but I wanted you to understand that the concerns you spoke of in terms of Adam leaving school and working on the farm will, one day, be laid to rest when you come to terms with his unique talent. In the meantime, thank you again for your company, your hospitality and your ability to reassure this lone traveller that in a world that is frequently portrayed as being evil and soulless there is goodness to be found everywhere by those who seek it.

I remain, I hope, your friend

W

Adam and his father were in Skipton, shopping for extra hurdles for penning the sheep in, along with cordless clippers. Luke had decided it was time the old cable-powered versions were pensioned off. The shearing season was almost upon them. Adam and his dad, along with Jack, who could still shear a sheep in three minutes (Luke could do the job in two and Adam, to his father's chagrin, in slightly less), would soon be bracing themselves for the annual ritual that saw the flock brought down from the hills and into the open barn where the mammoth operation would take place.

Bethany would leave this task to the men – she could certainly shear a sheep, but someone had to keep the workforce supplied with food and drink during the shearing season. She was happy to take on that role and leave the heavy work to her husband and son, with much unsolicited advice and only moderate assistance from Jack Knaggs. Not that they would be alone. They would be helped by a couple of strapping itinerant sheep shearers from New Zealand, who spent their summer in the Yorkshire Dales, going from farm to farm, relieving the flocks of their fleeces and the farmers of their funds.

Last year the sale of the wool had barely covered half the cost of the shearing, but from Luke's point of view, it made sense to invest in help at this time of year rather than at any other. His back was not getting any younger, and the company they enjoyed for the best part of a week would speed up the operation and keep them entertained.

But that would be next week. For now they needed to make sure all was ready for the complex and time-consuming operation so that the sheep could be marshalled, contained and shorn efficiently before being returned to the fellside to graze until they were taken to market in a couple of months' time. It was a tense time of year, but when was it not for a shepherd, dependent on the weather and the good nature of the workforce?

After the unseasonably warm weather of May, flaming June had, as yet, to prove itself worthy of the name. But the forecast was good, the weather set to improve, and the rain-washed streets of Skipton – such a contrast to the clarity of the swollen moorland becks – would hopefully be the last evidence they would see of torrential downpours this month.

The hurdles were loaded onto the trailer, the new trimmers strapped onto the middle seat of the Land Rover, as Adam and Luke began the drive back to Langstrothdale. Nip sat on Adam's knee, eager to watch what was going on around them. They drove across the top of Skipton High Street, past the dripping market-stall awnings, and by the church of Holy Trinity they pulled up at the temporary traffic lights. Nip began to bark.

He was looking out of the side window. Adam followed his gaze. There was some kind of skirmish on the pavement. Three youths in grey hoodies were setting about another teenager submerged in their midst. A young woman with a toddler backed away from them, panic on her face. An old man in a flat cap and lovat-green Puffa jacket steered his wife and her shopping trolley clear of the melee, fearful for their own safety. It was then that Adam recognised the figure being assaulted by boot and fist. It was Jakey Learoyd.

Adam opened the door and leapt from the Land Rover. He ran towards the group with Nip at his heels and tore at the clothing of the nearest youth, pulling him away. Nip barked wildly. Someone shouted. A fist caught him on the side of the head. He dodged a second punch and elbowed aside the other two youths before bending over Jakey who was clutching his side. His face was contorted with agony. Ready to shield himself from the blows about to rain down on him, Adam looked up in time to see the three youths scattering in different directions, their tightly tied hoodies still shielding their faces from view.

He turned back to the prone form of Jakey who was lying in the foetal position and emitting deep groans. His eyes were closed.

At first Adam did not notice the bleeding, not until the pool of blood extended beyond the line of Jakey's limp body. Nip had stopped barking now and was sitting at the kerbside, whining.

The whole occurrence had lasted seconds. Luke leapt out of the Land Rover and crouched beside Adam. 'Are you all right?'

Adam nodded, the wind temporarily knocked from him. Then he said, 'I don't think he is. Can you call an ambulance?'

'On its way,' said the old man, who had observed from a safe distance and was now lowering his mobile phone from his ear. 'And the police.'

The pool of blood was growing ever larger. 'We'd better get him into the recovery position,' instructed Luke. 'At least he's still breathing.'

They turned Jakey onto his side, and the cause of the bleeding became apparent – a knife wound in his side, just above his waist. It was pumping blood. Adam clamped his hand onto it in an effort to staunch the flow, and experienced a flashback of his own bleeding nose at the hands of Jakey six weeks earlier.

Father and son knelt there in silence for what seemed like an age, with bodies milling around them, and others passing without giving them a second glance.

'Well done, lad,' said the old man, whose wife – the one with the shopping trolley – had been standing as still as a waxwork as the events unfolded. She was clearly in shock.

From the other end of the high street they heard the wail of the siren. Closed to traffic on market day it might be, but the ambulance parted the stall-holders and shoppers in its path as it wove steadily towards them.

Jakey opened his eyes and gazed directly at Adam. 'You!' he said, before closing them again. His head fell to one side. All the while Adam kept his hand clamped to Jakey's wound.

Luke stood silently by, squeezing his son's shoulder by way of support.

The small crowd parted as two paramedics – a man and a woman – approached. 'All right, son. We'll take over now,' said the man. He was about forty, fresh-faced, keen to show that the cavalry had arrived and that there would be no further cause for alarm.

Adam looked up, but kept his hand on the wound as he did so. 'He's been stabbed.'

'Was it you? Come on, you can tell me. Some kind of argument?'

Neither Adam nor Luke needed to answer. 'Don't be bloody daft,' said the old man. 'It were three youths. They've buggered off now. This lad 'ere laid into 'em and they fled. 'E's a bloody 'ero 'e is. Would he be 'anging around if 'e'd done it 'imself?'

'All right, all right,' said the female, glancing at her colleague with a look that spoke volumes. She was older, clearly more experienced and less concerned about rank or dignity. 'Let's have a look at him.' She squatted and took in the pool of blood that had finally stopped widening. She noticed Adam's hand clamped to Jakey's side and said softly, 'All right, love, you can let go now.' She was reaching into a bag for sterile wadding to help staunch the flow, though it soon became clear that Adam's intervention had been astonishingly effective.

The wound had ceased to bleed. As Adam took away his hand he could feel the warm, sticky blood gluing his fingers together.

'Do you know him?' asked the woman.

'Yes. I was at school with him. His name's Jakey Learoyd.'

'Well, he's lucky to have you as a mate. You've probably saved his life.'

Adam glanced at his father who raised his eyes heavenward.

'Jakey! Can you hear me, Jakey? Come on, love.' The paramedic tapped gently on the side of Jakey's face. 'Come on now, stay with us . . . We'll get you off to hospital and sort you out. You're going to be all right . . . Come on now . . .'

Her companion eased his way through the crowd with a stretcher. Within minutes Jakey, an oxygen mask strapped to his face, had been lifted onto it and hoisted into the back of the ambulance as two policemen approached. One began to disperse the crowd: 'Come along, ladies and gents, nothing to see now.'

The other took out a radio and muttered some brief message into it, then asked Adam and Luke, 'So you saw what went on, then?'

The old man – whose wife still appeared to be frozen in time – was now feeling an integral part of the proceedings. 'I did. Three youths set upon the lad and this one came to 'elp 'im.'

The policeman turned to Adam. 'So you were involved, were you?'

Before either Adam or the aged onlooker could respond, Luke cut in, 'We were parked at the traffic lights. My lad saw the disturbance and jumped out to help. The three lads who'd attacked him . . . Jakey . . .' Luke could hardly bear to utter his name '. . . ran off and my lad, Adam, saw he was wounded. We put him in the recovery position while this chap here called the ambulance. Adam tried to stop the bleeding – that's why he's covered in blood.'

Until that moment it had not occurred to Adam that his appearance might indicate he had been the instigator of the attack.

'Are there witnesses?' asked the officer.

'Too bloody right there are,' said the old man. 'Me and my

missus for one. I mean, two.' He glanced at his wife, noticed her expression and added, 'She'll come to in a minute. And there's that lady with the toddler. She saw what went on as well.'

The policeman turned to the young mother. 'Is that right?'

'Aye, it is. He were brilliant, that lad. I wish I 'ad 'im for a 'usband rather than the useless article I 'ave at 'ome.'

He turned back to Adam and Luke. 'Right. Well, you'd better get yourselves off home and clean up. I'll just take some details so we can get you to drop by and make a statement later. Is that all right?' There was a note of concern in his voice now. He could see that the colour had drained from Adam's cheeks. He looked done in. Clearly in shock.

Adam nodded.

The female paramedic closed the ambulance's doors, the blue lights began to flash and its engine started. The officious colleague was clearly at the wheel, having been put firmly in his place, and the woman touched the police officer on the shoulder. 'Thank God for folk who know what to do,' she said, indicating Adam. 'Yon lad in there' – she nodded towards the ambulance – 'is hanging on. It's touch and go. If *this* lad hadn't done what he did, then *that* lad would have bled to death. Missed his vital organs by an inch, I shouldn't wonder. At least, I hope it has. Thank God for miracles, I say. And for . . . What did you say your name was?'

'Adam Gabriel.'

'Well, Adam Gabriel, you've just lived up to your name. Next time I need a guardian angel I'll give you a call. All right?'

Adam nodded and smiled weakly as the ambulance took off at speed towards the Airedale Infirmary.

The most admiring of glances came from Nip, who was sitting quietly at the kerbside, gazing adoringly at his master.

15

OLD JACK

Therefore my age is as a lusty winter,
Frosty but kindly.

William Shakespeare, *As You Like It*, Act II, Scene iii,
1599

'They tell me tha'll get a certificate,' muttered Jack Knaggs, as he and Adam were fastening together the new hurdles to direct the sheep into the holding pen.

Adam did not reply. The whole thing had become embarrassing and he just wanted to forget it and get on with his life. He avoided meeting Jack's eye as they linked the galvanised barriers together.

The old man was not to be deterred. 'Anyway, what was tha thinkin'? Trying to save the life of yon 'ooligan? Tha could 'ave got thissen killed.'

'Well, I didn't, did I?'

'No thanks to 'im. Daft bugger.'

Adam capitulated, explaining it to himself as much as to Jack. 'It was just something I did. Just something anyone would have done. I didn't really stop to think. I just saw someone being attacked and dived in to break it up. That's all. You'd have done the same yourself.'

Jack stopped what he was doing and laughed. 'Me? At my age? Don't be daft!'

'Well, if you'd been younger.'

'Nah. Steer well clear of trouble, that's my motto. Always 'as been. But you, you're drawn to it. I've seen it afore. Any time there's a bit o' bother, someone in difficulty, you're in. You just can't stop yourself.'

Adam shrugged. He hadn't really got an answer to that.

Jack's tone became placatory. 'Come on. Time for a cup o' tea.'

They parked themselves on a low wall of straw bales under cover of the open-ended barn, which in a few days would be a bleating hive of activity as the sheep were upended, relieved of their wool and turned out onto the fellside once more to face the summer five or ten pounds lighter.

Adam sipped his coffee from a black-and-white-striped mug with 'Happy Days' written on the side. Jack held a cracked pint pot that had once been white and whose inside was the colour of the dark sweet tea it now held, tipped in from a Thermos flask of dubious vintage that he kept in the small greasy tartan holdall that held his daily necessities – fags, flask, pint pot and *Daily Express*. Adam studied him as he drank his restorative brew. His hands were horny and calloused, the fingers like gnarled claws. His face was composed of a complex symphony of folds and creases through which grey whiskers erupted, and his cap was tilted over one eye, like a cockerel with an overlong comb. He gave the impression of being a man of few sensitivities and sensibilities, but occasional comments would give the lie to that. He was an astute old bird, a contradiction in many ways. He would frequently express an extreme opinion but, nevertheless, seemed to keep many of his thoughts to himself.

It was as though his often strident pronouncements were designed to create a reaction that would reveal the inner feelings of those to whom he expressed them. He was, like Adam, something of a loner, but cut from a different kind of cloth. Jack had been married, but his wife – a plump and comforting soul – had died young, and as long as Adam had known him he had lived on his own down in the village.

As Adam grew up the two of them had developed a mutual respect, and now that he was a capable sixteen-year-old, Jack had come to rely on him when certain tasks were simply too strenuous: the lad would cover for him without saying a word to his father. That counted for a lot in Jack's eyes – a youth who could keep his counsel and was not afraid of hard work on his own account. He respected it, but found the lad as hard to fathom as a bottomless well.

'Is he all reet, young Learoyd?' asked Jack. 'Will he live?'

'Apparently. The knife missed his liver and kidneys by an inch. So they say, anyway.'

'He didn't deserve to be so lucky.'

'Oh, he's not that bad. Just had a rough upbringing, that's all.'

Jack bridled at what he perceived as misplaced generosity of spirit. 'Rough upbringing? 'Is dad's an electrician. They've got enough money to live in a decent 'ouse. All reet so 'is mum and dad don't get on that well but . . .'

Adam fixed him with a steely gaze, under which Jack was stunned into silence. 'His mum left home last year. His dad's working all hours and Jakey's left on his own most of the time. With that and a bunch of mates who are a bad influence, what can you expect?'

'Ah, well . . .' There seemed no suitable defence, so Jack resorted to his original form of attack. 'I still think tha shouldn't

'ave got involved. It'll be the death of thee if tha's not careful.'
He took a gulp of tea and changed the subject. 'Any news of
yon monk, then?'

'Brother Wilfrid? No. I don't suppose we shall see him for
another year. You know how it is. He always turns up in May
– just after lambing – stays for a night and then goes on his
way.'

'Mmm.' Jack looked pensive. 'Funny bugger.'

'You think?'

'What's a monk doin' trampin' the Dales and singin' at the
top of 'is voice? Got a screw loose, if you ask me.'

Adam smiled. 'Just individual. He probably needs a break
from being cooped up in the monastery.'

Jack regarded him cynically. 'What monastery? Where does
'e come from? Nobody knows. I don't think there *is* a monastery. I reckon 'e's a tramp who nicked a monk's . . . What do
you call it?'

'Habit?'

'Aye. An' 'e goes around scroungin' bed and board from all
an' sundry.' He paused, then added as an afterthought, 'I used
to 'ave an auntie like that.'

'An auntie dressed like a monk?'

'No, yer daft bugger. An auntie who'd come for tea and stay
for weeks on end.'

'He only stays one night.'

'For now.'

Adam frowned. 'You've got a downer on everybody today,
haven't you?'

'Just sayin'.' And having delivered his valediction he drained
his pint pot, swirled a fistful of straw around its inside and
slipped it back into the tartan holdall beside him.

'What if he really is a monk?' asked Adam. He had never thought to question Brother Wilfrid's credentials. He acted like a monk, he dressed like a monk, and he was kind and thoughtful.

'Where from?'

Adam shrugged. 'Rievaulx? Ampleforth?'

'There 'aven't been monks at Rievaulx since 'Enry the Eighth saw 'em off. An' they've never 'eard of 'im at Ampleforth.'

'Sorry?'

'Edgar Bundy. 'Im what I 'as a pint with on a Friday. 'As a sister over at Coxwold. She says there is no Brother Wilfrid at Ampleforth.'

Adam became defensive. 'Maybe he uses a different name there. Anyway, he never said he came from Ampleforth and whenever we mention the place he shakes his head.'

'Maybe 'e was hexcommunicated . . . or whatever it is they do to monks what does things they shouldn't.'

'Are you saying he did something he shouldn't?'

Jack shrugged. 'I'm not sayin' anything. I'm just wonderin'.'

Adam looked irritated. 'He's been very nice to me, anyway.'

Jack eyed his companion warily. ''Ow nice?'

There was a note of anger in Adam's voice now. 'He's never been inappropriate . . . not in any way. Just kind and under-standing. He talked to me about my . . . well . . . my . . .'

Jack let Adam struggle for a few moments before coming to his aid.

'Your gift? That's what they call it, in't it? A gift.'

'Do they?'

'An' what did 'e say?'

'That it was as much a curse as a blessing.'

Jack looked thoughtful. 'Well, 'e's not wrong there, is 'e?' Then, seeing he was not going to get a response, added, 'I've oft thought that. When yer've done summat for one o' them sheep. Or the dog. An' it seems as it works wi' folk, too.'

Adam realised his own assumption that no one had noticed his ability to heal animals and, on occasion, people had clearly been nothing more than wishful thinking.

They sat mute for a few minutes, only the distant bleating of sheep and lambs breaking the silence. Then Jack said, 'Does it worry you? The fact you can do it, I mean?'

Adam nodded but didn't speak – just gazed off into the distance.

Jack patted his knee. 'You shouldn't. You should be grateful. And so should yon Learoyd lad.'

'Do *you* think it's a gift, then?'

'Too bloody right I do.'

Adam looked confused. 'But you don't believe in . . . well . . .'

'Things I don't understand? I go to church, don't I? An' I don't understand that. Just cos I don't understand summat dun't mean I can't believe in it. If that were the case, yon tractor would never move. Internal combustion engine? A mystery. But I see that tractor pullin' a trailer an' I 'ave to believe in it. Same wi' your gift. Oh, there'll be folks who think it's made up, who don't think it's real. But I've seen it for meself. It were tough at first. I tried to work out what were be'ind it. But I soon give over.'

He saw Adam's face, which bore an expression of surprise. 'Oh, I know tha thinks as I've no imagination. But I've worked in't Dales all me life and I know there's magic up 'ere. Every spring the magic of lambs. Every summer the magic of nature. I'm not so thick as to think I know everything. Dost tha know what I mean?'

Adam nodded and smiled. 'Thanks, Jack.'

'Anyway, it's time you 'ad a bit o' company. Got yourself a girlfriend.'

Adam coloured.

'Oh, I know you're only young, but you're stuck up 'ere wi' your mum an' dad. 'S not natural. You need folk your own age.' He reached into his jacket pocket and pulled out a crumpled piece of paper. 'Here y'are.'

Adam took it and unfolded it. It bore a telephone number.

'Young Farmers' Club,' explained Jack. 'That's the number of the secretary. They meet every Monday night in Appletreewick. Worth lookin' in. Take you out of yourself. And there's some nice young lads and lasses there.' He winked. 'Anyway, up to you.' Jack forced his weary body upright. 'Come on, then. We'd best be gettin' on or your dad'll think we're both skivin'.' And with that he made for the entrance to the barn, turning to deliver his final remark: 'Just be careful who you admit it to, this gift. There's some who'll make your life a misery on account of it. Just like young Learoyd.'

Whistling softly under his breath he ambled out into the farmyard, flicking aside with his boot a chicken that crossed his path. 'Gerrout of it, yer daft bugger,' he remarked, as he disappeared from view.

Adam sighed heavily. He'd felt quite bright about life when he had got up. Now Jack had disturbed his equilibrium. Perhaps it was a good thing. Perhaps he should be more questioning, more adventurous, get out a bit more. The very thought gave rise to butterflies in his stomach. He shook his head as though to order his thoughts. Maybe he'd ring the number. He could always find a way out if he needed to, if the people he met were not like him. But who was like him? Introspection was getting him nowhere, and perhaps that was part of his problem.

He was his own man now. He had left school. He was doing the job he loved. Why could he not just leave it at that, rather than forcing himself to broaden his horizons? And yet something inside him told him he must do so, at least in a small way. And what harm could it do, going to the Young Farmers' Club? Hardly as daring as a night out clubbing in Leeds or Bradford or York. The very thought of that made him shudder.

Jack was right. He'd call the number next week, when shearing was over and done. His reverie was interrupted by Jack's voice. 'Is tha comin' out 'ere or what? If tha stays in there any longer tha'll end up bein' sheared.'

16

THE BREATH OF FRESH AIR

We cannot bring ourselves to believe it possible that a
foreigner should in any respect be wiser than ourselves.
If any such point out to us our follies, we at once claim
those follies as the special evidences of our wisdom.

Anthony Trollope, *Orley Farm*, 1862

It felt like the calm before the storm. Adam was up early. Luke
and Bethany rose early, too, but Adam was dressed and outdoors
with his dog before the rising sun had breasted the top of the
fell. He wanted a few minutes to himself, to breathe in the cool
morning air, to savour the sharp tang of dew on heather and
grass, to listen to the echoing bleats of the flock as they greeted
one another at the dawning of another day.

The air was unusually still. Soon the youthful breeze would
send a gently shivering wave over the top of the cotton grass in
the boggy hollow that divided the hills, but for now all was
quiet. Halfway up the fellside Adam sat on a rock, Nip at his
feet, staring intently at his master's eyes, waiting for the inevitable
command. When it came it was nothing more than a nod, but

it was all the dog needed to spur it into action. Cutting a wide arc to the right of the sloping ground, Nip began the task of rounding up the flock and sweeping it down the hillside towards the farm. Before long the pastoral scene of calmly grazing ewes was transformed into a frenzied maelstrom of skittering live-stock, soon to be accompanied by the buzz of shears and the shouts of the team as they tackled their annual task.

The distant hum of an engine grew louder as the black pick-up truck hove into view. Noah was back. He had been coming to Langstrothdale for three years on his annual working holiday. The New Zealand winter coincided with the English summer, which was handy, since it meant – sun-worshipper that he was – Noah could avoid the worst of the weather in both countries. Well, at least that was the theory. He had come to realise that the weather in the Yorkshire Dales could deliver all four seasons in a day, never mind a week, but he loved the rolling hills and rocky crags, which reminded him of home, while Luke, Bethany and Adam had become like a second family to him, for one week in the year at any rate. He was Central Casting's idea of a Kiwi sheep-shearer – tall, rugged, dark-haired and – for most of the time – grinning from ear to ear. It seemed that nothing fazed him and he approached the task of shearing with a relish that left even the youthful Adam breathless. Bent over a plump ewe in his black singlet, shorts and hefty boots, he would have it trimmed of its fleece in under two minutes, then had a swig of water and called for the next candidate.

He made Adam laugh with his devil-may-care attitude, and down in the Blue Bell Inn of an evening, where he went to slake his thirst, his rippling brown muscles would set the Kettlewell ladies' hearts aflutter.

Noah always turned up with a mate – another itinerant New Zealand sheep-shearer – a different one each time, someone to whom he was showing the ropes, who would then go off and do his own thing in subsequent years. These mates varied in their shearing skills and their sociability but this year Noah turned up, for the first time, with a girl.

'Luke, Bethany, Adam, I'd like to introduce you to my sister, Isla.' As the two of them climbed down from their hired Mitsubishi Barbarian (which Bethany later remarked she thought was an appropriate vehicle, bearing in mind Noah's rugged charms), Adam was rendered speechless at the sight of the girl, who greeted them warmly, with a smile every bit as radiant as her brother's.

'Hello,' she said softly, in a tone that was the direct opposite of her strident sibling's. She was petite, with a bob of shining dark hair, far too delicate and fine-boned to be taken for a sheep-shearer.

'Don't be fooled,' instructed Noah, as Isla shook hands, first with Bethany, then Luke and, finally, Adam, meeting his gaze with a direct stare from clear green eyes. 'She might be slight but she can scare the pants off the toughest tup.'

Adam and Isla blushed simultaneously at the unintentional double-entendre, and Noah, realising the likely interpretation of his observation, laughed and said, 'Sorry, but you get my drift?'

Luke smiled. 'We get your drift.'

'Right,' said Bethany. 'Let's get you both settled into your rooms and give you some breakfast before we get started.'

It was a feeling Adam could not recall having experienced before. He had been in the company of girls at school, had even become friendly with one or two, but he had never felt such an instant attraction to any of them. He tried to put it out of his mind as the four – Luke, Adam, Noah and Isla – knuckled down to the job of shearing, but he couldn't deny that it was difficult.

He would glimpse Isla out of the corner of his eye as she manoeuvred a reluctant ewe onto its rump and began to slice off the fleece. She had a deftness and grace that he found mesmerising. But he was brought up short when, thanks to a momentary lapse in concentration, he nicked a ewe with the shears, causing her to bleat loudly. His father shot him a critical glance that indicated he should keep his mind on his work.

He did not make the same mistake again. Instead, he confined his glances towards her to moments when one sheep was being released and another upended.

When they stopped for lunch, brought out to them by Bethany and arranged on a trestle table at one end of the barn, Adam thought it safest to sit at the opposite end of the table to Isla, away from the hawk-like eyes of Luke and Jack. The latter had tackled the odd ewe but spent most of the morning grumbling about this and that and finding more than a handful of excuses to stop work and fetch some supposedly vital piece of equipment from a distant part of the farm. Nobody begrudged him that indulgence – he had, in his life, shorn more sheep than any of them. He was entitled to a lighter load.

They lunched on home-made bread, freshly baked pork pies ferried up the dale from Stanforth's in Skipton (for which Noah had previously expressed a particular liking), pickled onions, pickled beetroot and a salad cobbled together from the early summer harvest, courtesy of Adam's vegetable patch. There was a bottle of beer apiece (only the one, mind) or lemonade for those who were underage or wanted to keep a clear head.

Towards the end of the meal, when Luke and Noah were deeply engaged in comparing notes about the relative merits of Swaledale and Herdwick ewes, Isla got up from her seat and came to sit next to Adam. He did his best not to look awkward, offering her a smile, which he hoped gave nothing away.

'Noah's told me all about you,' she said.

Adam wondered just what she meant by 'all'. 'Oh dear,' was all he could say.

Seeing his discomfort she offered, 'No! All good. Honestly!'

He relaxed a little. 'That's all right, then.'

Isla looked out from the barn and across towards Yockenthwaite Moor. 'It reminds me of home,' she said.

It was obviously an olive branch, a means of making conversation.

'A bit colder,' offered Adam.

'Depends on the time of year,' she countered. 'It can be pretty chilly back home when it wants.'

'What sort of sheep do you have?' asked Adam.

'Romneys mostly. And Texels . . . no Swaledales. I rather like the Swaledales. Good mothers, Noah says.' She smiled and glanced in the direction of Bethany. 'A bit like yours.'

'She's not bad,' agreed Adam. Then, feeling braver: 'So how long have you been shearing?'

'Oh, a couple of years. Not seriously at first. Just to show my brother that he wasn't the only one who could do it or earn a living from it. Then I sort of got to like it. And it gave me an excuse to travel. So here I am.'

She grinned, and his heart melted again, but he made sure that neither his words nor his expression betrayed the fact. 'Will you carry on?' he asked.

'Probably not. I don't see it as a life. I'm doing it to see a bit of the world. I'm only seventeen. Plenty of time to decide what to do yet.'

'So you won't be back again?' Adam heard himself say. He hoped there wasn't too much disappointment in his voice. He had only met her hours ago – what was he thinking?

'Who knows?' she said brightly. 'That's my plan, but plans change, don't they?'

It was as if she could read his mind.

That afternoon he worked hard to concentrate, endeavouring – in vain for the most part – to keep up with Noah. He was faster than his dad, and Isla, but Noah sheared like a machine, with a seemingly inexhaustible supply of energy. As the day wore on Adam got into his stride, and his emotions calmed a little. He contented himself with simply being in the same space as the girl from the other side of the world who awoke in him feelings he had not experienced before. However much he told himself that they had only just met, that he knew little or nothing about her, that although she was the same age as him, give or take a month, and in a few days' time she would disappear from his life, it suited him to let his imagination run wild. Eventually he hauled himself back into the here and now, the reality that would settle upon him by the end of the week.

He would force himself to be rational and matter-of-fact, he thought – and then she would glance across at him and smile, and his equilibrium would be rocked once more.

There were no two ways about it. Adam realised that, for the first time in his life, he was in love.

THE FOURTH ESTATE

Journalists say a thing that they know isn't true,
in the hope that if they keep on saying it long
enough it *will* be true.

Arnold Bennett, *The Title*, 1918

At least the weather had stayed fair for them, and it looked as though the shearing might be completed with record speed. This pleased Luke, knowing that the shorter the time Noah and Isla were with them, the less it would cost him. Adam, for the first time in his life, was hoping that the operation would go on longer. In vain he would glance heavenwards, hoping for dark clouds on the horizon that would bring rain to slow them down. The sooner they finished, the sooner Isla would disappear from his life.

Lying in bed at night, knowing she was just a few rooms away, filled him with a mixture of excitement and unease. But what could he do? He certainly couldn't express his feelings, not least because he didn't know exactly what they meant, except that when she was close by he felt an excitement quite different from that engendered by anything else in his life, a kind of nervous power. And he had known her just three days. It was ridiculous, he told himself. It made no difference. The feelings did not go away.

They would breakfast all together around the farmhouse table, a hearty Yorkshire breakfast of bacon, eggs, sausage, fried bread, fried tomato, baked beans and hot buttered toast, slathered with Bethany's home-made marmalade and strawberry jam. Fuel for the day ahead. Adam would sneak furtive looks at Isla as she feasted on toast alone, while her brother piled his plate high with the fried offerings, which he washed down with a mug of sweet black coffee before rising from the table and declaring, 'Right! Let's get them little ladies shorn!' Then he would march out of the house and across to the barn, leaving the rest of them to down what was left on their plates and in their mugs before they followed in his unceasingly energetic wake.

That evening – probably their last together, weather permitting – would be spent in the dining room of the King's Head where Luke would treat them all to a slap-up supper to celebrate a job well done, and the following day, having mopped up any strays, Noah and Isla would be on their way to . . . where? Oblivion as far as Adam could see. He was already beginning to slide into despondency.

'Come on, Adam!' his father encouraged, as his son dawdled over a final slice of toast. 'You feeling all right?'

'Yeah. I'm fine. Just a bit tired.' He smiled weakly to cover his growing melancholy.

'Not long to go now,' Luke added.

'No', was all Adam could manage in reply.

*

They had been shearing for a couple of hours when the tiny yellow car bumped its way up the track. It was not a vehicle any of them recognised, except old Jack, who muttered under his breath, 'Oh, bloody hell. What does she want?'

Bent double though he was over a particularly stroppy ewe, Luke glanced across at him. 'Who?'

'Yon woman from t' *Craven Courier*. Reporter. Always puttin' her nose in where it's not wanted. Like a bloody Jack Russell rattin'.'

Luke frowned, trying to imagine what on earth such a character could want with them.

The car stopped twenty yards from the barn and out stepped a forty-something redhead in a floral-print cotton dress and high-heeled shoes — not the sort of get-up frequently seen in this part of the dale, except, perhaps, in the King's Head of an evening.

'Hello!' she shouted across the farmyard in their direction, at a decibel level necessary to overcome the cacophony of bleating sheep. 'Can I come over?'

Luke let go of the freshly shorn ewe, which made a run for it, only to be deftly diverted by a side-swipe from Jack, who sent her careering off in the right direction to join the rest of the newly coiffed flock.

Without waiting for an answer the vision in floral print picked her way carefully across the yard, avoiding the liberal scattering of sheep droppings, her flailing arms acting like those of a tightrope walker balancing on a high wire.

'Belle Barclay, *Craven Courier*. Might I have a word?'

Luke took a few steps towards her.

'Not with you, Mr Gabriel. With your son.' She had stopped walking now and pointed towards Adam and Noah. 'Which one is he?'

Adam had been quenching his thirst from a bottle of water. He stepped forward. 'Me,' he said, wondering what on earth he could have done to incur the interest of the local paper. Then, almost at once, he realised the likely cause.

'Can we talk?' asked the reporter. 'About the fracas in Skipton High Street.'

'Fracas'. What a strange word to use, thought Adam.

At this point his father cut in, alerted by Jack's remark and protective of his son. 'I'm afraid we're a bit busy, as you can see,' he offered.

'It won't take long, only I've come all the way from Skipton.'

''Ardly the other side of the bloody world,' muttered Jack, under his breath.

'Hello, Mr Knaggs,' she responded tartly. Belle Barclay and Jack Knaggs clearly had history, though its origins and significance were lost in the mists of time and, therefore, on the present company.

'Can you be quick, then?' asked Luke, aware that the woman was intent on getting what she wanted, and to prevaricate would be to delay things even longer.

Adam walked over to where she stood, while Luke, Noah and Isla carried on with the job in hand, and Jack regarded the woman with a scowl most frequently reserved for the opponents of the local darts team after a whitewash.

Belle Barclay reached out her hand to shake Adam's but quickly withdrew it when she saw its state of cleanliness. 'Ah! Best not,' she murmured. 'Now then, I've just heard about the altercation in Skipton.'

'Altercation', thought Adam. A bit like 'fracas' but different. 'The fight, you mean?'

'Yes. I gather you were very brave.'

Adam shrugged. 'Just did my bit.'

'But there were knives . . .'

'Well, there was *a* knife but I didn't see that until . . . well, I never did see it, but then I saw he was bleeding.'

'So you didn't see the knife but you saw the youths who were attacking – what was his name?' She glanced at the notepad she had pulled from her designer shoulder-bag. 'Jakey Learoyd?'

'Yes.'

'So you've no idea who his assailants were? You didn't recognise them?'

'No. They were wearing hoodies so I couldn't really see their faces.'

'And you knew Jakey from school, is that right?'

'Yes.'

'Were you close friends?'

Luke glanced across, about to answer when Adam beat him to it. 'No. We weren't friends. I just knew him.'

'And you saved his life?'

'I just tried to stop the blood. I mean, I tried to stop him bleeding.'

Belle Barclay was warming to her subject. Her orange hair (clearly the product of L'Oréal rather than reality) was tied back in a ponytail, the better to emphasise her hawk-like features as she homed in on her prey. 'And you succeeded. Thanks to you, Jakey Learoyd will live. There's talk of a police commendation, which is why I'm here.'

Adam looked at the droppings-scattered ground and shifted from one foot to the other, in his case not to avoid treading in the rural confetti of sheep shit but as a sign of embarrassment and unease.

'Where did you learn your first aid?' she enquired.

Adam shrugged. 'I didn't. At least, it wasn't really first aid. I just wanted to stop the bleeding, so I put my hand over where the blood was coming from. I mean, we did put Jakey into the recovery position but . . .' There his explanation came to an end. There was little else to say.

'And you did all this before your father arrived?'

Anxious to avoid his father being accused of inaction or, at worst, disinterest, he countered with 'No. I managed to get out of the Land Rover first. Dad was driving. I broke up the fight and they ran away, but it was Dad who said we should get Jakey into the recovery position.'

'So your father was on the scene by then?'

'Yes. Very quickly. I mean it was all over in seconds . . .'

Belle Barclay smiled weakly. 'Of course. These things usually are. I've spoken to the paramedics. They were particularly impressed by your actions, and surprised that you managed to staunch the flow of blood from what was really quite a serious wound. They said it was . . .' She shuffled through her notebook again to find the appropriate page. 'Ah, here we are. "Quite astonishing and something we have never encountered before in all our time in the ambulance service."'

Adam looked around, as if praying for reinforcements. Luke read the situation and came over towards them.

'If that's all?' he said, matter-of-factly.

'Yes. Yes, of course. I just wanted to meet the man . . . well, the boy really . . . who had so bravely leapt into the fray.'

Luke nodded. 'Well, there you are, you have.'

'Indeed.' She made to leave and then, after the fashion of a certain American TV detective, turned back to face them. 'Just one more thing, Adam . . .'

'Yes?'

'Some people say you have a gift. It's not simply that you're good at first aid, but that you have the power to heal. Is that true?'

That evening, in the smart surroundings of the King's Head dining room, the sextet of freshly scrubbed sheep-shearers met for their celebratory meal. It was one of those rare occasions when Jack took off his cap to reveal a thick thatch of grey hair – mercifully free of Brylcreem on this occasion – and when Bethany put on make-up and what she called her 'out on the toot' clothes – smart tailored trousers and a pale pink cashmere sweater that Luke had bought her two Christmases ago. Summer it might be, but there were few evenings in this part of the world when a cashmere sweater was not welcome.

Adam had thought long and hard about what he would wear, not that he had much to choose from. He settled for a pair of chinos and a white T-shirt topped with an open pale blue shirt. He couldn't recall ever looking at himself in the mirror for quite so long before he emerged from his bedroom.

From that first meeting over lunch, when he had taken care to distance himself from Isla, he was now intent on sitting as close to her as possible. This might, after all, be the last time he would see her. Without too much difficulty, he managed to interpose himself between Noah and his sister as they walked through from the bar into the dining room and sat round a table laid ready for supper.

Isla was positively glowing. The sunny weather had burnished her cheeks, and her fresh-washed hair shone like the flanks of a thoroughbred.

As they settled themselves at the table she gave Adam the

warmest of smiles and he fought hard to avoid blushing. Best to start up a conversation to take his mind off it.

'How do you think it went?' he asked.

'Well, I think. We were glad of the good weather. There's nothing worse than having to wait for sodden sheep to dry out. It takes bloody ages.'

'Yes. And they smell like . . . well, wet sheep!'

He was conscious of the pathetic nature of his response. He wished he was better at this sort of thing but consoled himself that he had had little practice. Well, in reality, no practice at all. He wished now that he had the nerve – if not the character – of a Jakey Learoyd. Jakey and his kind never seemed to lack confidence where girls were concerned.

Isla was polite enough to laugh. 'Does it happen often up here? Waiting for them to dry out?'

'Most years, yes. We sometimes have to keep them under cover for a day before they're ready. You should hear the racket in the barn.'

'I can imagine. We were lucky, then?'

Adam nodded and opened his mouth to speak.

Their conversation was interrupted by Luke who cleared his throat, raised his pint of Wharfedale Blonde and said, 'Can I just say a big thank you to Isla and Noah for getting the job done in record time? We were helped by the weather, of course, but thanks to good organisation' – this comment was directed towards Jack, who nodded curtly in thanks for the recognition – 'and a following wind, we can heave a sigh of relief and send them on their way.' His neck redder than ever from the ordeal of addressing a meeting even of this diminutive size, he lifted his glass higher to agreeable murmurs from the assembled company. After that Noah turned to talk to Bethany, and Luke to listen to Jack, who was already regaling him with previous shearing experiences, all of which would no doubt have been filled with incomparable difficulties and disasters.

Isla picked up their conversation. 'I was listening to that lady from the local paper.'

Adam feared the worst. 'Oh,' he said.

'Is it true? Do you have a gift for healing?'

He was surprised at the way she came straight out with it, but he should have realised by now that Isla and her brother were blessed with a refreshing brand of Antipodean directness, which should not be misconstrued as a lack of sensitivity.

'It's not something I really think about' – 'or talk about,' he wanted to add, but felt that to do so might make him sound stand-offish, and that was the last thing he wanted.

Sensing his discomfort Isla lowered her voice and said, 'If you have, then I'm lost in wonder and admiration.'

Now Adam really did redden.

'Oh, I'm sorry,' she offered. 'I didn't mean to embarrass you. It's just that I've never met anyone with that kind of power before. It must be one hell of a responsibility.'

'Well, I . . .'

'But it's a wonderful thing to have.'

Adam's brow furrowed. 'It is – and it isn't.' He saw the look on Isla's face, a mixture of concern and curiosity.

'How long have you had it?' she asked. 'I mean, how long have you realised you had the power?'

Adam looked her in the eye. 'The thing is, I try not to think about it. I mean, "power" makes me sound like Spider-Man or something. It's not like that. I'm not sure I even believe it. And there is this feeling that if I *do* believe in it, it will disappear. Sometimes I think that would be a good thing, but when I see what it can do . . . I'm sorry. I don't think I've ever talked about it properly before – except briefly to Brother Wilfrid . . .'

'Brother Wilfrid?'

'It's a long story. He's a monk.' He glanced across the table at Jack, who was draining his first pint. 'At least we *think* he's a monk. He comes to see us once a year just after lambing time – passing through on some sort of pilgrimage. He was here a few weeks ago and he mentioned it.'

'What about your mum and dad? What do they think?'

Adam looked uncomfortable. 'I know this sounds stupid, but we've never really talked about it. I've always liked animals, always been at ease with them.'

'But it's more than that, isn't it?'

'I suppose the truth is that none of us is sure it's real. It could just be a coincidence, except . . .'

'Except?' She was listening intently now, leaning towards him, so close that he could detect the light floral fragrance of her scent.

'When it happens – when I've . . . helped, I feel a bit weird, and afterwards I'm completely knackered.'

Isla smiled at his candour. 'It doesn't sound to me as though it's imagined. What sort of things have you done? Apart from stopping your schoolmate – who I heard was a bit of a shit anyway – bleeding to death?'

'Animals mostly. Apparently our old sheepdog Finn used to have a wall-eye. When I was little I would stroke that side of his head and it gradually disappeared. The vet said he'd never known that happen before. I can sense where sheep are in snowdrifts, and I've brought round lambs who've been at death's door – but lots of farmers and their wives have done that. All they need is an Aga.'

Isla ignored Adam's attempt to make light of it. 'Mainly animals, then?'

'Mainly but not always. I seem to be able to get rid of joint pain and speed up the healing of wounds. I've cured schoolmates of warts – but now I'm beginning to sound like a witch. Jakey Learoyd called me a weirdo. Perhaps he's right. That's all I am – a weirdo.' He offered a weak smile.

Isla shook her head. 'If you are, you're a kind and gentle weirdo.' She smiled at him and leant forward, kissing him gently on the cheek.

Their intimacy was curtailed by the arrival of a waitress. 'Duck breast? Who was the duck breast?'

The one-to-one conversation was interrupted and the table now fell into free-for-all revelry, but every now and then Isla would catch his eye and smile or wink. He could not get over how empowering it felt. Surely she could not now simply disappear from his life. Somehow, he had to make sure he would see her again. The thing was, did she feel the same as he did?

18

TENDER IS THE NIGHT

No, there's nothing half so sweet in life as
love's young dream.

Thomas Moore, *Irish Melodies*, 1807

And so, having dropped off a particularly merry Jack Knaggs, they journeyed back up the long and winding road, then the bumpy track that led to the farmhouse, each and every one of them aglow with the pleasant weariness of their week-long labours and the contentment enhanced by a fine meal and generous hospitality.

There were farewells at the door of the farmhouse before Isla and Noah went around the corner and up the stairs to the adjacent loft, leaving Adam, Luke and Bethany to enter through the front door. Their parting was brief and – in Adam's case – heartfelt. He gave Isla a hug and kissed her cheek before turning and following his parents. 'See you in the morning before you leave,' he whispered, in hope as much as anything.

'Of course,' she replied. 'I won't go without saying goodbye.'
And that, he thought, was likely to be that.

Adam lay awake for hours. The full moon flooded his bedroom with light, and through the open window he could hear the plaintive hoot of a pair of tawny owls and feel the gentle breeze of a summer night.

He slipped out of bed and crossed to the window. The fellside was bathed in silver light, the sheep, now silent, huddled down and dozing on the rolling dew-laden fields of close-cropped grass. He sighed and pulled on a sweater and jeans, then made his way quietly downstairs and out of the front door. He crossed to the edge of the farmyard, where the land dipped slightly and allowed the craggy boulders to nudge through the greensward. There he lowered himself onto the rocky outcrop and pulled his knees up under his chin.

There was a special atmosphere on his native hills in the middle of the night, an intimacy with nature that felt even more intense than he experienced during the day. The world was his and his alone, up there away from the influence of men and motors, where only the nocturnal activities of badgers and owls disturbed the stillness. In winter it had a rawness that served to remind a shepherd of his reliance on the elements and the fragility of nature up on the fells, so close to the sky, where the roaring wind could blow a man over and cause sheep to seek safety in the lee of a dry-stone wall. In summer it could be possessed of a beguiling gentleness, the rustle of leaves on the gnarled sycamore the only sound to be heard, save for the bark of a dog fox or the scream of a vixen. The eerie qualities of the night in the wilds did not alarm him. He had been born there; they were the native's sounds of home.

He was not aware of any ordered thoughts. More than anything he simply wanted to *be* and not necessarily to *think*. Just to savour the moment and let the cool night air work some kind of calming magic on his confused mind.

The voice at his side startled him. 'You too?' she said.

He turned to see Isla slipping her legs over the rock beside him. She did not look at him straight away, but gazed out across the moonlit moorland landscape and murmured, 'Beautiful.'

Adam was conscious of not breaking the mood. He said nothing, but allowed himself a quick glance at the seated figure beside him. She was wearing a thick white sweater and a pair of cotton shorts, which, he thought, must count as pyjama bottoms. Her feet were bare and her arms were wrapped around her knees, which, like his, were pulled up under her chin. He could feel his heart pounding in his chest.

For some time neither of them spoke. Then Isla lifted her hand and turned Adam's head so that he faced her. She still did not speak, but offered him the tenderest of smiles before easing forward and kissing him on the lips. He did not resist.

'Do you mind?' she asked.

Adam shook his head. Words did not seem to be an option. She kissed him again, longer this time, and he wrapped his arms around her and stroked the back of her neck.

As their lips parted she murmured, 'I've wanted to do that for such a long time.'

Words at last came tumbling from Adam's lips. 'Me too. Except I didn't know you would.'

'Oh, I wanted to from the moment I first saw you. Shame to leave without telling you.'

'Yes. Do you have to go?' He drew her towards him and

nestled her head on his chest, his arm protectively cradling her shoulders.

''Fraid so. Can't really stay. No sheep left to shear.'

'No. But . . .'

'Don't worry. I'm sure we'll meet again. Some day . . .'

'That sounds like a long time away.'

'Who knows?'

She seemed so calm, so philosophical about it, and all he wanted to say was, 'Don't go! Stay here! I want to spend the rest of my life with you,' but how stupid would he sound?

'Where do you go tomorrow?' he asked.

'Somewhere near Richmond. Noah has the details. I just go where he goes.'

'And when do you go home?' He tried not to sound too disappointed.

'In about a month. When we've shorn all the sheep in Yorkshire – at least, that's how it feels, Noah tells me.' She rose to her feet and took his hand. Then she looked into his eyes, said, 'It's been lovely meeting you, Adam Gabriel,' and kissed him again. They stood together on top of the rock, his arms enfolding her, gazing out over the valley where the merest hint of sunrise was beginning to stain the horizon with its amber light.

'I wish . . .' he said. But then he stopped. He didn't really know what he wished, except that she wasn't going.

She lifted her finger to his lips and with her other hand placed Adam's hand on her breast. 'I'll keep you here,' she said.

He had never touched a woman's breast before. It felt ridiculously, wonderfully intimate. Then she kissed his cheek, turned and walked towards the farmhouse.

He gazed after her for a few minutes, then got down from

the rock and went back to his room. His parents would be up before long and he wanted to keep this special moment to himself.

Luke backed away from the bedroom window, smiling. Then he felt a pang of guilt at having witnessed such intimacy. Bethany was still asleep. There was no reason to tell her what he had seen. And certainly no reason to tell Adam.

Humming to himself, he began to get dressed to face the dawning of another day.

19

FATHERS AND SONS

Father-like he tends and spares us,
Well our feeble frame he knows.

Henry Francis Lyte, 'Praise, My Soul,
the King of Heaven', 1834

'I don't know what's got into him. He's not been the same since shearing. Sort of distant.' Bethany was musing on the general wellbeing of her son as she and Luke rose from their bed and prepared for another day.

'Oh, he'll be fine. Probably just a bit knackered. Shearing takes it out of you even when you're young and fit.' He had kept the promise he'd made to himself and said nothing to Bethany about the dawn encounter he had witnessed just a few days before.

Bethany was sitting up in bed. 'He did seem rather taken with Isla.'

Luke was pulling on his jeans and tucking in his shirt. 'I think we were all rather taken with Isla.' Then, pointedly, 'Those of us who were not rather taken with Noah.'

Bethany grinned. 'Luke Gabriel, are you jealous?'

'Of course I am. A young, virile man like Noah . . . bound to make the rest of us feel we need to step up to the mark.'

'He did rather leave the rest of you standing.'

'Hey!'

'Well, you said so yourself.'

Luke frowned. 'It's one thing saying something yourself, and quite another to hear someone else say it.'

'Anyway, you'd better give Adam an easy day today, bearing in mind tonight's little ceremony.'

'I'd forgotten about that.'

'How could you? Honestly!'

'Well . . . not my sort of thing. I'll only get hot under the collar as usual and wish I could be somewhere else.'

'Aren't you proud of him?'

'Of course I am. It's just that . . . well, you know me and formal occasions.'

Bethany sighed. 'Only too well. So I've bought you a shirt with a size larger collar. I thought that might be more comfortable.'

Luke tried to look grateful, but his expression hardly conveyed the intended emotion. 'Will there be many folk there?'

'I should think so.'

'And that woman from the paper? Belle somebody . . . Jack seems to have had a run-in with her in the past.'

Bethany slid out of bed and walked towards the bathroom. 'I'm sure she'll be there. So best behaviour, please. She's only doing her job.'

'Isn't that the excuse they gave at the Nuremberg trials?'

Bethany turned as she reached the bathroom door. 'That's a bit political for you, isn't it?'

Luke frowned. 'Two insults already and the day hasn't even started.' He went to the bedroom door, opened it and, as he stepped through, delivered a parting shot. 'You'll miss me when I've gone.'

Bethany grinned. 'You reckon?' As he disappeared from view her parting words fell upon his ears: 'And put the kettle on.'

True to his word, Luke was gentle with Adam during the course of the day. The weather was capricious – a mixture of sunshine and showers – so rather than subjecting his son to an occasional drenching, Luke suggested to Adam that he saw logs in the barn. From time to time each year they would go through the small copse at the bottom of the fellside, hauling out fallen timber and thinning the canopy to promote the health of the remaining trees and provide fuel for the log-burner in winter. They would stack the trunks and heavy branches in the barn to dry out. Later, on days when the ground was too wet to do anything constructive without creating an instant quagmire, they would saw logs and store them at the end of the barn, ready for winter.

It was a job Adam enjoyed. It required little in the way of brain-power, and while the circular saw whirred he could let his mind wander over other things – provided he kept his hands clear of the rotating blade. It pleased him to create order out of chaos. There was satisfaction to be gained in watching the neatly cut log pile rising ever higher. His mind was far away when his father's voice brought him down to earth.

'I've made you a coffee,' said Luke.

Adam started. He had been exploring the possibilities of travelling to New Zealand and meeting a certain person with whom he could go travelling. No flies had been allowed to sully this particular ointment – such as his age (barely seventeen), or that his parents would never allow him to travel alone to the other side of the world. He had luxuriated in the flight of fancy that allowed no impediment to its accomplishment . . .

'You made me jump!'

His father smiled. 'I waited until your hands were away from the blade.' He handed him the mug and flipped the switch that turned off the circular saw. Slowly the singing note slowed to a gentle whine, until finally the shiny blade came to a standstill and all that could be heard was the sound of a pair of collared doves cooing from the ridge of the barn.

'Nice when it stops,' said Adam, half to himself.

Luke gestured to the towering stack of logs against the barn wall. 'Should see us through until next spring, that little lot. Well done.'

'Do you think I'm stupid?' asked Adam.

His father regarded him quizzically. 'What do you mean?'

'Well, it gives me a kind of satisfaction to turn this pile of timber into neatly sawn logs. Do you think I might be a bit soft in the head?'

There was a hint of irony in the question, which came as a relief to Luke. He sat down on a straw bale, took a sip of his coffee. 'If you're soft in the head, there's no hope for me. I could be sectioned any day now.'

Adam joined his father on the bale and the two of them gazed out of the open-ended barn at the freshly laundered landscape that was glistening under the emerging sun. 'Not a bad view is it?' remarked Luke.

'The best,' responded his son.

'People underestimate the pleasures of manual labour, you

know. They don't seem to rate practical skills the way they did in my dad's day. Without them – and the people who have them – we'd be lost. There'd be no food, no water, no electricity, no gas. However clever the scientists and the academics, the world would grind to a halt without people who are good with their hands.'

'Craftsmen, you mean?' asked Adam.

'Yes. And those who simply have the knack of being practical.'

'So you're not disappointed that I didn't stay on and go to university?'

'Not at all. University is fine for those with an academic turn of mind. But without people who can put theory into practice, and who gain satisfaction from a job well done' – he nodded at the pile of neatly sawn logs – 'we'd starve to death. If we didn't freeze first.'

'I suppose so.'

'Don't go knocking yourself for enjoying what you do. And when we're warming ourselves by that log-burner indoors and the January winds are whistling around the chimney, we'll thank our lucky stars that I have a son who can turn his hand to just about anything.'

Adam smiled at the compliment.

'And, anyway, you're bright enough. It's not as if you saw logs because you're not fit for anything else. You have a feel for things, you know that. Animals and humans alike. That's not the sort of thing you can learn at university, is it?'

'I suppose not.'

'Aptitude. Everyone is best at something, I reckon, and the ones who find out what that something is are the luckiest folk in the world.'

'Does that include me?'

Luke took another gulp of his coffee and turned to face his son. 'You more than most. You never cease to surprise me, you know.' He paused for a minute, as though weighing up whether to say anything more. In the end the comment was brief but heartfelt: 'I'm very proud of you, of what you've done, and what you can do.'

Adam blushed. He couldn't remember the last time his father had complimented him. It was not that Luke was surly, or ungrateful, it was just that, well, it had never cropped up in their conversations. It was not as if he had expected praise, or even felt deprived of it. The existence or absence of it had never crossed his mind.

Luke registered his son's embarrassment. 'Well. You know now, don't you? I don't think my dad ever told me what he thought about me. It was just sort of taken for granted. We got on all right but I was never sure what he really thought. Shame not to let you know.' He drained his mug and got up. 'So there you are.' He winked at Adam. 'I'd better let you get on. And just make sure you don't chop your hand off. You'd look a bit daft tonight without one. And you can imagine what the papers will say: "Certificate of Commendation given to Yorkshire lad who rescued his schoolmate singlehandedly".'

'Dad! That's dreadful!'

'I know. Sorry. Just make sure it doesn't ring true, eh?'

Luke was walking out of the barn when he turned. 'Oh . . . and last week, the shearing.'

'Yes?'

'Well done. You had fair competition from Noah, but I thought you handled it well. Kept up, you know.'

'Thank you.'

'And Isla . . .'

Adam looked at his father nervously. 'Yes.'

'Nice girl. Very nice girl.' And with that he turned the corner and left Adam alone with his thoughts.

20

THE FICKLE FINGER

Fate is not an eagle, it creeps like a rat.

Elizabeth Bowen, *The House in Paris*, 1935

The mayor's parlour was stuffy. The showery day had given way to a clammy evening and the mayor's secretary was busying herself opening windows in the small wood-panelled room that served as the office of Skipton's premier civic dignitary – Reg Bottomley. Councillor Bottomley was the epitome of a mayor who also happened to be a pork butcher: round and pink and swathed in Harris Tweed, his brow bedewed with perspiration on account of the temperature of the room and that, as befitted the occasion, his heather-mixture suiting was itself swathed in the scarlet robes of office, complete with gold chain and lace jabot. He looked as though at any moment he might go off pop. The bald dome of his head shone in the reflected light of the single chandelier (which had once graced the local saleroom and had been gifted to the town council by Councillor Mrs Oldroyd on her retirement from office some years ago), and every few minutes he would reach into his trouser pocket for a handkerchief with which he would mop his fevered brow. He looked nervous, rather than pompous, but the fact that Belle Barclay of the *Craven Courier* was present and he was endeavouring to cover up a covert relationship with a certain member of the Audit and Governance Committee added to his unease.

Luke, Bethany and Adam were ushered into the chamber by a small bird-like woman, who fussed over them in a manner appropriate to the grandeur of the occasion. The turn-out was nothing if not comprehensive: everyone from James Addison, Adam's old school headmaster, to a full complement of town councillors, paramedics, the local police inspector, Jack Knaggs in his Sunday best, minus cap, Fred Pennock the postman, Martin Hebblethwaite the vet (still achingly handsome, thought Bethany, even though his hair was now peppered with grey), and the obligatory photographer from the *Courier*, along with its star reporter. Standing in a corner, on his own, was Jakey Learoyd. Adam caught his eye as they were steered across the room and glanced back to see if his parents had registered Jakey's presence. It appeared they had not.

A young waitress, her fair hair tied in a ponytail, was handing round drinks from a silvered tray – a glass of red or white wine, a tumbler of orange squash or fizzy water being the choices of the day. Adam recognised her as a sixth-former from school. She smiled brightly at him and blushed before averting her gaze. Adam played safe and took some squash, his father looked relieved at the prospect of red wine and his mother, mindful of the drive back to Langstrothdale and the presence of the local police force, a glass of water.

The trio stood together in the middle of the milling throng while more late arrivals threatened to fill the room to bursting point. They were chatting to a lady councillor – or, rather, she was chatting to them, explaining the importance of being the sole Conservative member of a governing body composed mainly of independent members. Adam was all but overcome by the intensity of the woman's halitosis and the powerful aroma of mothballs that emanated from her fur-collared jacket. It was clearly brought out only on important occasions such as this, and the bald patches that dappled it suggested that, although the naphthalene in question might repel humans, it had been less effective against more robust Yorkshire lepidoptera.

Right now, he would rather be anywhere but here, a feeling that was exacerbated by a voice at his ear. He recognised it immediately, even though it uttered a word he had not heard it say before: 'Adam.' The last time he had endured its abrasive tone it had called him 'Weirdo'.

He turned to find Jakey Learoyd at his elbow. He half expected to be head-butted again, but realised almost immediately that such an action would, on this particular occasion, and in these hallowed surroundings, be inadvisable even when perpetrated by someone totally devoid of social graces.

'Hi,' said Adam, in response. Luke and Bethany stood silent and motionless beside their son as the two young men eyed one another nervously.

The rest of the room, unaware of the history of this particular relationship, continued to buzz with conversation, which avoided what might otherwise have been a deeply uncomfortable silence.

Lowering his gaze from Adam's, and appearing to focus on a spot somewhere around chest level, Jakey held out his hand.

Adam shook it warily.

'I just wanted to say thank you. That's all. It were good of you.' And with that, he turned on his heel and was gone – out of the door and away.

Adam glanced from parent to parent. Luke raised his

eyebrows, but before either could say anything a wooden gavel was banged on the desk in front of the mayor's carved wooden throne and the meeting brought to order.

Councillor Bottomley, determined to put aside his own matrimonial worries for the time being, puffed out his chest (which remained some distance behind his generous girth), cleared his throat and addressed the assembled company.

'Ladies and gentlemen, we are gathered here today . . .'

'Ooh, it sounds like a wedding,' Bethany murmured, her nerves getting the better of her.

'. . . to salute a young member of our community who showed conspicuous bravery in the face of grave danger.'

For a split second Adam wondered who they were talking about. Then he came back to earth and continued to wish he could somehow cause himself to dissolve into the ether and become invisible.

'Regardless of his own safety, he stepped into the fray and rescued . . .' Here the mayor cast his eyes about the room attempting to spot the victim of the assault. Failing to do so he motored on: '. . . a school friend who had been set upon by a gang of youths – with a knife I might add – and who would most certainly have died had not this young man intervened. With no thought of his own safety . . .'

You've just said that, thought Bethany, now managing to prevent her thoughts from being articulated.

'. . . he saw off the assailants and immediately attended to the youth who lay prone on the pavement bleeding profusely.'

Mr Bottomley was now warming to his subject, and warming bodily, too, for the river of perspiration was now emulating the copious flow of a moorland beck, running off his chin onto his lacy jabot.

'This is no ordinary young man,' intoned the mayor, giving extra gravitas to his vowels. 'This is a young man not only of great personal courage, but also with an exceptional gift. The gift of healing. There might be those who question such gifts, but I, as someone who has to deal with meat on a daily basis . . .' he paused for a laugh, which failed to materialise '. . . know that man – and beasts of the field – are made of more than mere flesh. They can be possessed of faculties and facilities that sometimes defy description.'

'A bit like your sausages,' muttered a man at Adam's elbow.

Several of the local councillors were now finding the pattern on the carpet and the glittering chandelier above them of rather more interest than their mayor, but out of respect for the object of his peroration they stayed the course and greeted the final line, 'a certificate of commendation for bravery is awarded to Adam Gabriel', with a hearty round of applause and shouts of 'Well done, lad!' and 'Good for you!'

Adam was pushed forward towards the mayor who descended from his throne, pumped Adam's hand vigorously and, still holding the framed certificate, put his arm around Adam's shoulders and grinned at the camera as the *Craven Courier*'s photographer snapped. 'This way!' he instructed, and 'Just one more', at least a dozen times, before Adam was finally handed the framed citation and allowed to return to his parents. It came as a considerable relief that he was not expected to make a speech.

And then, like the parting of the Red Sea, the crowd cleared to allow Belle Barclay through the throng.

'Well, there you are!' she hooted. 'What did I tell you?'

Adam couldn't think of a suitable reply. He simply smiled and, like the councillors before him, tried to make sense of the complex pattern on the carpet.

Realising the futility of her task, Belle Barclay turned to Adam's parents. 'You must be very proud?'

Luke nodded and managed a weak smile. 'Of course,' he said.

'And you, Mrs Gabriel. When did you realise that Adam was so gifted?'

It being something that was acknowledged only tacitly within the family, Bethany prevaricated. 'Oh, he's always been kind,' she said.

'But this was more than that, wasn't it? Yes, your son displayed bravery – and kindness – but it's the "gift" that Councillor Bottomley referred to that I'm interested in. We began to talk about it when I came to see you on the farm, but you were rather busy shearing and we didn't get time to discuss it properly.'

'No. Well . . .' Luke began, and as he did so he put out a hand to steady himself on Bethany's shoulder. She turned towards him, and as she did so she registered that the colour had drained from his cheeks and his lips were blue. Before she had a chance to react, Luke crumpled and he slid to the floor.

Time seemed to stand still for all of them. For several seconds no one moved, their eyes riveted on the form that lay at their feet. It was Adam who was the first to act, falling to his knees and whispering, with some urgency, 'Dad! Dad!' The image was of a child, explaining to his father that this was no time to sleep, that there was still something going on that needed his presence.

Gently but firmly Adam shook the shoulder of his slumbering father. He must have fainted: he had always become hot under the collar at events like this. School plays, village-hall gatherings and things outside Luke Gabriel's comfort zone had frequently given rise to the familiar symptoms – the reddening of his neck, the perspiration on his brow, the general discomfiture of someone happiest on the hills and ill at ease when confined to overheated rooms and stifling public meetings.

'Dad! Dad! Wake up. Come on! It's me – Adam.'

There was no response. Bethany dropped to her knees and offered soothing words to her husband. 'Up you come, love. Let's go out and get you some fresh air.' But there was no movement.

Adam noticed that his father's eyes were open. Then there came over him the familiar feeling of his whole body being taken over by some greater force. He massaged his father's temples, concentrated furiously on breathing life into the lifeless form. He must be able to do something to help his own father, surely.

His intervention was to no avail, and for the rest of his life Adam would feel that the one person in the world he would have given everything to save had slipped through his hands.

Luke Gabriel was pronounced dead on arrival at the hospital. It came as no consolation to Adam when the doctor confirmed that there was nothing anyone could have done to save him.

21

WE TWO

Sons are the anchors of a mother's life.

Sophocles

There had been no warning that Luke Gabriel had a heart condition. The fact that he frequently got hot under the collar had always been attributed to temperament rather than medical condition. A shy farmer, he naturally found himself discomfited in company he did not know, especially at formal events when he would feel lacking in the required social graces. It was nonsense, of course, for he had been brought up with good manners after the habit of many a Yorkshire man-of-the-land whose attitude to the upper classes had been refined by generation upon generation of tenant farmers. He knew how to behave, knew what was expected of him, and yet he still felt uncomfortable. Even his wife had put down his ability to colour at the slightest provocation to nothing more than unease in unfamiliar company. It seemed as though even she had underestimated the true complexity of the situation.

The paramedics were speedy in their response – they were

on the other side of the room after all – but even their proximity and the promptness of their actions could not save Luke. He had slipped away by the time the ambulance arrived at the infirmary.

The next few days passed in a blur for Adam and Bethany. Numbness and disbelief were followed by anger and sorrow in ever-fluctuating equations. Bethany seemed to be in a permanent daze, while Adam reproached himself for not being able to help one of the two people in the world to whom he was closest. The irony of the situation was not lost on him. There he was, being lauded for his courage in stepping into the breach to confront knife-wielding hooligans, and at its heart a growing belief in some quarters of his ability to heal. Why could he not heal his father, the person to whom he owed most? Why had it all happened so quickly?

Daily he would take himself off with Nip to the rock above the river and stare outwards as if hoping for some sign, some kind of comfort from the landscape that had nursed him. The dog would push his nose up under Adam's arm and lick the salt tears from his face. Each day Adam told himself that he must be strong, that the doctor had said nothing could have been done to counter such a massive heart attack, but that did not prevent him from reproaching himself. Neither did it stop the tears flowing – great racking sobs that left him feeling desolate and alone, emotions he was determined to hide from his mother. He knew he must be strong for her, that her containment of emotion was something he should emulate. He must not add to her burden of grief with the weight of his own. He could not, he would not, but at his very core there remained the feeling of failure to help when help was most needed by those he loved.

Jack Knaggs rose to the occasion. He said little, but made sure that from dawn to dusk he was a constant presence on the farm, seeing to the sheep and to the mother and son who had been left high and dry by the passing of their husband and father.

Adam gazed at the death certificate. 'Acute myocardial infarction'. It sounded such an impersonal, scientific way to describe a heart attack. When questioned about Luke's medical history, their GP had said that Luke's hot flushes were not necessarily an indication that such an event would be likely sooner or later. He had attended the surgery annually for what he called 'my MOT', and while his blood pressure was on the borderline of 'high' it had not been felt necessary to prescribe amlodipine. Both Bethany and Adam found little comfort in such an erroneous retrospective diagnosis.

For the most part, Jack kept his feelings to himself, confining his opinions to a lengthy shake of the head whenever the event was mentioned in the village. He had neither the heart nor the appetite to visit the Blue Bell and drown his personal sorrows. This was not a time for socialising. He took his comfort at home with a generous measure of Famous Grouse every evening when it was clear that he could no longer be of any use at the farm.

Bethany and Adam were astonished at the turn-out for the funeral. For a man who kept himself mostly to himself, it became clear that Luke was as widely revered in the local agricultural community as he was in the village. Hubberholme church was packed.

The two seemed to go around in a trance in the interim between Luke's death and his funeral, and only when his ashes had been scattered high up on the fellside did they turn their minds to the future, conscious that now the way ahead – however it might be handled – depended solely on them.

They walked back down the fellside in silence, Jack following slightly behind, out of a combination of respect and an inability to match the agility of his two employers. For that was what they were now.

It did not take Adam long to register the change in his position. His mother might be senior to him in years, but he was now the man of the house, and in this part of the Yorkshire Dales that still mattered. It was nothing to do with machismo, sexism or sheer bloody-mindedness, more a willingness to do his duty and shoulder the burden of responsibility handed down to him. He was determined to live up to the role carved out by his father, and equally determined to honour his mother, even if that phrase – which he turned over in his mind – seemed strangely old-fashioned.

'You should get out,' said Bethany to her son, over the breakfast table, a week after the funeral.

'I do get out. I'm out every day,' countered Adam.

'I don't mean fresh air. I mean fresh company.'

Adam pushed away the half-eaten bowl of porridge. 'Not yet.'

Bethany reached across the table for his hand. 'I'm not rushing you. I just don't want you to feel you have to be stuck here with me all the time.'

Adam looked crestfallen. 'But I want to be. I need to be here for you.'

'Of course you do, and you are. But I don't want the farm – or me for that matter – to be a millstone round your neck. Once we've got ourselves sorted we'll need to work out what we're going to do.'

Adam shook his head. 'There's no need. I know what I want to do. It's what I've always wanted to do. I want to run the farm.'

Bethany looked him in the eye. 'I know you've always wanted to, but your dad and I didn't imagine that you'd have to do it quite so soon – or so suddenly. You've had no time to grow up, Adam, no time to find out who you are. You're still young and you should be able to experience other things before you pin yourself down for the rest of your life.'

Adam shrugged, as if to make light of the matter. 'What sort of other things?'

'Well, you need to meet people for a start, people of your own age. You can't do that if you're stuck here in Langstrothdale.'

'There's the Young Farmers' Club,' offered Adam. 'I keep meaning to ring them. I've just not got round to it what with . . .'

Bethany smiled. 'That's hardly the big wide world, is it? I saw how your eyes lit up when you were with Noah and Isla.'

Adam looked surprised.

'I do notice things, you know. I'm your mum. And she was a very pretty girl. I want to see that light in your eye again, not feel that I'm holding you back in the dale when you should be out there experiencing things, broadening your mind.'

Adam was taken aback, not only by the fact that his mother had noticed his attitude towards Isla, but also that she had felt the need to show her approval. Her mention of the girl that he had fallen for did nothing to lift his spirits. If anything, it dampened them further.

'I don't suppose we'll meet again,' he said. 'She'll be going back to New Zealand soon.'

'There's always next year. If we're still here . . .' said Bethany.

Next year . . . It was all he could do at the moment to think of the next day and what it might hold, never mind the following week, month or year. And by next year Isla would be . . . where? Going to university in Auckland? Travelling the world? She was, in the balance of probability, unlikely to accompany her brother on his shearing sortie to the Yorkshire Dales.

He slumped forward on the kitchen table and cradled his head in his hands, then looked up when his mother's words finally sank in. 'What do you mean?' he asked.

'Exactly what I said. If we're still here.'

'Is there any reason why we shouldn't be?'

'Oh, Adam, it depends on so many things. It's down to the two of us, what we decide to do. And the last thing *I* want to do is, as I said, be a millstone around your neck.'

Adam shook his head. 'We don't need to have this conversation, not now, not ever. We belong here, both of us, and we're not leaving.' It dawned on him then that his parents had never discussed the security of their livelihood with him. He hardly dared ask the question. 'I mean, we can, can't we? Are we . . .' he sought the right words '. . . financially secure?'

Bethany smiled. 'Yes. We are. Your dad had enough sense to make sure that if anything happened to him we would be all right. He had an insurance policy that covers the mortgage, and I'll have a small income.'

Adam slumped back in his chair with relief. 'Thank God.'

Bethany smiled weakly. 'I don't think either of us really imagined it would happen – well, you don't, do you? – but your father was an archetypal Yorkshireman. He never wanted to come home and find the bailiffs at the door, carrying out his furniture and telling him that Langstroth Farmhouse was not his any more. He didn't believe in living on credit. The never-never. I used to tease him about it but in the end—' She stopped short, her eyes filling with tears.

Adam stood up and walked around to where his mother sat, putting his arms around her shoulders from behind and resting his head on hers. 'Don't worry, Mum. We'll be all right. And I'll be all right. There's no need to worry about me. I'll sort myself out, one way or another.'

The phrase echoed around Bethany's head. 'One way or another'. What did Adam mean by that? Perhaps he didn't know himself, and right now there were other things to occupy them both, the main one being grief. All these endless generations of people, all going through the same feelings of loss and anger and deep, gnawing sorrow. For that a cure had never been found. She had a lovely son with a strange capacity to heal others, but even he could not heal this wound, so deep and so raw as it was.

At night she lay in bed alone – the space beside her so empty and so cold. All she could hope for – hope for but not believe – was that in time the pain might lessen, not least because her only child was with her. At least for now.

THE MAN

22

OLD FRIENDS

When we honestly ask ourselves which person in our
lives means the most to us, we often find it is those who,
instead of giving much advice, solutions or cures, have
chosen rather to share our pain and touch our wounds
with a gentle and tender hand.

Henri J. M. Nouwen, *The Road to Daybreak:*
A Spiritual Journey, 1988

Grief takes many forms and runs wildly through all human
emotions. In a single day anger and sorrow may be overtaken by
irritation, frustration, loneliness and despair. There is no template,
no one-size-fits-all, no order in the catalogue of emotions that
ensues. Adam felt every undulation of the human spirit in an
unpredictable and seemingly endless tidal wave in the weeks
following his father's death, all the while watching his mother
closely and caring for her needs as much as his own. He was
conscious of a role reversal and found himself behaving as the
parent rather than the child. Aware that his mother could not
see past each bleak day ahead, he gentled her back to life with

a consideration and apparent understanding far greater than that expected of a boy of his years. And yet he was a boy no longer. He was seventeen now, and while unversed in many of life's experiences, he was familiar with other sensations of life – and death – that many of his age would find beyond their compass.

Like many a country child, Adam was content and comfortable in his own company. He could distinguish solitude from loneliness and learn to love the one without fearing the other. At least, he had been able to do so until now. In the aftermath of his father's death he could feel engulfed by sudden waves of isolation, not geographical – never that – but emotional isolation that found him staring into an uncertain future.

He found comfort in the companionship of Jack Knaggs, who seemed to know when to speak and when to keep his peace, when to let Adam wander off on his own, and when he would be better for company, talking about . . . what? Anything and everything that would momentarily take his mind off his loss.

With Nip at his heel he would wander down to the riverbank and sit, staring silently, as the dipper dabbled in the fast-moving eddies between the rocks, or as an otter nosed its way sinuously upstream, watched with unblinking avidity by the dog, who knew better than to dive in and chase his potential quarry. Maybe Nip knew which was likely to come off worst.

These early days of bereavement were deepened by another loss: Finn. Luke's old dog, now content to spend his days lying in the sun alongside the stone wall of the barn, or nestled close to the fire on chilly summer evenings, had quietly slipped away one night in his sleep. Jack and Adam had buried him at the foot of an old thorn tree where, through the tears, Adam had related to the old man his memories of growing up with his canine brother. Death was a frequent occurrence on the farm, but there was a world of difference between the death of a ewe or lamb – livestock and deadstock – and the loss of a lifetime companion. In the space of a few weeks, Adam had lost two of the beings dearest to him.

'Nah then,' said Jack, as they stood up from the grave. Adam fixed his gaze on the freshly made mound, dappled by the sun shining through the branches of the wizened thorn tree. 'I've summat in here for thee.' Jack ambled over to the barn and picked up from just inside the door an old sack that clearly contained some heavy object. He handed it to Adam, who laid it on the ground and tipped out a large flat stone. He turned it over and read the legend that had been neatly carved on its surface:

Finn

Good mate

Aged 16

'I 'ad it done when I could see 'e weren't right. Thought yer might like it.'

Adam placed the stone at the head of the mound, stood up, smiled, then turned and, for the first time in his life, wrapped his arms around Jack in a gesture of profound gratitude as his body shook uncontrollably and the tears flowed down his cheeks.

'Aye, go on. You 'ave a good weep. It's about bloody time.'

'I'm sorry,' offered Adam, a few moments later, easing away from the old man who, even through the veil of grief, gave off a distinct aroma of sheep and straw and honest toil. It didn't bother Adam. In a funny sort of way it was comforting, though not even the most generous-spirited would call it attractive.

'Come on. Time for a brew.' Jack led him into the barn for the customary mid-morning coffee. Adam glanced across at the kitchen window where he could see his mother going through the ritual of washing-up, her unseeing gaze directed at some distant vision across the valley. She seemed, as she had done for these last few weeks, to be going through the motions, present in body but not in mind. The colour had drained from her face and there was a listlessness about her. Adam hoped that soon she would reconnect with life and begin the long healing process.

Jack saw the direction of his gaze. 'She'll be all reet . . . Just give her time.'

'How much time?' asked Adam, the note of anxiety in his voice plain to hear.

'As long as it takes.'

'That's not very helpful.' Then, realising he had sounded ungrateful and unfeeling, 'Sorry . . .'

'Nay, lad. I know meself. There's nowt to be 'appy about when they goes. Nowt at all. Yer brain just goes round an' round in circles.'

Adam remembered now that Jack, too, had experienced his own personal loss. Adam had never known Florrie Knaggs, who had died long before he was born, but it was a reminder that Jack had more than an inkling of what his own mother was going through. Bethany was probably around the same age as Jack had been when he became a widower.

'What we need to do is to keep 'er goin'. Just let 'er know we're 'ere when she needs anything. An' don't you bottle it all up, neither. Yer allowed to let go. Nobody's goin' ter think any the worse of you, tha knows.'

'Thanks. I just don't know what I feel at the moment. Apart from being sad. And angry at myself for not being able to do anything about it. I mean, I just keep going over and over that day – every bit of it – and wondering why I couldn't help Dad – *my* dad – and why we went to that stupid ceremony, which he must have hated. It was all so . . . pointless.'

'There's no use thinkin' like that. None at all. It would 'ave 'appened sooner or later wherever yer dad was. Yer just need ter find something in yerself that lets yer move on.'

'But how can I?'

'Oh, yer will. In time. Don't rush it. Let nature take its course – and you know more about nature than anyone, what with yer naturalists an' all. You've not been for a bit, 'ave you? To meetin's an' that?'

'No. I'm not ready yet.'

'Well, there's plenty to occupy you round 'ere, I know, but it wouldn't be a bad idea for you to think about getting out a bit.'

'That's what Mum said.'

'Well, she's not wrong.'

'Young Farmers?' asked Adam, wearily.

'Or summat like, aye.'

Their conversation was interrupted by the sight of two distant figures walking up the farm track towards them. Jack screwed up his rheumy eyes to try to identify their unexpected visitors.

Adam followed the direction of his gaze and murmured, 'Walkers.'

And that was what the two appeared to be: an older and a younger woman, the former clearly having difficulty with the terrain. As they came closer Adam could see that the older of the two looked as though she were about to collapse. He walked towards them and indicated the old stone slab, once used as a shelf for milk churns when those who farmed there still found it worthwhile to have a dairy herd, now used daily by Jack to rest his weary bones.

'Sit down,' he said, taking the woman's arm and lowering her onto the sturdy seat. 'You look done in.'

Jack watched. He seemed uneasy.

Adam could see the woman had clearly overdone it. 'It's tough walking around here unless you're used to it. Let me go and get you a glass of water.'

As he walked to the door of the farmhouse, Bethany came out, drying her hands on a tea towel. 'What is it?' she asked.

'Walkers. One of them about to collapse, I think. Just getting her some water.' He brushed past his mother and went into the kitchen.

Bethany walked towards the pair – the older woman now sitting with her head between her knees and the younger stroking the back of her head. 'It's all right, Mum. We're here now. You'll be fine.'

Bethany cast a glance at Jack, who shrugged by way of reply. Adam returned and held out the glass of water to the girl, whom he recognised as the young waitress who had been present at the ceremony on the night of his father's death. He smiled at her and said, 'My turn to give you a glass today.'

The girl looked embarrassed. 'I'm sorry to come.' She turned to include Bethany in her apology. 'I mean, so soon after your loss. It's just that . . . I didn't know what else to do.'

23

THE KINDNESS OF STRANGERS

I will lift up mine eyes unto the hills:
from whence cometh my help.

Psalm 121

The significance of the remark did not sink in at first. Bethany, Jack and Adam all assumed that the girl and her mother had been out walking and had stumbled upon Langstroth Farmhouse by happy accident when the mother was in need of sustenance.

The girl pressed the glass of water into her mother's hand. Her mother looked up, then sipped the water slowly as the colour gradually returned to her cheeks. She managed a weak smile before she, too, began to apologise.

'I said we shouldn't come, but Jess insisted.'

The daughter smiled. 'It's my mum, you see.'

The mother put a hand on the girl's arm. 'I really don't think this is right.' Then she looked towards Adam and Bethany. 'It's really very kind of you to give me a glass of water, but we should be on our way.' She made to get up, wobbled a little, then sat down again. 'In a minute or two, perhaps. You've been very kind. Please, do get on with your day. We'll just rest for a bit and then be off.'

Bethany asked, 'But you were coming *here*?'

The daughter nodded. 'It's just that I thought you might be our last chance and I didn't want to . . . I mean . . .'

She directed her words at Adam. Bethany and Jack exchanged glances.

'I should explain,' she said. 'I'm Jess Hartley, and this is my mum, Sarah. She's been ill. There's a lump in her tummy and the doctors have said there is nothing they can do for her. Not any more. They've tried all kinds of things and . . .' She sat down next to her mother and took hold of her hand. 'Well, I'd heard about you, Adam, and I just thought that what you've done is so wonderful.'

Sarah Hartley tugged at her daughter's arm in an effort to get her to stop speaking, but Jess carried on regardless. 'I was going to talk to you that evening in the mayor's parlour but . . . it wouldn't have been right after what happened—'

Her mother interrupted. 'And it's still not right now, Jess. Please . . .'

Jess looked up at Adam. 'I can't just sit by and do nothing, can I? I know I shouldn't ask, and I feel bad that I have, but if *your* mum was ill, and the doctors said they couldn't do anything, what would *you* do?' She stopped speaking, her eyes brimful of tears.

Sarah smiled at Adam. 'I wouldn't have come if it hadn't been for Jess. She's all I've got, you see, and I'm all she's got since her dad died last year. You understand that, don't you?'

She spoke directly to Bethany now. 'I do understand how you feel, Mrs Gabriel. And I know that so many people will say that to you, but I *do* know. I've been there. It's still raw, even after a year.'

Bethany nodded and attempted a reciprocal smile. 'Thank you.'

'So you see,' said Jess to Adam, gulping back the tears, 'you're our last hope.'

Adam looked horrified. 'But I don't know what I can do. I mean, I've never—'

'I know you never boast about or even admit your gift,' said Jess, 'not openly, but everyone at school knows about it.'

Bethany cut in: 'But Adam doesn't . . . well, he doesn't make a point of—'

'I know, I know. But if he could just help . . .' She ran out of words and simply looked pleadingly at Adam, who glanced at his mother with bewilderment.

'Why don't I run you two back home in yon Land Rover,' offered Jack, 'and give Adam time to think, eh?'

Sarah rose unsteadily to her feet. 'Of course. I'm so sorry to have bothered you both, particularly at this difficult time. If it were up to me, as I say, we wouldn't have come but Jess is very persuasive when she puts her mind to something.'

Jess lowered her eyes. 'I suppose I am.' Then she looked again at Adam. 'I probably shouldn't have asked. But what else could I do?'

She took her mother's arm and the two of them, shepherded by Jack, walked unsteadily across to the Land Rover. Jess helped her mother climb into the cab and as she followed she turned and spoke again. 'I didn't mean to impose. I'm sorry.'

Her pale blue eyes shone and her face bore a look that Adam would never forget.

The Land Rover growled into life, and before either Bethany

or Adam could say anything, it lurched off down the track in the direction of the village.

Jack did not return that afternoon. It was getting late, and since Luke's death, he had taken to using the Land Rover as a taxi. Bethany had encouraged him to do so, and knew it would not be long before Adam, too, would be at the wheel. Now that he was seventeen how could she stop him? He was adept at driving on the fellside tracks on both quad bike and Land Rover. He had been proficient at it since he was fourteen, and when he passed his test she would have to sit at home while he was let loose on the road with traffic and pedestrians and— There was no rationale to her worries as far as Adam's proficiency at the wheel was concerned. But now he was all she had, and the prospect of him coming to grief at the hands of some idiot was more than she could bear. It was best to put it to the back of her mind. It was another worry that lay ahead. Right now there was a different ordeal to face. What should her son do about Sarah Hartley?

They sat at either side of the kitchen table for their evening meal. Not that Bethany had been eating much since Luke's death. It worried Adam that she was wasting away, and he had nagged at her until he realised the futility of such an approach. Instead he had taken to making sure he was as good a source of company as he could be, putting aside his own grief when he was with her, and only allowing himself to give way to his deepest emotions in the confines of his bedroom. The time would come when they would be able to speak openly to one another of the husband and father whose absence had left a gaping void. For now it was simply a matter of bumbling through as best they could. Adam tried to get

Bethany out of the farmhouse kitchen and into the fresh air where, he hoped, the land and the flock could work their magic. If she ventured out once a day he was lucky. He must work on that, he knew.

But now there was another thing to be considered.

'Have you thought about what you'll do?' asked Bethany.

'What *can* I do?' asked Adam, the note of desperation clearly detectable in his voice.

'You could go and see her.'

'But I'm not a doctor.'

'No, you're not, but if you can help . . .'

'I'd feel weird about it. Like some sort of quack. It seems wrong somehow to go into somebody's house and pretend that I can make them better.'

Bethany forced a smile. 'But you can, and you do. Or, at least, you have.'

'Yes, but quietly. I don't really think about it. It just sort of happens.'

Bethany fixed him with a mother's look.

Adam persisted, 'Supposing it didn't work. Supposing I raise her hopes and nothing changes.'

'Supposing you don't go and Mrs Hartley dies. How will you feel then?'

'That's not fair.'

'But it's a pretty fair assessment of the situation, isn't it?'

Adam looked pleadingly at his mother.

Bethany reached across and took his hand. 'I know it's difficult, and had it been anybody else, in any other kind of situation, I think I'd have felt like you. But you heard what the mother said. She's all Jess has. And you could see from the girl's face how worried she is – terrified, even. She stands to lose everything. Like you, she's lost her dad, and now her mum is ill.' Bethany looked out of the window and said, almost to herself, 'I wouldn't wish that on anybody.'

She turned back to Adam. 'You don't have to tell anybody about it. You could just go there quietly and see if you can help. Perhaps just talk to them. Explain that it's not something you do regularly, that you don't even know how you do it or if what's happened in the past has simply been a coincidence. But you and I know that's not true, don't we?'

Adam turned to meet her eye.

'I know we've never really talked about it, not together. But your dad and I did sometimes. Not that we understand it.' Then, correcting herself, 'Understood it. But we both acknowledged that you seemed to be able to heal things – whether it was Finn's eye, or a sickly lamb or even that wretched boy Jakey Learoyd. Look how you used to find sheep lost in snowdrifts. Just because you don't understand your gift doesn't mean it doesn't exist.'

'That's what Jack said.'

'And he's right. One day you're going to have to acknowledge that you're special.'

Adam made to protest.

'Oh, I know you'll say, "We're all special," and, of course, we are, but your gift is rare. I might be your mother, and mothers often think their children are special. But I don't know anyone – I've never heard of anyone – who can do what you have done. You can either pretend it doesn't exist or try to use it for good – not in a way that shouts it from the treetops, but quietly when your particular talent is most needed.' She let go of his hand and sat back in her chair. 'That's all.'

'But if I go, and I do . . . whatever I can and it doesn't work, haven't I raised their hopes for no good reason?' He paused. 'I couldn't help Dad.'

Bethany looked at him sternly. 'Never say that. Not ever. Your father was beyond being helped, even by you, and if I thought you blamed yourself for his death . . . Well, please don't even go there. Jess's mum is a different story. There's still a chance for her, and what other hope do they have? They've exhausted them all. As Jess said, the doctors have done all they can. There's no other avenue left to explore.'

'Except me?'

Bethany nodded. 'Except you.'

24

BEST ENDEAVOURS

You never know what you can do until you try.

Nineteenth-century proverb

The weather was vile. Jack pulled up the Land Rover outside the end-of-terrace house – larger, but not much, than his own – and turned to Adam. 'Go on, then. I'll be 'ere.' He nodded by way of encouragement and tacit support as Adam left the cab and walked down the short path to the front door.

Jack had told him where the Hartleys lived, but Adam needed to get his head around what he was being asked to do. He found all kinds of reasons to avoid committing to a particular date or time – the care of the flock, his lack of belief in his own ability and the fact that his mother needed him (even though she had encouraged him to offer what help he could). In the end, on a day when the rain lashed sideways in swathes across the fellside, and sawing logs seemed too painful to contemplate (that being the last time Adam had enjoyed a one-to-one conversation with his father), he took the bull by the horns and asked Jack to run him into the village.

The short path leading up to the front door was bordered by white-flowered Japanese anemones – a sure sign of the summer reaching its height, even though today they were dripping with diamonds of water. The door was painted pale blue, the colour the August sky should have been, rather than the unseasonal slate grey of the tumbling clouds that lowered above him.

Fred Pennock, the postman, had just pushed an envelope through the letterbox next door and was retreating up the path. 'Mornin', Adam,' he called cheerily. Adam barely registered. His mind was elsewhere.

There was silence for quite some time after he knocked. A feeling of relief was beginning to creep over him. They weren't in. He could go back and say to his mother that at least he had tried. Then he heard a key being turned. The door opened to reveal Jess, whose initial reaction was to step back into the house, almost as though she had seen a ghost. Then came recognition, swiftly followed by delight. She stepped forward and flung her arms around Adam who, taken aback, found himself lost for words.

'Thank you so, so much for coming,' said Jess. 'I honestly didn't think you would.'

Still Adam said nothing.

'Come in, come in!' Then, turning and shouting through to the back of the house and the kitchen, 'Mum! It's Adam. He's come!'

Mrs Hartley emerged from the kitchen, wiping her damp hands on her apron. Her face bore a look of incredulity that swiftly turned into delight. 'I didn't think you'd come,' she murmured. 'I really didn't.'

Adam smiled at her nervously and shrugged. 'I'll do my best, Mrs Hartley. That's all I can say, really. I'll do my best.'

*

The next half-hour passed in a blur, and when Adam left the house, with the thanks of mother and daughter ringing in his ears, the familiar feeling of total exhaustion descended upon him, like some invisible shroud. He could barely speak on the journey home. Jack was content to leave him to his thoughts, saying nothing until he pulled up outside the farmhouse. The rain had eased now, and a strong breeze was shunting heavy clouds across the horizon.

'Go and get thissen a drink,' suggested Jack. 'Tha's earnt it.'

'We don't know that yet, do we?' murmured Adam, sliding down from the cab and treading wearily to the door of the farmhouse. His mother was chopping vegetables at the kitchen table. On seeing her son she rose, walked across and wrapped her arms around him. 'Well done.'

Adam shrugged. 'I think I'll have a shower.'

Bethany knew better than to tax him about the morning's events. He would tell her in his own time. But whatever transpired in terms of Sarah Hartley's health, at least Adam had done his best, and there was no need for anyone else to know.

Adam spent the afternoon walking the fellside with Nip, talking to his dog, sharing his thoughts. 'Am I mad?' he asked himself – and his companion. 'Am I making it up? Have I any idea what I'm doing?' To all three questions the dog made no reply, but his own answer was a clear 'No.' Not that it eased his mind much.

The sky was clearing, the sun winning the morning's battle with the rain. The wind was easing, too. It was as if the elements were in tune with his thoughts and the clouds above him began to lift. The total sapping of energy caused by the morning's activities was replaced by a strange lightness of being. He felt almost heady with relief as he and Nip tumbled down the hillside towards the river.

His favourite rock was damp from the rain, but he didn't care. He climbed up it, sat down and surveyed the view across the bend in the infant Wharfe, whose amber waters were freshened by the earlier rainfall. Nip sat beside him and nudged his arm, hoping for attention or a titbit. He bent down and ruffled his companion's glossy coat, looking out across the narrow valley and wondering – not for the first time – what Isla would be doing. She would be back in New Zealand now. Did she still think of him? He certainly still thought of her, even though the loss of his father had pushed most other things from his mind. The remembrance of their brief time together filled him with welcome warmth.

He wondered if she would know about his father. She couldn't, he supposed. Being so peripatetic and not staying anywhere for more than a few days, it was unlikely that the news would have caught up with her. She might well have been on her way home on that fateful evening.

From Isla his thoughts turned to a girl nearer home: Jess Hartley.

He had been taken aback by the extent of her gratitude. She had hugged him again as he left, and kissed his cheek. He could still detect her fragrance although he had showered and changed in the meantime. What was it about scents that made them linger, long after they had first been experienced? Of all the senses, it was smell that had the power to transport you to another place, another time, and the company of another person. Isla's fragrance did the same. It was fading a little in his memory now, but he knew that the moment he detected it again he would feel the butterflies in his stomach and the sensation of her presence would be reawakened.

The scent of grass being cut at haymaking and the thick, sickly aroma of silage were capable of heightening the senses and giving those who recognised them a sense of place and time.

He was woken from his reverie by niggling thoughts of tasks left undone, of those that needed immediate attention and which, God willing, would help take his mind off the recent tragedy, offering respite from the sorrow. There were ewes to get to market, grass to cut, hay bales to store, walls to repair and the general day-to-day running of the farm, which Jack seemed to have been shouldering alone for weeks. He couldn't let him go on doing the lion's share of the work. And he really must find a way of getting his mother out of the house, not least because they were short of manpower. The loss of his father was compounded by the withdrawal of Bethany from the workforce. Thank God it had not happened at lambing time. And then he felt dreadful for even having that thought, although he consoled himself that Luke would have felt just the same about the flock he had built up and cherished.

Sitting on the rock, overlooking the river, an awareness of the ongoing power of nature enveloped him. Luke had taken over from his own father, and now Adam must take over from Luke. There was an inevitability to it, yes, but also a choice. He could let things drift or grasp the nettle and move on. He knew that he had chosen a life on the land, a life in the dale, but was that it? The yearly round of lambing and shearing, haymaking and market, with one year being much the same as the last? It was a life he relished, but should he – as his mother had encouraged – seek more?

At the moment how could he? No. He would run the farm and the flock and run them well. There was time enough to decide what the distant future held – if, indeed, he would have any control over that. Perhaps Isla would come back next year. Perhaps not. Should he be realistic about the brevity and intensity of their encounter, or would he give way to the daydream he had toyed with of going to New Zealand? No, that was not an option. Not now, at any rate. His work, his duty and, if he were honest, his heart were here in the Yorkshire Dales. He must prove his worth and his mettle by stepping up to the plate and making a decent fist of the life that Fate had so far dealt him.

As for the thing they called his 'gift', he would simply let that lie. What could he do? Deny it existed? He could not. But neither could he claim that it *did* exist, that he was in possession of some hidden power. Oh, it was all so confusing for a boy of seventeen, though he admitted to himself that he did not feel like a boy any more. Boys were carefree, boys were irresponsible, boys were into computers and mobiles. That word 'weirdo' began to sneak into his consciousness again. If only life were straightforward. If only he could be given a sign that he was choosing the right path to follow. But as recent events had proved, nothing in life was certain and, as his mother frequently reminded him, in this life you simply have to go where Fate dictates.

He had found that hard to believe when he was younger. He had even looked up the word in the dictionary. He had never forgotten the definition. It was as if it were engraved on his heart. 'Fate: the development of events outside a person's control, regarded as predetermined by a supernatural power.'

25

NEW BLOOD

'Pipe a song about a Lamb!'
So I piped with merry cheer.
'Piper, pipe that song again';
So I piped: he wept to hear.

William Blake, *Songs of Innocence*, 1789

The summer wore on. The leaves on the sycamore turned brown at the edges and rattled like paper bags in every passing breeze while the weary river slid by, its water low and seemingly irritated by the rounded boulders that broke its surface. It grumbled gently, impatient to be filled by autumn rains.

At last Bethany had eased herself back into the landscape, had left the confines of the farmhouse kitchen and felt once more the healing power of earth and sky, wind and rain, river and moorland. It was as if she had deliberately put herself through a period of deprivation, a withdrawal of privileges to purge herself of grief. Somehow she needed to isolate herself from the world, from any kind of distraction that would impair her ability to brood on what had been. Slowly, so slowly, she came to and took the late summer air. There were days when she would retreat back into the house, like a tortoise withdrawing into its shell, but those lapses became less frequent, and she began to come to terms with the guilt that followed any momentary relaxation of her overwhelming sense of loss. How long was one meant to grieve? What was normal? She would mourn Luke for ever, but she owed it to her son, and her land – Luke's land – to pick up the threads of her former life and weave them into some kind of pattern that would honour him and help soothe her anguish.

Adam knew she was turning a corner when, for the first time since his father's death, she came down to the water's edge and shouted at him across the river, 'Are you coming in for your breakfast or what?'

He had been moving sheep, Nip doing most of the work and Jack content to bring up the rear and corral any strays. He had lost all track of time, as he frequently did when out on the fellside. It was one of those calm September days, the weather settled, the wind too weary to bother getting up speed.

'On my way,' he shouted back. He turned to Jack, who was ambling towards him. 'Mending,' he said.

'Aye. It's time,' was the old man's reply.

Over breakfast – for Jack had been invited in to partake of the kind of meal he would never dream of making for himself – the three of them talked over the jobs for the day ahead. Adam had got into the habit of watching his mother's every move, every twitch of eyebrow, every furrow of brow, steeling himself not to overreact, but noting the ups and the downs. He was registering that gradually, little bit by little bit, there were fewer downs and, if not more ups, certainly days when Bethany seemed more level in her outlook and less weighed down.

'There'll be more of 'em off termorrer, missus,' said Jack, referring to the lambs he was to take to market. 'An' are we goin' for that new tup or what?'

'Oh. I'd forgotten.' Bethany turned to Adam. 'What do you think?'

Luke had intimated that they could do with a new ram. Along with several other initiatives, it had been put on hold after his death. But with the autumn coming, and the ewes needing to be covered, Jack knew that if no new ram was purchased at the livestock sales over the next few weeks – the ram having to be introduced to the ewes in autumn – the window of opportunity to introduce new blood would be missed.

Adam was positive in his reply. 'We'll have to wait another year if we don't do it now. I think we should.'

Bethany nodded. 'Shall I come with you?'

The question made Adam's heart leap. It would be the first time Bethany had left the farm since the funeral almost three months ago. 'Yes, please!'

'Aye, missus. A grand idea,' confirmed Jack, through a mouthful of scrambled egg and bacon. He was anxious to get his employer back into the fold, mainly because he was pleased to see Bethany rediscovering her old self but also because his old bones were wearying of the increased labour her absence had necessitated.

'Tomorrow morning, then?' said Adam. 'If Jack can hold the fort here.'

'No problem,' said the old man.

Bethany nodded. 'Fine.' That was all. Adam hoped that when the day dawned she would not change her mind.

*

True to her word, the following morning Bethany travelled with Adam to market at the wheel of the Land Rover. She was silent for most of the journey, but Adam noticed she looked about her as though seeing the landscape for the first time. The clumps of trees, the sinuous river and the towering fells burnished copper by the ripening fronds of bracken she looked at with fresh eyes. It was as if Nature was refuelling her. By the time they arrived at the Craven Cattle Mart Adam was sure he could detect the faintest sign of a smile on her lips.

They moved their twenty-five lambs from the trailer into the designated pen, and once they had seen to the paperwork they went for a coffee. How strange it seemed, to be there without Luke. It was he who would be the guiding hand at auctions. Now they must manage on their own. Both felt nervous at the prospect, not that there was anything they could do. The lambs would fetch what they would fetch, but still it seemed like some out-of-body experience. Adam was aware of feeling protective towards the mother who, until so recently, had been protecting him.

They sat at a table overlooking the mart. The auction was already in progress and the tumble of words, no discernible gaps between them, spewed from the auctioneer as he knocked down lot after lot to a motley collection of bidders – some local, some from far afield – clad in tweeds and waterproofs, flat caps and jaunty trilbys, men and women alike.

There was a brisk tang of business in the air, and for a few minutes the two sat silently until Adam enquired, 'Are you all right?'

Bethany nodded, still gazing out over the ring as one small flock replaced another and the auctioneer began his monotone litany, sounding for all the world like some robotic alien from a science-fiction movie. 'Strange,' she murmured.

'What do you mean?'

'It's been so long. I haven't been here for years. I wondered what it would be like, without your dad. And it's just . . . different.' Then, conscious of her words, 'Does that sound stupid?'

Adam shrugged. 'Obvious, I suppose.'

Bethany heaved a sigh. 'Thank you.'

'I didn't mean—'

'Neither did I. Thank you for looking after me. That's what I meant. I know it's been difficult for both of us, but I couldn't have hoped for a better son.'

Adam looked embarrassed.

She reached across the table and took his hand. 'We're just going to have to get on with it, aren't we? No point in sitting inside that house thinking what might have been. This is it. Got to crack on.' She managed a brave smile.

Adam smiled back. It seemed the right thing to do. Telling his mother she was right would have seemed as though he had been impatient for her to realise as much, and he didn't want that. It came, though, as a relief. A corner turned, a statement of intent for which he was grateful.

Bethany took another sip of her coffee and changed the subject. 'Have you heard anything from the lady who came to the farm? Mrs Hartley?'

'No. I'm a bit worried.'

'You shouldn't be. You did your best and you were right to go.' She thought for a moment. 'You could drop in to see how she is, I suppose.'

'What? Like a doctor paying house calls?'

Bethany realised her mistake. 'Yes. Sorry. Silly idea.' She paused. 'I rather liked her daughter. Nice girl.'

'Yes.'

Bethany met his eye. 'I'm not doing very well this morning, am I?'

Adam smiled. 'You're doing fine. You're out, that's the main thing. Now, shall we go and see what we got for those lambs? And we need to look for a decent tup, too.'

'Are you bossing me about?'

'Just a bit.'

Bethany lifted up her hand as if to strike him. 'You're never too old for a clip round the ear, remember!'

Adam grinned. 'No. But I'm quicker than you are. Come on. Let's go shopping.'

26

THE MATING SEASON

Man's love is of man's life a thing apart;
Girls aren't like that.

Kingsley Amis, *A Bookshop Idyll*, 1956

He was a hefty beast with a mind of his own, but he was certainly handsome.

'So 'e bloody well should be at that price,' muttered Jack, as the new tup butted and tumbled his way out of the trailer and into the pen beside the barn to be given the once-over and tagged before being allowed out with his new flock.

'They can go for more than he did,' offered Adam, defensively. 'Some of them fetch five grand.'

'I remember when we used to borrow one,' reflected Jack, grudgingly. 'Still, 'e's a looker, I'll give 'im that.'

Their conversation, as so often of late, was interrupted by the sight of a figure coming up the farm track. Jack was busy at the back of the barn sorting out the tag for the new ram so it was Adam who saw Jess Hartley. She was alone, her face cast down.

His heart beat rapidly, a sickening feeling in his stomach, waiting for what he suspected was the inevitable.

He walked across the farmyard towards the top of the track. As he did so she lifted her head and he saw the tears coursing down her cheeks.

'I'm sorry,' he said.

'Why? Why are you sorry?'

Her face broke into a wide smile. The tears were of joy. 'She's better. You did it!'

'But I didn't do anything. I just—'

'You just did what you can do. And it's wonderful. Thank you so much.' She came up to him, put her arms around him and kissed his cheek. Then she gave him an enormous hug. 'I can't tell you how relieved we are.'

For the second time today Adam was struggling to find the right words. Eventually he managed, 'That's great news. Really great. I mean, have you . . .?'

'Mum was at the doctor's yesterday. He couldn't believe it. He said the lump's almost gone, and Mum's feeling so much better.'

'Perhaps it was—'

Jess interrupted him. 'The doctor says it happens sometimes. "Spontaneous regression" it's called, or "spontaneous remission", where a lump reduces in size and eventually disappears of its own accord without any scientific explanation.'

'Yes. Yes, of course.'

'But we know it wasn't that. We know it was you. Mum said she could feel it straight away – the healing process.'

'Well, whatever it was, it's great news.' Adam turned towards the house, as if looking for reinforcements, but his mother, now relishing her new-found freedom, was out with the sheep.

'Would you like a coffee?' he asked.

'Thank you. That would be lovely.' Jess looked around her. 'I do love it up here. So far from the village. So peaceful. So other-worldly. A bit like you.' Then, realising her remark might be misconstrued, 'I mean – special. Not weird.'

Adam smiled. 'Oh, don't worry. I've been called that before. But I think I prefer "other-worldly".'

They sat on the same stone slab as Jess and her mother had when they had come to the farm. The late-summer sun caught her blonde hair, tied back in its customary ponytail. Her skin was delicately freckled, her eyes the colour of the sky. She seemed to be bursting to talk – about her mother, her life in the village, her future, which, it seemed, was far from certain.

'Will you go to university?' he asked.

Jess shook her head. 'No. Can't afford it. Not with Mum . . . and, anyway, I don't think I'm cut out for an academic life.'

'So what, then?'

'Something local. Outdoors preferably. There's a small nursery just outside Skipton. I thought I might see if they needed any extra hands, even though the pay will be rubbish.'

'When will you leave?'

She laughed, a light, rippling laugh. Adam realised he had not heard laughter in a long time.

'I left in July. I'm a free agent.'

'Wow!' was all he could say.

Jess gazed about her at the rolling hills and fells. 'How do you get any work done up here? It's all so beautiful.'

'Oh, it's a bit different in winter. Perishing cold. And when the snow comes, or the biting easterlies, you need more than a vest to keep them out.'

She laughed again. 'You are funny.'

'Funny and other-worldly. What a combination.'

'How old are you?' she asked.

'Seventeen.'

'You don't talk as if you're seventeen.'

'Older or younger?' he asked.

'Older. Wiser.'

'Maybe I've had to grow up fast. Over this year at any rate.'

'Yes. I'm sorry.'

'No. Don't be.' He hesitated. 'It's nice to see you again.'

'And you. Perhaps we could . . .'

Adam was aware that she felt she might have said too much. He surprised himself by offering encouragement. 'See each other again?'

Jess nodded. 'If you like.' Then, by way of teasing him, 'Of course, I'm much older than you.' She saw the bewilderment on his face and gently dug him in the ribs. 'Eighteen. Positively ancient.'

Adam grinned. 'I've always liked older women.' And then, realising the rashness of his remark, he felt himself blushing.

Jess smiled. 'Well, that's all right, then.' She drained her mug. 'What about tomorrow night?'

'Fine.'

'Shall I come and collect you?'

'Er . . . yes, if you like.'

She grinned. 'You see, being older than you, I've passed my driving test and I'm using my dad's car. It's a bit ancient, and it's very small, but it does mean I have my own wheels.'

He took the teasing well. 'Sounds great.'

'Shall I pick you up about seven, then? There's a nice little bistro down by the canal in Skipton . . .'

He could think of no reason to demur. 'Right. Fine. I'll see you tomorrow at seven, then.'

Jess put down her mug, turned towards him and kissed him lightly on the cheek. 'Till tomorrow.' She got up and began to walk down the track, then turned and said, 'And thank you. For everything.'

He had not experienced such a feeling since Isla had left. He had not expected to feel it again. Funny how unpredictable life could be, in so many ways.

'You're going out?' his mother asked, looking up from the book she was reading. It was by Georgette Heyer. She had found solace in Regency England since Luke had died. She had read the books in her twenties and now found it comforting to immerse herself once more in their protective blanket.

'Yes. If you don't mind?' The concern was genuine. It had not occurred to him that since his father died he had been under the same roof as his mother and seldom left her alone, except to work the sheep.

Bethany smiled. 'Of course I don't mind. It's about time.'

'I won't be late back.'

'Am I allowed to ask where you're going? Only my dad always needed to know where I was and who I was with and I can't tell you how much I resented it.'

Adam shook his head. 'I don't resent it. I'm going to a bistro in Skipton with Jess Hartley.'

'How nice.'

'She's driving.'

'I'm sure she's very careful. And very grateful, too, I should think. For what you did.'

'I'm not sure I did anything. According to the doctor . . .'

'Yes, I know. You said about the "spontaneous regression". Well, whatever it was I doubt we'll ever know for sure, and I'm so pleased for her. And her mum.'

Adam grabbed his jacket from the back of the door. He turned. 'Mum?'

Bethany looked up once more from her book.

'Do you think we could do with another pair of hands? On the farm, I mean.'

27

HIRED HELP

Immature love says: 'I love you because I need you.'
Mature love says: 'I need you because I love you.'

Erich Fromm, *The Art of Loving*, 1956

'I thought you might call me and say you didn't want to come,' said Jess, as she drove him down the farm track.

'I don't have your phone number,' countered Adam.

She glanced at him quizzically.

'And, anyway, why should I not want to come?' he asked.

'Oh, it happens.'

'A lot?'

She dug him in the ribs with her left elbow. 'No. Not a lot. I just thought you might have second thoughts.'

'No. Not at all.' He fought for some more words, anxious not to mess things up. Finally he managed, 'I've been looking forward to it.'

'Me too.'

Gradually Adam began to relax. There was more talk about what each of them had been doing during the day, about the weather, the respective health of Jess's mum, Adam's mum and the flock of sheep, until they finally arrived at the café on the edge of the canal. It was only when they got out of the car, a battered little Peugeot that had once been bright red, that Adam got a good look at – well, yes, he supposed she was – his date. She wore three-quarter-length caramel-coloured trousers, flat brown shoes, a white sloppy Joe sweater, and her hair, which he had hitherto seen only when it was tied back, was now loose. It shone like gold in the evening sun as it brushed her shoulders. Her skin had a rosy freshness, and there had been no attempt to hide the freckles that dusted her nose and forehead. She seemed to float in a cloud of delicate floral fragrance that gave him butterflies in the pit of his stomach. He remembered experiencing the same sort of feeling when he'd met Isla. This time it was slightly different, just how he couldn't explain.

She locked the car, came round to his side, said, 'Hello,' and kissed his cheek. He was surprised at how open she was, and found himself comparing her with Isla, until some inner voice told him that was neither wise nor fair. He must put Isla out of his mind, for tonight at least.

'Are you hungry?' she asked.

'Starving.'

'They do a great spaghetti carbonara. And kombucha. Have you tried kombucha?'

'We don't go in for puddings much,' confessed Adam.

Jess laughed. 'It's not a pudding. It's a drink. A sort of fizzy tea.'

Adam frowned.

'No, it's delicious, honestly. And non-alcoholic, so you can have as many as you'd like. And it's very good for your gut.'

'Oh, well, if it's good for my gut . . .' he teased.

He was warming to her. Not that he hadn't done so earlier, but he was beginning to get her measure. He liked the way she teased him, and the way her eyes twinkled when she smiled. Her presence made his heart beat faster, lifted him out of himself in a way he hadn't experienced since he had lost his father. He was suddenly able to relax and say what he felt, when he felt it, rather than keeping things to himself, which he seemed to have done for most of his life. Every few minutes he would check himself, would wonder if he was being too open, but it was good to let go – a little anyway – and try to match her mischievous sense of humour with his own personality, whatever that might be.

They ordered the spaghetti and the kombucha – much better tasting than he had imagined – and fell to talking about the future: he about taking on the farm, she about finding some outdoor job that would allow her to be at one with nature, rather than stuck in some office where she wouldn't see daylight from nine till five.

'Have you done anything about that nursery?' he asked. 'The one near Skipton.'

For the first time that evening she looked downcast. 'Yes. They've no vacancies. There's a little nursery by the river at Ilkley but it's just too far to travel. So I'm still looking. I'm determined not to take the path of least resistance and settle for something I'd hate. I want fresh air and I'm not afraid of hard work.'

'What about being a shepherdess?' he asked.

'Me?'

'Yes. You'd be outdoors in the fresh air, not stuck within four walls.'

Her eyes widened. 'I know a bit about growing plants – I

look after our back garden, and Dad's old greenhouse – but I don't know anything about sheep.'

'You could learn. If you're willing.'

'Well, yes. I'm always happy to learn but how would I start? *Where* would I start?'

'There's this little farm in Langstrothdale. You wouldn't have to travel far. You could probably walk to work if you wanted.'

At first she didn't twig. 'But would they take on someone who knew nothing about it, even if she wanted to learn?'

'Well, I asked the boss lady and she said that if you wanted to give it a go – a trial period she called it – then she'd be prepared to take you on.'

'Oh, my goodness.' Jess sat back in her chair, and simultaneously the reality of the situation dawned. 'You mean . . . *your* farm?'

Adam nodded.

'And the boss lady, she's your mum?'

He nodded again.

'Goodness!' She sat quite still for a few moments, her brain clearly spinning. 'A shepherdess,' she murmured. 'But with you?'

Adam feared that the situation was clearly too much for her to take in. 'You don't have to give me an answer now. Think about it. It's just that you said you wanted to work outdoors, and we could do with some more help. It's been a bit of a struggle since Dad died, and an extra pair of hands would make a real difference.'

'No . . .' she murmured.

'Well, I thought it was worth asking. Just in case . . .'

'I mean, no, I don't need to think about it. I'd love to.' All this was said as though her mind was elsewhere and the words were being dictated by some hidden force. Then she came to and looked at him directly. 'There's just one thing.'

Adam looked at her questioningly.

'I don't want you to think I'm doing this out of gratitude. For what you did for Mum. I mean, I *am* grateful – we both are – you know that, but I'm doing it because I want to. Because the thought of being a shepherdess . . . Well, it's never crossed my mind before – Lord knows why not. I've been surrounded by sheep since I was born but I suppose it's easy to overlook the obvious. I love the countryside, I'm not afraid of hard work, I'm happy to learn and – oh!'

'What?'

'Are you offering me the job because you feel sorry for me?'

'No!' Adam's reply was so emphatic that it almost knocked her back in her chair.

'OK, OK! I just needed to ask, that's all. If we're going to do this, we need to get off on an even footing. You need a shepherdess – I can't believe that's what I'm going to be, it sounds like something made out of porcelain, with a crook in one hand and a lamb in the other – and I need an outdoor job, so it makes sense that we both get what we want.'

Adam smiled. 'You don't know if it *is* what you want yet. You might hate it.'

'I'll take that chance. And I have to warn you that I'm a sticker. I don't give in easily.'

'You'll be cold, you'll be wet, you'll be tired –'

'And I'll be outside in the Yorkshire Dales,' she interrupted.

'– and winter's coming,' concluded Adam.

'Do you want me to do this job or not?'

'Yes, I do. Very much.'

'Oh dear,' she said.

'Why "Oh dear"?'

'It's just that we were getting on so well . . .'

'And you don't want to spoil it?'

She nodded.

Adam reached across the table and took her hand in his. 'We'd better try hard not to, then.'

Jess sighed. 'I think that's going to be very difficult.'

28

COMPANY

Friendships begin with liking or gratitude –
roots that can be pulled up.

George Eliot, *Daniel Deronda*, 1876

Neither of them thought it would be easy. Not the physical work – that kind of difficulty was a given. But to keep their friendship going – and perhaps something deeper and more meaningful – would be testing in the workplace where they saw each other every day. And they were both so young.

But there was a matter-of-factness about Jess, which surprised Adam. For someone so delicately boned and slight of stature she had an inner strength that seemed to power her slender body.

Bethany was surprised at the girl's willingness and adaptability, and relieved, truth to tell, to have another pair of hands on the farm.

Jack, on the other hand, was sceptical. How could some slip of a girl cope with the demands of a flock and the ruggedness of the fells? Like as not it would end in tears. The lad was besotted by her, that much was clear, and who was Jack to burst the bubble? Adam had had enough to deal with over the last few months and he doubted that anyone would have handled things as well as the boy had. Added to which, having watched him grow from a toddler to, well, a man now, it had to be admitted, he had more than a little respect for the lad's resilience, tenacity and general attitude.

Jack would watch the young shepherd and putative shepherdess as they went about their work. Try as he might to disparage the girl, it was clear that she was made of stern stuff. But she had not yet worked through a Dales winter, when the tips of your fingers throbbed so violently that you could have happily taken a knife to cut them off and relieve the pain. When the icy rain ran down the back of your collar in a never-ending torrent, and when the sheep were so bloody-minded and recalcitrant that you didn't care whether they lived or died out there on that blessed fell. All of this would run through his mind, day after day, and day after day the girl would return, plodding up the track in her boots and her windcheater, cheeks red from the exertion, but the light in her eye never wavering for a moment.

The three of them were out on the fell – Adam on the quad bike, Jess with Nip at her heel (the dog was learning her ways and had warmed to her rather more than Adam would have liked), Jack muttering to himself and bringing up the rear. They were sweeping their way down the fellside towards the river with two dozen sheep in front of them, bleating wildly and careering this way and that, as they were rounded up for market. It was early morning and Bethany had come down off the fell before them to make coffee and breakfast.

This was not the normal course of events, except on market

day when a bacon roll and a steaming coffee would fuel them for the ride into town, the sheep pulled behind in the trailer and hopes high – always high – of a decent price. Sometimes those hopes and aspirations were realised, at others not, but there was no point in being a shepherd unless you had faith in the future.

Over breakfast Jess fired off questions like a machine-gun. How old were the lambs they were taking to market? Why were they taking that number and not more? How much would they get for them? Would it be enough? When was lambing time?

Adam made to reply, but it was Bethany who gave the answers: the lambs were around six months old; she and Adam preferred a steady flow of income, hence the small numbers that were taken each time – added to which there was always the hope that prices would rise for the next batch; they would probably get just over a hundred pounds per head; it was never enough; and lambing time was in April and May.

Jess sat back in her chair taking it all in. She was about to make further enquiries when Bethany rose from her seat and said to Adam, 'Right. You ready?'

Adam nodded, and looked enquiringly at Jess. 'Are you sure you'll be all right?'

'Of course,' she answered brightly. 'I've got Jack to look after me.'

The old man nearly choked on the last mouthful of bacon roll, but hastily washed it down with the dregs from his ancient mug before muttering something that even Bethany and Adam found impossible to translate. He seemed acutely uncomfortable and Bethany found it hard to suppress a smile at the prospect of the gnarled old Yorkshireman having to work with a bright young teenage girl: being left in charge with Jess would challenge not only Jack's powers of diplomacy, but also his ability to get on with an outsider. He had not worked with anyone other than Bethany, Luke and Adam for the last twenty years.

As the Land Rover and trailer bumped off down the track, Adam looking anxiously over his shoulder, Jack turned to his new charge. 'Reet. Is tha feelin' strong?'

Jess nodded.

'See that dry-stone wall o'er theer?'

Jess glanced in the direction of Jack's outstretched arm. 'Yes.'

'It's brocken. Dost tha think tha can repair it?'

Jess looked at the collapsed section of the six-foot-high wall, which was now little more than a jumbled heap of boulders, revealing a ten-foot-wide gap through which sheep and hikers alike would have little trouble in passing. She shrugged. 'I'll have a go.'

'Tha'll find a pair o' gloves in the barn. If tha feels tha'll need 'em.' And with that he wandered off in the direction of the outside lavatory for his morning ablutions. After a few steps in that direction he turned. 'And don't think tha's the first girl he's set his eye on.' The observant passer-by would have noticed a wry and rather mischievous smile on his lips as he headed off for his morning ritual.

It was lunchtime when Bethany and Adam returned with the empty trailer and rather more in their pockets than they had anticipated. Their mood was bright: there was nothing like a good morning at market for lifting the spirits and encouraging you to think you had the best job on earth – a feeling magnified by the emergence of a watery autumn sun that glinted on the fine dew-laden grass of the lower pastures.

Bethany parked and went into the house. Adam went in search

of Jess. He did not have to look far. She was standing beside a neat stretch of dry-stone wall, adjusting a wobbly cope stone until it seemed anchored to her satisfaction.

'Have you been learning at the hands of the master, then?' asked Adam.

'What do you mean?' asked Jess.

'Dry-stone walling. That broken section. He's clearly been showing you how to put it back together.' Adam glanced around him. 'Where is the old man?'

Jess shrugged. 'Don't know. He left me here . . .' she glanced at her watch '. . . about four hours ago. Haven't seen him since.'

'But the wall!'

'I know. Not bad, is it? I could have done with some better copes but I had to make do with what was here.'

'But how do you know . . .?'

'My cousin Geoff. He does it for a living. Up in Cumbria. I used to go there for my holidays and help him.'

'You never said.'

'Well, you never asked. And when we first went out I wasn't going to spend the entire evening boasting about my dry-stone walling technique, was I? That would have been a real turn-off.'

Adam grinned. 'Oh, I don't know.'

Jess laughed. He loved her laugh – light and free and rippling. It never failed to lift his spirits.

Before either of them could say any more, Jack appeared from behind the barn. 'How are you—' He stopped in his tracks and surveyed the scene. He walked slowly forward as if advancing on a dangerous beast. First he crouched and looked along the line of the wall. Then he approached it and patted the coping to check its stability. He stepped back once more, scratched his head and took in the way in which the fallen section had been rebuilt and toothed into the walling on either side.

Slowly he turned to Jess. He looked back at the wall, then at Jess once more. His expression was one of incredulity, and his words were few: 'Well, bugger me.'

29

THE BAD PENNY

All newspaper and journalistic activity is an intellectual brothel from which there is no retreat.

Leo Tolstoy, in a letter, 1871

'Bloody 'ell,' said Jack. 'Not 'er again.' He leapt to his feet from the stone slab outside the barn as fast as age and rheumatism would allow and beetled off down the track towards the advancing figure. Only as the individual loomed closer did Adam, emerging from the barn, recognise their visitor: this time, instead of being swathed in a floral print dress and teetering between the sheep droppings in high-heeled shoes, she was wearing a brand new Barbour jacket and a pair of Le Chameau wellington boots.

Belle Barclay was having none of it, however much Jack remonstrated with her. From a distance Adam could see only gestures and hear raised voices, rather than the precise conversation, but she remained fixed to the spot and unwilling to retrace her steps, which appeared to be what Jack was suggesting.

'No!' she boomed, her words clearer now, thanks to an

increase in volume and diction, and an inexorable advancement up the slope. Jack was shuffling backwards, clearly fearful of getting too close and becoming contaminated with the infection he evidently believed the woman possessed.

Eventually he threw up his arms in despair and retreated towards the barn as his aggressor marched resolutely on, coming to a standstill a few yards from Adam, whose expression was a mixture of mistrust and incomprehension.

'Adam!'

He didn't reply, uncertain as to the nature of the visit, the mood and temper of the visitor.

Belle Barclay attempted to disarm him with her best smile, a confection woven of guile and malicious intent in equal measure. 'I wonder if we could talk?'

Adam shrugged. 'What about?'

'Shall we sit down over there?' She gestured in the direction of the stone slab adjacent to the barn, and began to walk towards it, assuming that Adam would follow. He did not.

She sat down and patted the space beside her, indicating that he should join her. Adam walked over, but resolutely refused to do as he was bidden.

'What's this about?' he asked levelly.

'It's about you.' Belle Barclay beamed, the better to show off her expensive orthodontistry and to encourage the sharing of confidences.

'What about me?' asked Adam.

'Let's not be coy, Adam. I want to talk about your gift. Your gift of healing. We were interrupted last time we talked.'

'My father died.'

Belle Barclay's face became a picture of sorrow. 'Yes. Terribly sad. And so sudden. Such a shame for you and your mother.'

She looked about her. 'And for the farm, I shouldn't wonder. How are things? Financially, I mean.'

The question was answered by a figure at the farmhouse door. 'I don't think that's any of your business,' said Bethany, with more than a hint of irritation in her voice.

Belle Barclay brightened, oblivious to any implied criticism. 'Mrs Gabriel. How lovely to see you again. I came up to talk to Adam.'

'Really?' Bethany was advancing after the fashion of a ewe protecting her lamb, but she had reckoned without the newspaper reporter's skill at ignoring any verbal and physical obstacles placed in her way.

'Yes. You see, I want to produce a positive piece about the wonderful work that Adam has done. "The miracles that he has wrought in these hills" in a manner of speaking.'

Bethany drew breath to interrupt. To no avail.

'You see, it's clear to me,' Ms Barclay went on, 'that Adam has a gift, and a remarkable one at that. There was the boy whose life he saved after the stabbing, and before that there were numerous reports from his school friends about his "healing hands", which had cured them of everything from pulled muscles to mysterious rashes, to all kinds of things, too many to list.'

'Well, if it's all the same to you,' said Bethany, 'we'd really prefer not to talk about it. It's just one of those things. Adam is very young and—'

'Oh, Mrs Gabriel I think he's quite capable of answering for himself, don't you?'

The colour rose in Bethany's cheeks, but before she could respond, the *Craven Courier*'s chief investigative reporter motored on to deliver her *coup de grâce*. 'And then, most recently, we have the amazing cure he effected on Mrs Hartley, down in the village. I mean that's just remarkable, isn't it? The doctors failing to do anything for her – writing her off as incurable – and then Adam intervenes and her lump miraculously disappears. It really is an astonishing turn of events and one worth celebrating, I would have thought.'

The annoyance that both Adam and Bethany had felt was now translated into something more complex: a mixture of anger and betrayal. Neither of them had spoken to anyone about the situation involving Jess's mum. How could Belle Barclay have come to know the details? There was only one possible explanation: Sarah Hartley, or her daughter Jess, must have told people about it, explained about Adam's powers of healing. How could they have expected that Sarah and Jess would keep it to themselves? They had been naïve to assume such a thing. Of course mother and daughter would have told people. Why would they not? And now here they were being interviewed by the local paper with a view to . . . what?

The ceremony in the council chamber all those months ago was predicated on Adam's speed of response to an attack that might have resulted in the death of one of his fellow pupils. The paramedics had acknowledged that the swiftness of his actions had saved Jakey Learoyd's life, and there was a certain magical quality about Adam's ability to staunch the flow of blood, but that was really all it amounted to. Wasn't it? And now here was the local newspaper reporter, who not only knew Adam had 'cured' Sarah Hartley but also about the various schoolmates he had 'healed' over the years. This was clearly an investigation that the terrier-like reporter had been working on for some time. Belle Barclay's words might seem to be encouraging, but her reputation as a build-them-up-to-knock-them-down reporter preceded her by some years.

Like a dog with a bone, she continued, 'Why are you so cagey about it, Mrs Gabriel? Isn't this something worth celebrating? Adam has a wonderful gift for helping others. Shouldn't more be made of it?'

Bethany stepped forward to confront her. 'For a start Adam's "gift", as you call it, is something for him to come to terms with. Nobody else. The fact that he can help people is wonderful, yes, but he's never boasted about what he does. We've barely even spoken about it in the family. Who's to say if these gifts are real or just a matter of luck? Or Fate? Who knows if they'll last or simply fade with age? If you write about him in the papers, all manner of people will come to our door asking to be cured. Can you imagine what that will mean? We are farmers, Ms Barclay. We work the land and we raise sheep. We have a job to do. I'm not going to put any more pressure on Adam than that which is already there. He's had to take over as head of the family from his father, that's hard enough, and to eke out a living from these fells. You're asking us to talk about a gift we don't understand in the hope of what? Selling a few more newspapers? And when you've done that, then what? What happens to us? We have to cope with all and sundry trekking up here to the farm in search of cures for Heaven knows what. And we certainly won't see you again until somebody claims that Adam is a charlatan and needs to be made an example of. And what then?'

Belle Barclay sighed.

Bethany took a step closer to the reporter, who steadfastly refused to budge. 'Well, I'll tell you what. You'll be back up here telling my son that he's a fraud.'

The words flowed like water off a duck's back.

'But you cannot deny, Mrs Gabriel, that Sarah Hartley was cured of a lump that doctors had said was incurable.'

Bethany smiled in exasperation. 'But that could have been the result of . . . What do they call it?'

'Spontaneous regression?'

'Yes. There is no knowing that Adam was responsible.'

'Nevertheless, you let him go and try to effect a cure.'

'Because we were asked to by . . .' Bethany paused, unwilling to bring Jess's name into the conversation, even if she was now concerned that she and her mother were responsible for this unwanted visitation. 'Because it would have been unkind not to.'

'So you do accept that your son has a gift?'

Bethany realised she was cornered. She tried in vain to find a response. It was Adam who came to her rescue.

'Sometimes there's a chance I can help,' he said. 'And if there is then I try.'

Belle Barclay was surprised at the degree of steeliness that seemed to have crept into his voice and his demeanour.

'I've never understood what I have, or what I can do, but sometimes it makes a difference.'

'Ah, so you admit—'

'I admit that I have been able to help but I've absolutely no interest in talking about it. Or profiting from it. I help out friends. I'm not a doctor and I make no claims for my . . .' he hesitated before saying the word '. . . gift. I don't want to be defined by it, and I don't think it's fair that you interrogate my mother on my account. If you have any bone to pick it should be with me, not with my family or my friends.'

Belle Barclay was impressed by Adam's forthright approach. So, too, was his mother, who looked silently on, quietly astonished at this new-found assertiveness in her son. But Adam had not yet finished.

'You seem to know everything that has happened since I was at school.'

He shrugged. 'I have nothing more to add. If I do have a gift, I suppose I'm lucky to be able to use it to help people, but I don't see why it should define me or govern my life. I'm a shepherd's son and I'm now a shepherd myself. I just want to be allowed to get on with my life as best I can, raising sheep on the hills where I was born. That's all. And now, if it's all the same to you, we have a flock to look after.' He motioned Belle Barclay towards the farm track. This time she took the hint, but there was a smile on her lips as she said, over her shoulder, 'You're a lucky woman, Mrs Gabriel, having such a capable – and gifted – son.'

As Belle Barclay walked down the track away from the farm, she murmured to herself, 'Seventeen? Mmm. Going on forty. I've had husbands more juvenile.'

30

PRESENT TENSE

Good women always think it is their fault when
someone else is being offensive. Bad women never
take the blame for anything.

Anita Brookner, *Hotel du Lac*,
1984

It was as if the world had settled once more on its customary
axis, in terms of the sounds of nature at least. Birds sang, albeit
in a desultory fashion since it was autumn, and the river, filled
with October rain, chattered by in the bottom of the valley.
Adam and Bethany watched in silence as Belle Barclay wended
her way down the track, astonished that she had not come by
car, and that she had finally capitulated in the face of Adam's
forthright dismissal of her intentions. But she had what she
needed. They both knew that.

Jack came round the corner of the barn. 'She's buggered off,
then?'

Neither felt the need to answer, and the question was left to
hang in the air until, after a few seconds, Jess appeared, running

down the fell with Nip at her heel. For the first time since they had met, Adam felt a rising sense of irritation.

She came towards him, beaming. 'Who was that?'

Adam glanced at his mother, who nodded. 'You'd better tell her.' And with that, Bethany went into the house and closed the door. Jack shook his head and disappeared around the back of the barn – after years of avoiding domestic disputes he had perfected the art of melting into thin moorland air.

Jess could feel the frost in the atmosphere. 'What is it? What's the matter?'

Nip walked across to Adam and sat at his heel. It was as if he was aware of the need to be on the right side of the argument.

'It was the reporter from the *Craven Courier*.'

'What did she want?'

'She wants to write about me and my "gift" as she called it.'

'Oh?'

'She tried to interview me at that presentation – when you and I first met, remember?'

Jess nodded, clearly unaware of the direction the conversation was taking.

'Then, with Dad and all that, she didn't get what she wanted. Until today.'

'So she talked to you about Jakey and the stabbing?'

'Yes. And about your mum.'

'What?' There was total surprise on Jess's face.

'Apparently she knows about every single thing I've ever done – from healing sprains at school to making a difference to your mum.'

'How?'

'You tell me.' The look on Adam's face made his feelings clear.

'You don't think . . .?'

Adam shrugged.

Jess made to reassure him. 'I mean, we've not said anything to anybody. Well, *I* haven't. Not about your visit to see Mum. Neither of us has spoken of it.'

'Somebody has.'

'Adam! Honestly! I've no idea how that woman would have found out.' She looked thoughtful, as though scouring her mind for some clue as to how Adam's intervention might have become public knowledge.

'Well, she has, and now it'll be in the local paper, and then, who knows?'

Jess could see the dejection on Adam's face. 'You do believe me, don't you?'

'Well, yes, but . . .'

'You don't sound very sure.' Her face fell. It was clear that Adam was struggling to believe her. 'How can I convince you? I knew you wouldn't want anybody to know so I deliberately kept your visit quiet. I told Mum not to say anything either. I said we owed it to you.'

'What about the doctor?'

Jess looked confused. 'What do you mean?'

'When he examined your mum and found that the lump was going down, did your mum say anything to him?'

'No. At least, I don't think so. I'm sure she wouldn't. She's told her friends the lump has gone – how could she not? – but nothing about why.'

'Well, it's out there now.'

Jess reached for his hand. 'Adam, I'm so sorry. I really didn't mean for this to happen. I tried to make sure that we said nothing. I can't believe Mum would have said anything to the doctor, really I can't.'

Adam pulled his hand away and turned to go. 'I'd better get on. Have you given some water to that ewe in the barn?'

'Yes. Oh, please don't change the subject. Can't we sort this out?'

'How?'

'Just by talking about it. By working out what could have happened. And is it such a bad thing, anyway, that people know you're special?'

'You don't get it, do you? When this story appears in the paper it's obvious what will happen. You came up here asking me to help because you heard what happened with Jakey. Nobody else really thought much of it, just a young lad doing his bit to help. What happened – my being able to stop the bleeding – was really lucky. But when people find out I can make lumps go away, well, that's a whole new ball-game, isn't it? Who wouldn't want to come and see if they could be cured?'

'Is that what you thought when I came up here? Just a nuisance?'

'No. That was different,' said Adam, defensively.

'How different?'

'Because it was *you*.'

Jess shook her head. 'But I was the start of it all, wasn't I? The reason it's all gone horribly wrong. Mum may have been cured, but she and I have clearly mucked up your life.'

'Hang on a minute.' There was a note of alarm in Adam's voice. 'That's not what I said. I'm just saying . . .'

Jess bit her lip and Adam saw that her eyes were filling with tears.

'I should never have come,' she said softly.

Adam realised that things were getting out of control. 'No. I mean, yes, you should. This isn't your fault . . . well, not exactly . . . I mean . . .'

'I only wanted to help Mum.' Jess turned away and walked towards the barn. Then she stopped, thought for a moment, wiped away a tear that, irritatingly, had escaped and trickled down her cheek, before turning in the opposite direction and walking away down the track.

'Where are you going?' Adam shouted after.

'Home,' she replied. 'I'm going home.'

Supper at Langstroth Farmhouse that evening was a low-key affair, not that any meal had been a bundle of fun since Luke had died. Bethany and Adam ate quietly each evening, talking of this and that, of sheep and feed, of auctions and the weather, with occasional references to Jack and, lately, to Jess, who had brought at least a glimmer of light into their lives. And now she was gone and neither of them was sure whether she would return.

The plates were cleared, the dishwasher loaded, and mother and son, driven to stay indoors by the torrential rain that was hammering against the window, sat down in front of the fire to watch the least demanding offering among the few TV programmes that were available so high up in the dale.

They flipped through the channels: the choices were limited to exotic cookery, a documentary about dysfunctional families, and a group of overweight people being taken to a tropical island to lose weight. None held what either of them would call irresistible appeal.

'Do you want any of these?' asked Bethany. She was sitting in an armchair with her legs tucked underneath her, a plaid blanket around her shoulders.

'No. I think I'll go and read,' said Adam, as he got up from his chair and made for the staircase.

'What's happened to us?' asked Bethany.

'Mmm?'

'Look at us. We could be a couple of OAPs.' She pulled the blanket from around her shoulders. 'This is ridiculous. Since your dad died we've been nowhere and seen no one, apart from going to market and a weekly shop in Skipton. I used to have a few friends, but I haven't seen them since . . .'

Adam was unsure where the conversation was going.

Bethany continued, 'And now this thing with Jess has blown up.'

'I'm sorry.'

'Come and sit down.'

Adam did as he was bade, albeit warily.

'I'm sure she didn't mean anything by it,' offered Bethany.

'I know, it's just that—'

His mother interrupted, 'We've got to get a grip. Got to come to terms with it. Quite a few people know anyway, don't they, even if they've always been kind enough to leave things unsaid?'

'I suppose.' Adam was slumped in his chair, disconsolate.

His mother continued, 'Either we get on with our lives and take the consequences of your ability, or we up sticks and move away. What's it to be?'

'What?' Adam was shocked at the bluntness of her suggestion.

'Do we stay or do we go?'

'We stay, of course. Why would we go? *Where* would we go?'

'Anywhere that doesn't know who we are, and we just keep quiet about your ability. We can farm sheep anywhere.'

Adam was unsure how serious his mother was being. It was unnerving. He found himself silenced by the unexpectedness of her suggestion.

Bethany fixed him with a look. 'Are we up to coping with this or are we going to give in and be forced out of here?'

Adam did not hesitate. 'No. I mean, we have to cope.'

'Right answer. And if we're coping we need to crack ourselves out of this inertia and get a life.'

'But we have a life!'

'Oh, we have a life on the land, and that means a lot to you and to me. We wouldn't change what we do, but we could stop being frightened of our shadows, which we seem to be at the moment. You are who you are, and I don't see why you or I should apologise for that. Your dad certainly wouldn't have done. Not now. We've been going through life trying to pretend your gift isn't really there. I'm not saying we should make a big thing about it, but the sooner we reconcile ourselves to the fact that it's a part of our lives, the better.'

Adam was taken aback by his mother's candour. She had never spoken like this before and it was deeply unsettling. 'So what are you saying? That I should advertise?'

'Don't be silly, Adam. And don't overreact. You just need to have a bit more confidence in yourself, and stop being so apologetic.'

Adam made to protest, but his mother was having none of it. 'I know you can do it. I saw how you handled that reporter woman. I was very proud of the way you stood your ground.'

'So what do you want me to do?' he asked.

'First thing in the morning you go down to Jess's house and tell her how sorry you are.'

'But supposing she doesn't want to hear?'

'Oh, I think she will. She's very fond of you and she'll have had a good night's sleep in the meantime. It's clear that she loves working here and, frankly, we need her manpower, or womanpower, or whatever I'm meant to call it.'

'And then?' asked Adam, unsure that he could work such magic.

'And then we carry on as normal, and if that wretched woman's story comes out in the *Craven Courier* on Thursday we brace ourselves for whatever happens.'

Adam stood silent as his instructions were clearly enunciated.

'We've tried to ignore it for as long as we can, Adam, but the time has come when we have to face up to it. There will be those who try to catch you out, and those who find it hard to believe in your ability, but you and I know what we know and we'll just have to be resolute and get on with our lives. OK?'

Adam nodded. 'OK,' he said, though he was far from sure that things would pan out as his mother hoped. Time would tell, one way or the other.

31

BUILDING BRIDGES

It is a good rule in life never to apologise. The right sort
of people do not want apologies, and the wrong sort
take a mean advantage of them.

P. G. Wodehouse, *The Inimitable Jeeves*, 1923

At least the weather was brighter, even though a stiff easterly
breeze served as a reminder, if such a reminder were needed,
that the summer was over and done and autumn's armoury
firmly in place. Adam decided to walk down to the village, the
better to clear his head and order his thoughts. He nodded at
a few acquaintances on the way, finally reaching Jess's house
and noticing that the Japanese anemones that lined the path to
the front door were all but spent. Faded flowers . . . symbolic
of a fading relationship?

He had made up his mind to apologise, to say that he had
overreacted, that it was time he faced up to his situation and
learnt to live with it, without taking it out on others who referred
to it in any way or asked for his help. It was what it was, and
he was who he was, and that was that.

'Checking the progress of the patient, are you?' asked a voice from the garden path next door.

It was Fred Pennock, the postman. The man who knew everybody's business and not just because he delivered their mail. Rumour had it that Fred Pennock had been born with antennae that he carefully concealed beneath his clothing. They said that if somebody coughed in Kettlewell, Fred Pennock would be first in the queue at the chemist – he had feelers out everywhere.

And then the epiphany occurred. Adam remembered that Fred Pennock had been delivering post the day he had visited Sarah Hartley. He had registered that Fred was walking down next door's path that day as well. He had obviously put two and two together when Sarah's condition had improved, and assumed that Adam had been the cause. It seemed so obvious now. It would not have been Jess, or her mum, or the doctor – whose Hippocratic oath would have prevented him from discussing details of his patient with the wider community – but Fred Pennock would have had no such qualms. It was a piece of gossip, and a juicy one at that.

Adam watched him go, and was unsure whether he felt relieved that it was not Jess and her mother who had talked about his ability, or guilty that he had assumed such was the case. He thought of shouting after the postman, but confined himself to a heavy sigh. He knocked on the door. There was no reply.

He was unsure what to do. He did not want to let matters lie – not for much longer anyway. He needed to see her, to straighten things out. Slowly he began the long walk home. On the edge of the village, he caught sight of her, walking towards the little red car parked outside a farmhouse. She was carrying two pints of milk. He wanted to shout, but no words would come. Instead, he quickened his pace, hoping she would see him and stop what she was doing.

She got into the car and shut the door, started the engine and pulled out into the road. He did the instinctive thing and leapt out in front of the advancing vehicle. The car screeched to a halt as Adam toppled gently forwards onto the bonnet.

Jess leapt out. 'Adam!'

For a few moments he didn't move, but lay spread-eagled across the front of the car. He was winded, but unhurt, though it took him some time to communicate that fact, thanks to the stuffing having been knocked out of him.

'What were you thinking? Stupid idiot!'

'I'm sorry. I was looking for you,' he blurted out, between gasps for breath. 'I went to the house. Nobody there. Was going home . . .'

'Sit down' she instructed, pulling him by the arm and leading him to the rough grass verge that rose up at the side of the road. 'Can you move everything?'

He nodded, then put his head between his knees.

Jess sat beside him and looked into his eyes. 'Silly boy,' she murmured.

He managed a smile. 'I came to apologise. I was stupid. Not thinking straight. I know it wasn't you.'

'What?'

'Who talked about your mum. It was Fred Pennock. Obvious when you think about it. Knows everything. Keeps nothing to himself. He saw me when I came to see your mum. He was delivering next door's letters. Nothing escapes Fred Pennock. When your mum got better he put two and two together.'

Jess began to laugh.

'I'm glad you think it's funny,' said Adam, weakly.

'But it is. Don't you see? What number do we live at?'

'Number twenty-two . . .' He realised as he spoke the words. 'So am I forgiven?'

Jess put her arm around his shoulders. 'Of course you are. You shouldn't have jumped to conclusions and I shouldn't have been so sensitive. I'm sorry.'

'So will you come back?'

'Course I will. Tomorrow. Got to sort Mum out with her shopping this afternoon. I'll be back in the morning. If you'll have me.' She leant forward and kissed him on the lips. 'I missed you,' she said.

'Not as much as I missed you.' He surprised himself by saying it, but knew that he meant it. She was a bright light in his life. When he was with her he felt lifted somehow. And safe. How could he have doubted her? But that was yesterday, when events had conspired to stop him thinking straight. Today would be different.

The *Craven Courier* came out on Thursday. On page seven there was a photograph of Adam's award ceremony at Skipton Town Hall and beneath it a feature headlined: 'Local Lad With Power of Healing'. Bethany and Adam read it with trepidation:

High up in the Yorkshire Dales, above Yockenthwaite, is a sheep farm managed by an unusual shepherd and his mother. Adam Gabriel (17), whose heavenly name is something of a clue as to his character, is not only a dab hand at sheep farming, but seems to have a gift for healing not only ewes and rams but humans as well. Readers will recall

Adam's heroic efforts during the summer when he went to the aid of local lad Jakey Learoyd (17) who had been set upon by youths in Skipton High Street and who would have bled to death from stab wounds had not young Adam intervened. He saw off Learoyd's attackers and proceeded to staunch the flow of blood until the ambulance arrived. 'He's a miracle worker,' said paramedic Wayne Cawood (41) when questioned by your reporter. 'We've never known such a thing to happen before. How Jakey did not die is a mystery.'

The subsequent awards ceremony was blighted by the tragic death of Adam's father, Luke Gabriel (57), who collapsed and died at the event, causing the celebrations to be curtailed and subsequent enquiries into Adam's particular gift to be postponed.

Such an isolated incident as the saving of Jakey Learoyd's life could have been treated as a one-off case where a working knowledge of first aid proved invaluable, were it not for Adam Gabriel's track record during his schooldays when, according to various sources, his 'laying on of hands' cured everything from aches and sprains to warts and bruises.

More recently, Adam attended Mrs Sarah Hartley (46) who would seem to have been cured of a lump in her abdomen, which had steadfastly refused to respond to the treatment of doctors and surgeons.

When questioned about his powers of healing Adam is remarkably reticent. 'If I do have a gift, then I suppose I'm lucky to be able to use it to help people' is as much as he will say.

There is no evidence to suggest that Adam uses this

'gift' for profit, or that he claims to understand it. Indeed, it seems to be something of a burden to the lad, and one can understand why.

Did Mrs Hartley's lump disappear as a direct result of Adam's 'laying on of hands' or was it, as the doctors would say, most likely due to 'spontaneous regression', a catch-all expression used to encompass occurrences that leave the medical profession baffled, and defy rational explanation?

Whatever the case, there can be no denying that Mrs Hartley is now in good health and that the lump would seem to have disappeared.

Adam Gabriel and his mother Bethany (47) continue to raise their flock on the Langstrothdale fells, regardless of Adam's remarkable gift, and gave short shrift to your reporter when questioned about his ability. Perhaps they fear being inundated with people seeking relief from hitherto incurable conditions, or perhaps they are unsure themselves of the reliability of such unorthodox methods of treatment.

Readers will have their own opinions as to the believability of 'faith healing'. Some will consider exponents of the art to be nothing more than quacks and charlatans; others will take a more open-minded view.

Either way, the evidence of Adam Gabriel's ability is clear for all to see in this neck of the woods, and there are many locals who will vouch for it.

Time will tell if it is real or imagined. In the meantime, this young Yorkshire shepherd and his mother continue to contribute to the picturesque beauty of this part of Yorkshire with their flock of Swaledale sheep safely grazing the moorland fells.

THE GIFT

In spite of Adam and Bethany nervously scanning the horizon for pilgrims in search of cures for an assortment of ailments, the rest of the day passed pretty much as any other.

32

CLOSER

It is one of the superstitions of the human mind to
have imagined that virginity could be a virtue.

Voltaire, 1694–1778

The leaves had fallen from every tree except the gnarled oak by
the bend in the river, and those that remained on its twisted
boughs were dry and coppery, crisp as parchment. The river
was full now. Autumn was mustering her troops for the onset
of winter, and the fear of a steady procession of invalids arriving
at the farm had, to everyone's relief, proved groundless. They
would be unlikely to come now, and there would soon be days
when the mud and mire, the snow and ice would conspire to
discourage all but the most determined adventurers. Perhaps
they had overreacted after all.

Adam had been chivvying his mother to spread her wings,
to renew contact with the few good friends she cherished and
had all but withdrawn from over the months since Luke's
death. It was she, after all, who had bemoaned the fact that
their lives were becoming increasingly reclusive. Finally, she

capitulated and agreed to visit a friend in Richmond – a doctor's wife. She would even stay the night, but only if Adam felt he could cope without her. On that particular point he was adamant.

'I might just about manage,' he reassured her, with a wry smile. 'Anyway, Nip will take care of me.'

'You will ring if you need me?'

'Of course. Now go. And stop worrying. I'm quite capable of looking after myself.'

'Yes, well . . .'

Failing to find any other reason to delay her departure, in spite of various attempts to do so, Bethany kissed her son lightly and made for the door.

'Are you sure you can manage without the Land Rover?'

'I've got the quad bike. And I can't drive it on the road yet, remember? I've passed my theory test but I'm still waiting for the practical.'

'It seems daft. You've been driving it up here since you were fourteen and you're a better driver than me.' She was hesitating in the doorway.

'Go!' instructed Adam. 'And be careful.'

Bethany smiled. 'That's what I'm supposed to say to you.'

Adam raised his eyebrows.

'I'm going, I'm going . . .'

He stood at the doorway as his mother drove off down the track, relieved that she had finally plucked up the courage to see friends again. She talked to them on the phone quite frequently – the three or four she regarded as close. The doctor's wife in Richmond was one of them, a kindly woman who seemed able to juggle admin for a busy practice and three teenage children in a surprisingly unflappable way. Seeing them again, sharing their company would, he hoped, ease her mind, give her some kind of comfort.

He knew that he could help soothe his mother's pain simply by being there, by being her son, her companion. But it frustrated him that he could do no more than that. He could heal physical pain, or so it seemed, but mental anguish appeared to be beyond his compass.

When he was younger he did not question his gift. He took it for granted. It was just what he did, who he was. It was only in adolescence that he began to wonder what it was that made him so different, that enabled him to make a difference. It troubled him sometimes, frightened him even, but he had managed to come to terms with the strange burden most of the time, just occasionally being unnerved by its very existence and wondering if it would be better to ignore it. If he did, would it disappear? Would it fade with age? If he thought about it, would it vanish as though it had been no more than a figment of his imagination? It was a kind of mind game that left him exhausted. Better to accept the status quo and just get on with life, allowing Fate to intervene as far as the bigger picture was concerned.

All his life he had been a reader, eschewing the opportunities offered by mobile phones and other forms of technology, but always with his head in a book, reading about everything from nature and astronomy to Dickens and Austen, du Maurier and Agatha Christie, while his schoolmates were engrossed in more contemporary forms of amusement. In the early days he had tried to conform – albeit half-heartedly – but had swiftly come to the conclusion that there was more solace to be had in those works of natural history and fiction with which he felt greater personal affinity. Being honest with himself seemed more important than fitting in, though it took a deal of courage to do so.

An hour after his mother had left he came indoors and banked up the fire. Nip was at his heel. Like Finn before him, Nip had been allowed to sleep in the house, rather than the barn – one concession that had been passed down from senior dog to junior but only on Finn's demise. Before that the older dog would growl if Nip put his nose through the doorway. As a result, Nip knew his place and stood patiently outside until Adam emerged each morning.

On the evening of the day of Finn's burial, Nip had crossed the threshold unbidden, looked up at Adam and Bethany as if to seek their approval, then quietly walked to Finn's bed, lay down and closed his eyes.

He lay there now, dreaming as the flames licked around the logs and Adam sat at the table eating a bowl of spaghetti Bolognese.

The grandfather clock struck seven. It was dark outside and the wind played gently on the rattling window frame. He would fix it in the morning. For now he mused on how his mother was getting on. Then his mind turned to Jess. He could see her smiling face and feel her lips on his – a vivid memory of kissing her goodnight on that first date and subsequent closeness walking the fells. There were evenings together when she stayed for supper and increasingly frequent suppers in the café by the canal that had become 'their place'. How warm he felt when she was with him. How safe. And Isla? He smiled at the memory and realised he would probably never see her again. That prospect did not hurt as much as it once had. But he would be grateful for ever that she had awoken in him feelings that showed he could fall in love.

His pleasant thoughts were interrupted by the sound of a minor explosion from the scullery next to the kitchen. He leapt from the chair as Nip barked and shot up from his bed. Adam ran through the doorway to see a plume of water shooting upwards from the tap above the old porcelain sink where poultry feeders and the like were washed. The room sported a collection of well-worn boots and waterproofs, orderly hanks of orange baler twine, Luke's collection of shepherd's crooks and walking sticks, dog leads and buckets – the domestic minutiae of farming life.

The water was cascading on to the floor in a copious cataract and swirling across the stone flags towards the main kitchen. For a moment Adam stood and stared at the spectacle, surprised at its occurrence and also by its velocity. The water was bouncing off the ceiling, and the tap, which normally controlled its flow, was hanging limply to one side. The pressure must have proved too much for the old joint and was now flexing its muscles.

The stopcock. Where was it? Under the sink, obviously. To reach it Adam had to duck underneath the fountain of water and into the cupboard. It was dark down there. He groped towards the back of the shadowy void, screwing up his eyes against the spray of water and attempting to locate the tap that would stop the flow. He found it. Tried to turn it. It wouldn't budge. Nip had scuttled back to his basket now. Having discovered the source of the commotion, and realised he was ill-equipped to assist, it seemed sensible to be in bed by the warm fire.

Adam pulled himself out of the cupboard and stood up, dripping with icy water. He made for the back door, dashed across to the barn, flipped on the light, ran to the tool bench for a wrench and returned with all speed to the scullery. The water was two inches deep now and rising. One more inch and it would be over the threshold into the main kitchen with its rugs and furniture and— Panic welled inside him. Here he was, left in charge and – disaster.

He ducked under the waterfall once more, applied the wrench to the stopcock and put his shoulder behind it, fearful of the entire apparatus breaking off. Then what? Where was the next cut-off point? But the tap yielded, albeit slowly, and the flow of water gradually subsided to a trickle, which obligingly made its way down the plughole. One final half-turn and the flow stopped.

Adam stood up, shivering. God, that water was cold, but a half-mile journey through moorland soil was hardly guaranteed to bring it up to room temperature. How it managed to retain as much pressure over such a long journey was a mystery, but one best accepted for now. He glanced behind him towards the kitchen. The water was trickling over the step that led into it from the scullery. He grabbed the mop and bucket from the corner and attempted to staunch the flow.

It was at this precise moment that the phone rang. Adam cursed. He'd let it ring. But what if it was his mother? If he didn't answer she'd only worry. He must sound unperturbed. 'Yes, everything's fine. Stop worrying', that sort of thing. He dropped the mop, went through into the kitchen and picked up the phone.

'Hello?' He tried to sound calm and level in spite of the aquatic mayhem that surrounded him and the need to get back to mopping up.

'Adam? It's Jess.'

'Oh!' The relief that it was not his mother came through in the tone of his voice.

'What's the matter? Is everything OK?'

'Yes. I mean, no.' He spoke rapidly. 'I thought you might be Mum and I've had a bit of a disaster.'

'Is your mum not there?'

'No. She's gone to stay with a friend in Richmond. I finally persuaded her. And then this happens. I know she'll think I'm not fit to leave alone.' There was a hint of irony in his voice.

'What sort of a disaster?'

'The tap in the scullery's blown and there's water everywhere. It's all right now – I've managed to turn it off – but there's such a bloody mess.'

'I'll come up!'

Her response took him by surprise. 'What – now?'

'Of course.'

'But—'

'Has the water gone through into the kitchen?'

Keen to avoid sounding feeble, Adam offered, 'It's trying to but I'm doing my best to catch it.' He looked over his shoulder to see a menacing trickle forcing its way over the step between the two rooms. 'Look, I'd better go. I don't want it spreading, OK?'

He put down the phone, hoping he hadn't sounded too rude, and began pushing back the water with the mop and squeezing it out into the sink. Slowly the level began to drop. The kitchen, it would seem, had now escaped the threat of inundation, but his feet, clad only in a pair of thick socks, were numb.

He had been mopping and swabbing and wringing out the mop for ten minutes when a voice called through the open door, 'Are you there? Adam? It's me.'

He turned to see Jess carrying a mop and bucket. Her feet were encased in wellies, her body in a waterproof jacket and her hair tied up in a scarf.

'You look like someone out of *Coronation Street*,' was all he could think of to say.

*

It took them the best part of two hours to mop up the water, dry out those items of rural life that were retrievable and to restore the scullery and the fringes of the kitchen to a picture of domestic harmony that even Bethany Gabriel would have struggled to identify as different from normal. The only casualty was a pile of *Farmers Weekly* stacked on the floor by the sink that Luke had kept and even Bethany would have admitted were now surplus to requirements. Adam would have felt sentimental about them were it not for their sogginess and the putrid smell they gave off.

The cleaning operation finished, they looked around to check that nothing had been missed and, satisfied that all was as it should be, aside from an all-pervasive aroma of damp, Adam said, 'I think you've earnt a glass of wine.'

'I think I probably have,' said Jess, with a twinkle in her eye.

Adam walked over to her and gave her a hug. 'Thank you. I don't know what I'd have done without you.'

'Oh, you'd have managed. That's the thing I like most about you, Adam Gabriel. You're capable.'

'Is that your best commendation? The fact that I'm capable?'

'Not *just* that. But it's certainly a contributory factor.'

Adam shook his head at the back-handed nature of the compliment. 'I'll get you that glass of wine, and I'll put another log on the fire.'

'A log on the fire and a glass of wine. What could be nicer?' Jess took off her jacket and her wellington boots, placing both by the back door. Then she pulled the scarf from her hair and crossed to the fire, crouching and warming her hands by the orange flames that licked ever higher around the dry and crackling wood.

Adam returned and handed her a brimming glass.

'Oh, thank you! Worth coming,' she murmured.

Adam flopped into a chair at the side of the fire, his socks steaming as the heat began to dry them out.

'That's attractive!' remarked Jess, as the misty plumes rose from the damp knitwear.

'Sorry!' said Adam. 'I'll go and change them.'

'No! Don't be silly.' Jess turned and began to peel off his socks. Adam felt slightly embarrassed. 'Why are you blushing?' she asked. 'They're only soggy socks. I've seen them before. Well, not yours, but my dad's. And his *really* smelt . . .'

'Yes, but . . .'

Ignoring his pleas, Jess pulled off the socks and draped them across the fender so the steam could rise up the chimney. 'There you are. Now you'll warm up.'

It seemed futile to protest. 'Thank you for coming,' he said, sipping from his glass. He felt strangely empowered. It was a sensation not unknown to him. Something similar happened when he was involved in healing, but this was different. It seemed to come from without, rather than within, less under his control. Here he was, by his fireside with a beautiful girl, who seemed to enjoy his company, and a glass of wine in his hand. A wave of contentment mixed with elation swept over him.

Jess was sitting at his feet, her arm draped over his legs as she gazed into the flames. 'This is nice,' she said, putting down her glass and turning to face him. She took his own glass and put it down by hers before kneeling up towards him.

Adam looked into her eyes. They were paler blue than ever, shining like sapphires, but the flames imbued them with a piercing quality, like some kind of supernatural ice. She smiled the familiar warm smile, and the amber flames highlighted the freckles that dusted the soft skin of her cheeks. Slowly she leant into him and kissed him. She had never kissed him like that before. Oh, she had pecked him lightly on the cheek when they had been out together, but never actually kissed him on the lips. Properly. He should have felt unsure of himself, uncertain of what to do, yet it all seemed so perfectly natural, so perfectly . . . perfect. He was not the slightest bit nervous now. Instead a kind of relief flooded over him. He had spent so many years convincing himself that he was different from other people – and he knew he was in some ways – but this feeling came as a kind of vindication. It was reassurance that although he might be possessed of talents that were far from the norm, that had caused him to feel isolated on many occasions, he was capable of feeling love towards another human being and could be loved in return.

He had spent his entire life being told that he was different, being labelled 'weird' and 'strange' by unfeeling schoolmates. Meeting someone who could accept all that and still want to be with him, to love him, filled him with a hitherto unknown confidence.

He'd had some inkling of that possibility with Isla, but her visit to the Dales was so fleeting he had barely had time to come to terms with his feelings, and then she was gone.

Jess stroked the back of his head and pulled him towards her. He lowered himself onto the hearthrug beside her and caressed her body, then slipped his hand up inside her shirt and ran his fingers over her breasts. There was no resistance. Jess's response made her feelings perfectly clear.

Whatever else that evening had promised when his mother had left the house, he could never have imagined it would end in the way it did.

33

UNDER THE DOCTOR

I do not like thee Dr Fell,
The reason why – I cannot tell;
But this I know and know full well,
I do not like thee Dr Fell,

Tom Brown, 1680

Adam was ready to inform his mother of the events of the previous evening on her return, those that directly concerned her, which could be described as being of a domestic nature. He had already rung the plumber who had promised to get up to the farmhouse that afternoon to repair the faulty water pipe. The other events would remain known only to himself and Jess.

By the time his mother returned late morning there were other things on her mind, not least that the Land Rover had broken down and Dr Blackstone had driven her home. He had a morning off from the surgery and insisted that it would be no problem at all.

Adam had met the man only rarely. His mother had known the doctor's wife since their children were at playgroup together, but Adam and the other boy had gone on to attend different schools so their continued association had been complicated. Mrs Blackstone, on the few times Adam had encountered her in the intervening years, had always seemed pleasant enough, but the doctor was a shadowy figure of whose character and personality Adam had little recollection.

'You probably don't remember Adam,' offered Bethany, as she invited the doctor in for a cup of coffee and took in the slight smell of damp and airlessness that Adam had briefly attempted to explain.

'Not really, no. But I'm aware of his reputation.'

It was the kind of comment that made Adam's heart sink, but he did his best to be polite and if he offered a smile that was less than effusive at least his handshake was firm.

After the customary pleasantries the doctor, at Bethany's suggestion, took his mug of coffee outside and sat alongside her on the stone slab by the barn. The watery sun was doing its best to warm things up, though it seemed to be fighting a losing battle.

'I wonder if I might ask a favour of you, Adam,' asked the doctor.

Adam made no reply but looked at him questioningly.

'I've been charged with arranging group meetings for the local medics, a handful of doctors getting together to discuss this and that and share our findings with one another. We're looking into alternative methods of therapy. Homeopathy and suchlike. Acupuncture and naturopathy. Most of us are involved with what you might call orthodox or conventional medicine, and feel we should be better informed about other courses of treatment. I was talking to your mother last night and asking her about your apparent gift.'

Adam tried not to bridle at 'apparent', which conveyed more than a hint of scepticism. He hesitated. 'I don't know . . .'

'You can rest assured that it will be handled carefully. We are not coming at it with any preconceived notions. Well, other than those that occur as a result of indifference or ignorance. We'd just like to explore other avenues. As I'm sure you're aware, there are many different kinds of treatment and therapy on offer nowadays, and old sticks-in-the-mud like me who've been at it for years need to keep an open mind – as much as we can, anyway.' He laughed. It was something of a forced laugh and Bethany looked every bit as uncomfortable as her son.

Adam took in the scuffed brogues, the well-worn tweed suit, the gravy-stained tie, the florid complexion, which, judging by the slight aroma emanating from his breath, most likely owed its colour to a fondness for Famous Grouse. As doctors went, Dr Blackstone was no shining beacon of alcoholic moderation, personal hygiene and sartorial elegance.

'I'm not sure I . . .' offered Adam.

'Oh, do say yes. The members of my practice have been hugely . . .' he searched for the right word. then decided upon '. . . impressed with what you've achieved. We'd just like to try to understand it more.' His accent was posher than those of most folk in the dale, thought Adam, but in this part of the world the doctor was still regarded as something apart, referred to as 'doctor' without the definite article. 'Doctor says . . .' was the usual beginning of any sentence relating to a personal experience at the surgery.

Adam shook his head. 'The thing is, I don't really understand it myself.'

'But you feel a need to help people?'

'Well, yes, when I can. But it only happens occasionally, when I'm called on . . . or however you want to put it.'

The doctor kept pushing. 'Ah, but, you see, that's what we need to understand. Most of us chose medicine as a career, studied it at university, in hospitals and general practice. It was a conscious decision either on our part or our parents'. In your case it seems medicine chose you. Quite the other way about, you see.'

'Well, I suppose so.'

'If we're to understand that approach, to build on it and value it, we need to know more about it from those who are possessed of such a talent and able and willing to use it.'

He smiled, and Adam could feel that this was a well-practised bedside manner. Dr Blackstone was clearly used to getting his own way.

'You do see what I mean, don't you? If we can't ask people like you questions, or discover how you achieve the cures you seem able to bring about, then we'll never understand how such things happen and how best we can improve our own approach to medicine.'

'Well, yes, but—'

'And where there is ignorance there is fear and – worse still – suspicion.'

Adam felt trapped. 'But I've never made any claim to be anything other than helpful.'

'Indeed not. Which is exactly why you'll be such a valuable help to our group of doctors. We want to understand, in order to respect, value and evaluate these alternative methods of healing, rather than simply plodding along on our conventional route.'

The doctor took a deep breath, surveyed the view of the

windswept dale, returned his gaze to Adam and went in for the kill. 'You will help us, won't you? In the interests of those souls who live in this glorious part of the world who deserve our help on every level, not just that of orthodox medicine?'

As the doctor's car wove away down the track Bethany made to placate her son.

'I'm sorry. I was cornered, you see. I knew you wouldn't be happy but I didn't feel I could say no on your behalf.'

Adam was looking out over the dale, his jaw set firm. He said nothing.

34

THE INEXPLICABLE

Most men make little other use of their speech than to
give evidence against their own understanding.

George Savile, Lord Halifax, 'Of Folly and Fools',
comment published in 1750

'So how would you describe this feeling?'

Adam sat on a hard wooden chair in front of the panel of
four doctors. He felt like a criminal. He also knew that the day
would not end well. How could he explain something of which
he himself had no understanding?

There were four of them – two men and two women. Adam's
own doctor, the kindly Dr Senior, had retired the previous year
and, as yet, he had not met Dr Senior's replacement. He
wondered which of the quartet it might be.

Dr Blackstone seemed to be in charge of the group and
presided over the proceedings with a crumpled yet proprietorial
air. On his right was a young doctor, introduced as Gary
Westlake, dark and good-looking in an open-necked shirt and
corduroy jacket. Adam could imagine his female patients

swooning. On Dr Blackstone's left sat Dr Scarlett, aged about thirty-five, Adam guessed, neatly turned out in a white blouse and dark jacket, her copper-coloured hair swept back into a French plait. She was the only one of the quartet who appeared keen to put him at his ease. She smiled a lot and nodded encouragingly, which contrasted sharply with the plump, severe-looking older woman next to her who gazed at him incredulously over a pair of half-moon spectacles as though he were an insect in a bottle. Dr Cruickshank's grey hair was drawn back into a bun, held in place by an elaborate construction of tortoiseshell combs she frequently pulled out and repositioned as though to improve her concentration.

'Mr Gabriel?' Dr Blackstone realised the need to attract his subject's attention.

'Sorry?' Adam's mind had wandered, not through inattention, but because he was trying hard to articulate what, up until now, he had not been required to explain. How did you rationalise something that was instinctive?

'How would you describe the feeling you have when you are healing?'

Adam did his best to clarify his state of mind whenever he found himself in such a situation. 'It's a kind of heat. A sort of welling up inside me . . .' He struggled to be more precise. 'It's as if there is a power source that I can latch on to and which I have to give myself up to.'

Dr Cruickshank asked, with more than a hint of cynicism in her tone, 'So you go into a sort of trance?'

'Not exactly.'

There was a note of impatience in her voice. 'What then?'

Adam tried again. 'I'm still conscious, but I kind of have to give myself up to the feeling. Let it take me over.' He stopped, looking from left to right at the row of faces, hoping for some kind of acceptance, some kind of understanding.

The younger female doctor offered an olive branch: 'So you're used to it happening, used to it taking over?'

'Yes.'

'Does it make you feel afraid?'

Adam felt slightly more confident. 'No, not at all. It's been happening for so long now that I know I won't come to any harm.'

'What about your, er, patients?'

Adam was unnerved. 'I wouldn't call them that. I mean . . . I haven't harmed anybody. Ever.'

'I'm sure.' The doctor nodded. 'And how do you feel afterwards?' she asked.

'Tired. With no energy. Just worn out.'

'And how long does that feeling last?'

'A couple of hours.'

'And then you're fine again?'

'Pretty much.'

'You have a banana and your nutrient levels are restored?'

Adam was not sure whether he was meant to answer. Was her response sarcasm or practical advice? It could have been either.

She wrote down something on her notepad as Gary Westlake cut in, pressing buttons on his mobile phone at the same time: 'How do you decide when to exercise these remarkable powers?' He seemed to be only half interested in Adam's reply, as though he was reluctant to be there but felt he had to go through the motions.

'I don't. I mean, it's not something I think about. If friends come to me with something wrong with them and ask me if I can help, I do.'

Gary Westlake looked up. 'Always?'

'Yes. I suppose. Why would I not?'

The doctor sat back in his chair and smiled. 'Of course.' But the smile was not friendly. It lacked warmth. He went back to fiddling with his phone.

Dr Cruickshank leant forward now, as though to get a better view. 'Young man, I am curious to know *when* you discovered you had what you call "this gift" and *when* you decided to use it.'

'I don't think there was a particular moment, and I've never been aware of making any decision about it. It's just something I've always been able to do, something that's always been a part of me.'

The doctor looked frustrated. She tapped her pen on the pad in front of her. 'Were you encouraged by your parents?'

'No. I mean, they didn't encourage or discourage me.'

'They just took it as a normal part of your life?'

'Well, they knew it wasn't normal but . . .'

'They did nothing to foster it?'

'No. But then they didn't stop me using it.' Adam felt frustrated by the wave of negativity that seemed to emanate from a woman who clearly had no concept of his ability or that it might even exist.

She confirmed his suspicions with her next question: 'You have heard of spontaneous regression? Sometimes called spontaneous remission?'

'Of course.'

'And you don't think that such cases have been the cause of your . . . successes?'

'It's possible that some of them might. But there have been too many for them all to be explained that way.'

Dr Cruickshank smiled for the first time. 'So you admit that you might just have been lucky?'

'Sometimes, yes. But not always.' Adam took a deep breath. 'I can't see how everything I've done . . . everything that's happened . . . could just be a coincidence – from sprains and warts and rashes to . . .'

'To cancerous growths in the case of Mrs Hartley?'

Adam shrugged. 'If that's what it was. I just knew it was a lump.'

She sat back in her chair. 'You are aware that the finest surgeon in Bradford had declared that Mrs Hartley was incurable?'

'Well, not exactly . . .'

'That she had only a few months to live?'

'I knew that the doctors had said there was nothing more they could do. Jess told me that. Mrs Hartley's daughter. It was she who asked me . . .'

'So where the most accomplished surgeon in the county had decided that Mrs Hartley's cancer was inoperable, you thought you'd have a go.'

'It wasn't really like that. I mean, it didn't seem . . .'

'That's how it seems to me, Mr Gabriel. That you feel your own gift is superior to those of a trained surgeon.'

'No! Not at all!'

Dr Blackstone glanced in the direction of his colleague, who shrugged off the implied censure and busied herself writing copious notes on her pad.

Gary Westlake finally put down his mobile phone and made to clarify the situation. 'You see, Mr Gabriel, those of us who have undergone extensive training and who have' – he glanced at Dr Cruickshank – 'many years of experience in conventional medicine, find it difficult to believe, I mean, to understand, that someone with no medical experience or even rudimentary knowledge of human anatomy and physiology is able to cure people of ailments that have resisted the endeavours of those whose lives have been devoted to curing the sick.'

Dr Blackstone cleared his throat and bestowed on Adam one of those indulgent smiles that he had so successfully used in persuading him to face the ordeal by fire that this 'pleasant chat' had transformed into. 'Ladies and gentlemen,' he intoned, 'I think we're being rather harsh with Adam, who has come here today of his own free will to help us to understand what he has achieved and to what he attributes his skills.'

'Which is why I didn't want to come,' blurted out Adam. 'Because I don't attribute them to anything. I don't begin to understand them. I just know they're there and I've come to trust them.' There was emotion in his voice now. 'I know no one will understand, especially those trained in what you call "conventional" medicine. How can you understand it when you haven't felt what I feel?'

Dr Cruickshank interrupted: 'Now, young man—'

'No! You have no idea what I can do. You believe in what you do yourselves but when something . . . someone . . . comes along and you don't understand their ability you try to pretend it doesn't exist. People who want to heal the sick should be encouraged, not attacked.'

Dorothea Cruickshank was having none of it. 'And there, young man, you are quite wrong. To allow all and sundry – with no training – to treat the sick would be disastrous. Heaven knows what state the health of the country would find itself in. One has only to look to the United States of America and the scandalous activities of their television evangelists to recognise the dangers inherent in such activities. I and my colleagues went to great lengths to learn about and to practise medicine to heal the sick and to understand the complexities of the human condition. You must not be surprised when we try to safeguard our profession by protecting it from fly-by-night practitioners who raise people's hopes with their quackery, only to have them dashed and, in many instances, to lose their life savings in the process to some charlatan who offers them some magic potion or "laying on of hands" to cure their ills. That is why we approach such people with suspicion and wariness – because we know that in every case there will be some kind of rational explanation for these miracle cures. So-called "faith healing" when it *is* effective can invariably be attributed to some rational medical explanation.'

'And when it cannot?' enquired Dr Scarlett, speaking softly and regarding her senior colleague with a questioning glance.

'Then we are back in the territory of spontaneous regression.'

'Which cannot itself be explained.' The younger doctor laid down her pen. 'Adam, thank you for coming to see us today. I understand that it must be upsetting for you to be questioned so closely about your apparent talent by four apparently mistrustful people – well, three, since Dr Blackstone has very kindly left the job to us.'

Her glance at the convenor of the interview was not without a hint of reproof. 'The fact that we find it hard to understand just what someone in your position can achieve or, rather, *has* achieved should not be taken as a criticism.'

Dr Cruickshank did not look up but gave voice to a muted 'harrumph'. Gary Westlake took up his phone once more to check the time, clearly anxious to get on with a day that contained what he considered to be more important appointments than this one.

Dr Blackstone looked uneasy, as if aware that his handling of the situation had been less than authoritative. 'Yes, well, I think we'll leave it there, shall we?'

Having run his eye over the panel of inquisitors he turned to Adam. 'Very good of you to come. I hope it hasn't been too much of an ordeal.' He stood up and smiled at his fellow panellists, who also rose to their feet and made to leave.

'I think we've learnt a lot,' said Dr Blackstone, by way of consolation.

'Do you?' asked Adam. His eyes shone and the colour rose in his cheeks.

His interlocutors stopped packing their bags and pocketing their pens and turned towards him.

'I don't think you've learnt anything at all. You're like everybody else, whatever your medical training. If you can't understand something you can't believe it exists. You can't take anything at face value. Unless you have a scientific explanation for a situation then it simply can't have happened. It's easier that way, isn't it?'

Not one of the doctors seemed capable of replying.

'I just think it's sad, that's all. Sad that you can't believe there's more than one way of making people better. I've tried to help people, tried to understand why I can do what I can do but I just can't. The only thing that keeps me going is that sometimes I can make a difference.'

The image of his father lying on the floor at his feet swam into his mind. He paused. His voice became softer, his words more measured. 'Not all the time, but sometimes. But . . . well . . . it just doesn't seem worth it any more.' His eyes were glazed, his mind in another time, another place. Then he came back to the present and looked directly at the doctors with fire in his eyes. 'I've gone through my life – and I know I'm only seventeen – with everybody thinking I'm weird. Odd. A misfit. It's no fun, you know.' There was a crack in his voice as he spoke, but he steeled himself as he glanced at the sea of faces – Drs Scarlett and Westlake now looking embarrassed, Drs Blackstone and Cruickshank staring at the floor.

'Why should I bother when all I get is strange looks? Even from people whose lives are devoted to healing the sick. I've tried to help, that's all. To use a gift – an unusual gift, yes, but a gift I was born with. I've never asked for money, never forced myself on anyone. I've not advertised my services. I've just done what I've been asked to do, by people who wanted me to help them. Well, I'm done with it now. I shan't be doing whatever it is I do any more. It's time I realised there really is no point. I hope that makes you feel better. Less threatened. I'm sorry to have taken up your time. Goodbye.'

He nodded at the little group, paused as if thinking of something else to say, then walked out of the room.

On his return from the fateful meeting, Bethany had found it hard to get anything out of Adam. He had gone straight out onto the fells, taking Nip with him, and had not returned until it was almost dark. She had questioned him about the experience, but it was clear that he was unwilling to share his feelings. She did not press him, but noticed over the days and weeks that followed he remained more introspective than usual, keener than ever to spend time on his own. She reproached herself for having not been more discouraging of Dr Blackstone. But what could she do? Adam was old enough now – or so he kept telling her – to make decisions for himself. Yet still she felt guilty at not protecting her child, like some diligent ewe with her lamb.

35

CONSEQUENCES

We all make choices, but in the end our
choices make us.

Ken Levine, *Bio Shock*, 2007

As the months passed the cloud lifted, very slowly, and Adam became more like his normal self, but there was a knowingness about him now, as if the last vestige of his childhood innocence had slipped away, thanks to the unkindness of strangers, and revealed to him a world that was less than perfect, less kindly disposed to inexplicable occurrences.

Bethany knew, in her heart of hearts, that it was inevitable, that in growing up all children must lose the magical wide-eyed wonder that is sooner or later eroded by life's experiences. She hoped that Adam could retain at least some of the passionate individuality and enthusiasm that made him so special, that the cynicism he had encountered in his meetings with journalists and doctors would not sour his once positive outlook on life. She would continue to blame herself for introducing him to Dr Blackstone; for persuading him to meet that group of medics.

She could guess what had happened, but was fearful of admitting it even to herself.

Jess seemed to know when to step back and let him brood. At least he made an effort to avoid inflicting his mood on the two women who mattered most to him. When he was with them he did not speak of his change of heart, if such it was, and both knew to allow him time and space to process what was clearly a disappointment engendered by the attitudes of others towards him. They made sure they were there, to support, to encourage, and to foster within him the sense of worth they suspected had been eroded by those disposed to distrust his ability and his motives.

A bitter winter – with searing winds that tore across the moor and flurries of snow that stung the eyes – came and went to nobody's regret. Spring was slow to arrive but worth the wait, with a good crop of lambs, though there was no sign of Brother Wilfrid. This the family did not take amiss. It had happened before. It would doubtless happen again. Brother Wilfrid was a law unto himself. It made no sense to brood upon his absence.

The summer was capricious, as if to mirror Adam's life of late, and in a year of absences there was no visit from Isla and her brother. Noah had sent a missive a month before his predicted arrival, saying that neither he nor Isla would be over from New Zealand this year and would they be able to manage with local labour? Some kind of domestic hiatus had made their life a little complicated but they would be back in a year's time if that would still suit the Gabriels.

Their absence, Adam was forced to admit, came as something of a relief. The prospect of being in the same space as Jess and Isla, however much he had reconciled himself to his current affections, would have made for an awkward atmosphere. Jess was uneasy enough about that past relationship without putting her emotions to the ultimate test.

There was little time to dwell on such things – the shearing, the marketing, the managing of the flocks and the maintenance of walls and fences took up not only time but headspace, and before he knew it, winter was upon them once more. Alternating periods of thunderous clouds and snow flurries; brimful becks and searing winds.

Throughout the time since his father's death the understanding between Adam and Jess deepened. Little was said but much was acknowledged. There were moments for both of them when the spectre of Isla and all she had meant to Adam would come to the fore in their minds, albeit at different times.

From Jess's point of view her ghostly presence was an occasional flash of worry. Had Adam really got over the girl who had first stolen his heart? Jack had seen fit to mention Isla, to warn Jess that she herself wasn't the first – was there more to it than Adam was willing to tell her? Then she would reproach herself for falling prey to such thoughts. He was with *her* now, wasn't he?

Adam would always cherish the memory of that first fleeting love affair, if such a brief dalliance could qualify for such a description. The sudden discovery of combined physical and mental attraction – albeit on one brief moonlit evening – was too great a sensation to be denied or put from the mind. It lifted his spirits in a way that was impossible to deny without feeling hypocritical. Did that make him disloyal to Jess, for if he were not honest with himself about his feelings, then how could he hope to be honest with anyone else?

He knew, deep down, that Jess was the one he wanted to

share his life with. Why? Was it because she was a safer bet? A steadying influence rather than a globe-trotting adventurer? And yet how could he traduce the memory of Isla with such a dismissive epithet? All of these things he gradually processed, eventually coming to terms with the fact that life was not nearly so neat as he would like, that opinions, loves and beliefs were subject to adjustment and evaluation throughout the years. He was eighteen now. Surely such changes in feelings did not amount to disloyalty, simply to growing up.

Christmas saw the Gabriel and Hartley families pooling resources and celebrating in each other's houses, the two widows grateful for the presence of the other's child in their lives, and the positive attitude that Adam and Jess seemed to share. Their love for each other was clear to see, but both mothers had the sense not to make too much of it, while being glad of the convivial company it provided. Adam at eighteen and Jess a year older were mature for their years, certainly, but they were still young and their lives, God willing, stretched in front of them, with whatever vicissitudes lay in the days, months and years ahead. For now, it was enough that they were together and enjoying each other's company.

On Christmas Eve the party of four made their way from the Hartley household in the village up the hillside to Langstroth Farmhouse, where 'the stockings were hung by the chimney with care' and Adam was pleased to see a flicker of her old spirit begin to manifest itself in his mother. She smiled more nowadays, even if, from time to time, he would catch her gazing wistfully out of the window, her eyes filled with tears. She had been a widow for the better part of two years now; the various anniversaries had been lived through and were occuring once more

– Luke's birthday, their wedding anniversary; Adam's birthday and her own, marked by Adam and Jess with a cake in the shape of a particularly portly ewe, with a generous pelt of dripping white icing. The tears on Bethany's cheeks that day were of gratitude and love, rather than sadness and haunting memories.

Now, in her second Christmas without the man she had loved, a kind of resignation came over her. It was not born of depression or futility but built upon the innate practicality that had first attracted Luke to her: the ability to get on and not waste time yearning for what might have been. She was learning to remember without mourning, to relive the happy times and use those memories as a way of lifting her spirits rather than lowering them. It was, she told herself, what Luke would have wanted. If he had been admiring of her pragmatic approach to life, then what she had admired in him was his ability to live and cherish every moment, except those that involved him wearing a thick tweed jacket and a collar and tie that caused his neck to go red. She could smile even at the memory of that now. She had moved on. As much as she cared to.

Spring came early to the dale that year: the willow wands down by the river erupted with their golden curls and the sheep relished the early bite from the lower meadows. On this particular day Bethany was away shopping in Skipton and Sarah Hartley visiting a friend in Richmond.

It was a bright but blustery morning when Jess came into the kitchen of the farmhouse for her morning coffee.

Adam looked up from the steaming kettle. 'You look dreadful!'

'I don't feel so good. A bit fluey.'

'Why don't you go home? No point carrying on if you're not right. It'll only get worse.' He moved to comfort her.

'No. Don't come near me. I don't want you catching it.'

Adam did as he was bade, but with a downcast face.

Jess zipped up her windcheater. 'I'll get home to bed. I'll give you a ring later, all right?'

Adam nodded. 'You sure you don't want me to run you down?'

Jess smiled wanly. 'You might be driving now but your mum's got the Land Rover and I can't really face a journey on the quad bike or that little grey Fergie you're determined to restore.'

'Point taken.' He felt dreadful just standing and looking at her. 'Go on then. But walk slowly, and sit down if you feel funny.'

Jess tilted her head on one side and said, 'I don't feel at all funny.'

'You know what I mean . . .'

She nodded, turned and slipped out through the farmhouse door. It was the first time she had ever shown any sign of illness and it made him uneasy.

It wasn't as if he could do anything about it. The will to heal had all but left him. He wouldn't know where to start, had blocked it from his mind for so many months now that he could hardly remember the feeling.

A few weeks before he had come across a pregnant ewe in distress. He found himself looking at her, either unable or unwilling to intervene, he was unsure which. An invisible hand seemed to hold him back, to tell him that this was no business of his: this was something for Martin Hebblethwaite, the vet.

Martin had come as quickly as he could. Pregnant ewes and their offspring were valuable to farmers – their main source of income, a key to their livelihood. When Martin had said that it was too late to save either ewe or lamb, the two looked hard into each other's eyes. Adam's direct gaze was momentary. He looked down almost at once, aware that a year ago he would, like as not, have managed to save both ewe and unborn lamb. Martin Hebblethwaite's gaze was unwavering. He remained staring at Adam, wondering why the lad who seemed to have such a gift for healing animals and people was now so reluctant to use it. He patted Adam's shoulder. 'I'm sorry,' he said. The sentiment, while referring in the main to the current circumstance, was also a reflection on times past.

And now, all these weeks later, it was Jess who was feeling unwell. He shook his head, despairing at his lack of ability to make a difference. He worried about her. What if it was something serious? They had all had their flu injections, as was the norm nowadays. But what if she was one of the few who did not respond?

He took his mug of coffee, went out and sat on the stone slab beside the barn.

Jack ambled past him. 'Seen Jess?' he asked.

'She's gone home. Not feeling very well.'

Jack raised an eyebrow. 'Not like her.'

'No.'

Then, realising he might have worried the lad, 'Something and nothing I shouldn't wonder. Women's trouble probably. You know how it is.'

Adam nodded.

'Anyway, when you've a minute there's a ewe in the barn that's limping. You want to take a look at her?'

Adam smiled weakly, then shrugged. 'Better send for the vet. Martin Hebblethwaite will know what to do.'

Jack regarded him thoughtfully then muttered, almost to himself, 'Bloody stupid doctors . . .' before ambling off in the direction of the privy for his morning ritual. It rattled him that since the fateful day when Adam had been persuaded to meet with the local GPs he had lost not only his willingness to help any ailing human soul but also his ability to treat sick animals. Even if he still possessed such a gift he was clearly reluctant to make use of it. It was a bloody shame. More than that, it was scandalous.

Adam got up from the bench, returned the mug to the kitchen, beckoned Nip to follow him and walked up the pathway behind the farmhouse towards the upper reaches of the Gabriel acres where the heavily pregnant ewes were peacefully grazing the welcome growth on the grassy slopes.

'What a thing, eh, Nip?' He addressed the dog as was his custom, from one end of the day to the other. Nip listened to his random thoughts without question or criticism, but also, it had to be admitted, without bringing anything to the table other than an attentive ear. But there were days when that in itself was useful. It helped somehow to hear his own voice asking questions out loud without fear of recrimination, and he had had enough of that during the previous year to last him a lifetime. He sighed and moved his thoughts from himself to Jess and her current state of health. Not that the transition was a comfortable one. Half of him wanted to put it out of his mind, not because he didn't care but because he cared too much. The other half sought for some way of making a difference, though he knew that was impossible.

'Perhaps it's just a tummy-bug,' he explained to Nip. 'A twenty-four-hour thing. She'll be back tomorrow, her usual self. Smiling and happy.'

Nip let out a gentle whine.

'Yes, I know. It's not the same without her, is it? Not much fun, even with a view like this.'

He surveyed the scene – the silvery river snaking across the bottom of the valley, the sheep bleating as they grazed the velvet grass, and the higher heather-covered fells beginning to shed their dark winter livery. The turn of the year.

A different year. Another year in which his father would not play a part. There seemed to be so many sadnesses to dwell on, so many disappointments, unwanted changes in circumstances. But the spring would help – the annual sense of renewal Nature offered to all those who cared to partake of it. And Jess. Jess always helped. When she was there . . .

Perhaps Brother Wilfrid would call by. Would he know about his father's death? There was no reason why he should, but maybe, somehow, it would have got through to him on his travels. And yet there had been no letter, not since the one his mother had told him about: the one she would not let him see because she said it was personal and private.

He had not pressed her. He was sure it was for the right reasons: why else would she be so secretive?

Soon it would be lambing time, then summer, and the sheep would need shearing. Would Isla return with Noah? Had his mother remembered to ask them? Then he recalled that it was a standing arrangement and only in the event of cancellation would they need to let Noah know they did not require his services. Two or three weeks before his arrival in Langstrothdale he would telephone to tell them when he was coming. It had always been like that. A gentleman's agreement with his father.

His father . . . Had Bethany informed Noah of Luke's death? The thought gave rise to panic in the pit of his stomach. Why had he not asked these questions before? Why were they now tumbling through his mind in such profusion, and why were so few answers forthcoming?

The jumble of thoughts unsettled him and he began the climb down the fellside with Nip at his heel, resolved to clear such things up when his mother returned that afternoon.

The following morning, in the doctor's surgery in Skipton, Jess had an appointment with Dr Emma Scarlett.

She had rung the health centre, describing her symptoms to the receptionist who confirmed that Dr Scarlett would be happy to fit her in since Jess's doctor, Dorothea Cruickshank, was indisposed.

Jess had been a patient of the older lady doctor all her life and, although she was a fierce old bird, Jess had a sneaking admiration for her fortitude – rising to the top of her profession in spite of the preference among farmers, in particular, for being attended to by a man.

Dorothea Cruickshank had seen Jess Hartley through chicken-pox, tonsillitis and other complaints that were part and parcel of growing up. She was sorry not to be examined by her now, but Emma Scarlett, whom she had heard about though not met, seemed kind and welcoming when she entered the consulting room.

'So what seems to be the problem?'

Jess wondered how many times any doctor would say that during the course of a lifetime, but proceeded to explain her symptoms and offered her own opinion that it was probably some kind of tummy bug.

Dr Scarlett smiled indulgently at her patient's self-diagnosis and politely asked her to remove her shoes and her jacket and lie on the padded examination table opposite her desk. While the doctor washed her hands, then checked the patient's blood pressure she asked various questions designed to assess the general health of the patient: regularity of motions, dietary preferences, frequency of periods and the like.

Lying back on the padded table Jess's head began to swim. 'I'm so sorry,' she said. 'I think I'm going to be sick.'

With the swiftness of a winged messenger, Dr Scarlett produced, seemingly from thin air, what looked like a grey cardboard top hat, into which, obligingly, Jess deposited the breakfast she had last seen only one hour previously.

'Pop your shoes back on,' instructed the doctor, having completed her examination and skilfully disposed of the rejected refreshment.

'It's just a tummy bug, isn't it?' asked Jess, expecting confirmation of her suspicions.

'I'm afraid not,' responded Dr Scarlett. She smiled at her patient, in the hope of softening the blow. 'From what I can see – and feel – you're round about three months pregnant.'

36

SPRING FEVER

Spring is the time of plans and projects.

Leo Tolstoy, *Anna Karenina*, 1878

How could she tell him? When *should* she tell him? What would he say? What would his mother say? What would *her* mother say? Would he think that she had trapped him? Would his love for her – for he did love her, didn't he? – turn into hatred? She sat in her bedroom and sobbed as the multitude of muddled thoughts whirled in her head. Some tummy bug!

Her mother was out shopping. She'd be back soon. She needed to order her thoughts, decide what to do. She would go away, not tell anyone.

No, that was cowardly. But there was so much to take in, so much planning needed for a life that would change for ever within just a few months. Two lives. Three lives now. Four. Aside from herself there was her mother, and Adam, and a new-born child. And Bethany. What on earth would Bethany say to this young hussy who had trapped her son?

Jess tried to formulate some kind of plan. She would bring

the baby up on her own, with her mother's help. She would not expect anything of Adam: he need have no responsibility for the new arrival. She was older than him. She was nineteen. He was eighteen: far too young to commit to the kind of responsibility and obligations that came with a new-born baby. She would face the consequences of her actions and let him get on with his life. It was only fair.

But the prospect frightened her. What had she thrown away? They had been so happy together and now it was all spoilt. It was love; she knew that. Love that she felt whenever they were close; love that she felt for him daily. But he was a man – a *young* man: how could she possibly believe that his feelings towards her were the same? Yes, he was different from other men – she admired that in him – but at heart he was still a man and, at eighteen, not nearly ready to commit to such a change in his circumstances. What if this propelled him straight back into the arms of Isla? Love without ties: a chance to choose and to live a life of freedom rather than be committed to raising a family. Her heart beat faster at the prospect of losing him, yet she could not bring herself to – as he might see things – trap him.

Oh, it was all such a mess. Of course, she could always change things. Change her state of health. No, the thought was dismissed with the speed at which it had arrived. That was simply not an option, and she could not imagine that Adam would ever agree to it. But what if she took certain steps without telling him? She felt ashamed that such thoughts should even enter her mind. She was carrying a child and she would see it through. She stroked her tummy, round and round, caressing what she knew was within, and vowing that whatever happened she would be a good mother. The very word made her tremble.

Two hours ago such a thing would never have crossed her mind. True, she had mused on the future and on being the mother of children, but that future was comfortably at arm's length by a good ten years. Now it was here, it was now, it was . . . barely six months away. Twenty-eight weeks. No time at all.

The heart palpitations continued. She breathed deeply in an attempt to alleviate them. But at least she did not feel quite so sick. Not at the moment. Why had she not realised? The nausea that had started around a month ago came mostly in the mornings. It was obvious when she thought about it. Her periods had always been irregular. It was nothing out of the ordinary when she missed a month. Oh, *why* had she not been more careful?

She lay back on the bed and closed her eyes. Then she heard the front door open and her mother call, 'I'm back. How are you feeling? I've brought you some Lucozade.'

She ran to the bathroom and threw up again.

Adam worried that it was more serious than Jess had anticipated. The twenty-four-hour bug had clearly morphed into something more protracted. He didn't want to call her, lest it should seem that he was fussing or, worse, chivvying her back to work. He went to bed that night promising himself to call in on her after work the following day. In the event it became unnecessary, for at lunchtime, three days after she had absented herself, Jess appeared at the door of the farmhouse. She was shaking.

'I thought I told you not to come back until you were right?'

Jess didn't speak. Instead she looked down at the ground and her shoulders began to heave.

'What on earth's the matter?' he asked. 'Is it serious? Are you really ill?'

She shook her head. 'Not ill, no. Not exactly. Can I come in?'

Adam stepped to one side and motioned her into the kitchen. 'Of course. There's only me here. Mum's out shopping. But what is it?'

Jess blew her nose on a fistful of tissues she pulled from the pocket of her jacket. Then she took several deep breaths. 'When we were alone that night, all those months ago, in front of the fire, that was the first time. And since then, most of the time we've been careful but . . .' She hardly needed to say any more.

Adam's face fell and the colour drained from his cheeks. 'Oh, God!'

Jess's eyes filled with tears once more. 'I knew I shouldn't have come—'

'No. I mean . . . of course you should. It's just that . . .' He held on to the door jamb to steady himself.

'I didn't mean it to happen. I tried to be sure of my timings. I didn't want to – I mean I didn't think it would . . .'

Adam shook his head. 'You don't have to say that. I know you wouldn't have . . .'

'If you want nothing to do with me I'll understand. I'll go away. You needn't hear from me again. I'll ask nothing of you. And I don't blame you at all. The last thing I want is for you to feel trapped. You have your own life to lead. This is the last thing you need . . .'

Then, very softly, he said something she never expected to hear: 'It's wonderful.'

At first she thought she must have misheard. 'What?'

'I mean . . . it's a surprise – a shock even – but it's happened. It's real. There's no point in me pretending otherwise. I'm not going to change my mind about you. It's my responsibility as much as yours and, well, I can't think of anyone I would rather bring up a child with.'

'But you're eighteen! You're meant to be horrified. Your feelings might change. You might get tired of me. You might want to spend time with someone else.'

'And so might you,' he countered. 'You're only a year older. How do *you* feel? Do you want *me* around? Do you want to . . .?' He paused, fearful and reluctant to say the words.

'Keep it?' she asked.

Adam nodded.

'Of course I do. How could I not? It's just that I have to ask you . . .' she sat down on a stool by the kitchen sink and looked up into his eyes '. . . do you love me?'

Adam smiled. 'How could you even *ask* me that? Of course I love you.'

'More than a New Zealand sheep-shearer?'

For a moment he was unsure how to reply. Then he answered as truthfully as he could. 'I only knew her for a week. Yes, I was smitten, but then she left and went home to . . . I don't know what. I haven't heard from her since.'

'But you did love her?'

'Yes, I did. Or I thought I did. I was certainly bowled over by her. And it was the first time I'd had such feelings.'

'And then I came along, and it happened all over again.'

'But it was different.'

'How different?'

Adam struggled to explain. 'Just . . . different . . .'

'Not second best? Not just convenient because I was around and she wasn't?'

'No! Not at all. I did still think of her, but as you and I grew closer it happened less and less.'

'So I had the advantage of being here when she was across the other side of the world?'

'Yes, but . . . no!'

'And if she comes back, what then?'

Adam reached forward and took her hand. 'Everyone's allowed to fall in love. You can call it attraction, or infatuation or whatever you want. It's a part of growing up. Everyone goes through it – or, at least, they should. But then something different happens. If you're lucky the attraction turns into something deeper. That's what happened with you. I was attracted to you physically, then I got to know you, to admire you . . . to love you. Nothing will change that. Not you, not Isla, not anybody. I've never told anybody I love them before. And, yes, I might only be eighteen, but I know in my heart the things that are important to me in another person and they'll never change. I've watched you learning about the land, seen your feelings for the animals and the way you relate to people. You're a good person, a kind person, and that counts for so much. Plus the fact that, in spite of everything, you care for *me*.'

Jess was looking at him with wide eyes now, and tears were rolling down her cheeks, one after another in a steady flow. 'And you don't hate me for not being more careful?'

Adam sighed. 'What about me? Shouldn't *I* have been more careful? But what we have isn't just lust or passion – well, they were both a part of it that first time, but it was more than that. I wanted . . . to be a part of you, I suppose. And to make you a part of me. Perhaps we should both have been more careful, but what's happened has happened.'

'And you don't feel angry?'

'No. A bit . . . strange but not angry. I don't think I could be angry with you.'

'But I'm older. I should have been wiser.'

'Look, it's down to both of us. The fact that you've come here and told me— But wait a minute. What about you? What do *you* want to do? This isn't all about me, it's much more about you. You're carrying . . .' he was aware of the gravity of the moment '. . . a baby.'

Jess wiped away the tears and blew her nose once more. '*Our* baby. I want us to sit down, talk about it and think it through properly. Do we want to commit to one another? Where will we live? What will people think? What will your mother say?'

'I don't care what people say or think. I've had enough of that to last me a lifetime. You've given me more love and under-standing than anyone except my parents. We like the same things – well, a lot of the same things. We share the same values. We laugh together, we're comfortable in each other's company . . . aren't we?'

'Yes.'

'So what do you think?'

'Honestly?' She asked the question coldly.

Adam looked fearful, as though he were about to have the earth pulled from beneath him.

'I can't imagine a world without you. I love being with you. But I don't want to trap you. I don't want you to think that this', she pointed to her tummy, 'is my way of hanging on to you. I want us to be together because we *want* to be together not because of circumstances that make us feel we *ought* to be together.'

Adam thought carefully for a moment. 'Does your mother know?'

Jess nodded. 'I told her just before I came up here.'

'What did she say?'

'Very little for a few minutes. She walked into the kitchen, put the kettle on, then asked me to come and sit down.'

For the second time in as many minutes, Adam feared the worst. 'And?'

'She gave me a telling-off for not being more careful, and then asked me what I planned to do about it.'

'What did you say?'

'I said I'd come up here and talk to you. That it would have to be a joint decision since it affected both of us.'

'Did you consider . . . the alternatives?' He looked away for a moment.

'Briefly. But then I knew I couldn't . . . not have it.'

He smiled. 'No.'

'You do feel the same, don't you?'

'Of course.'

'You're not just saying that?'

There was a degree of intensity in his voice now. 'I've been helping people get better ever since I could walk. I might have stopped all that now, been put off by . . . you know . . . attitudes. But it doesn't alter my feelings towards those I love, those I care for. Including . . .' He gestured towards Jess's tummy.

Jess stood up. 'Come here.' She wrapped her arms around him and laid her head on his chest. 'I'm sorry I got you into this.' Adam made to protest but she interrupted: 'I could have fended you off but I chose not to since it seemed that it was something we both wanted to do. I could have been more careful but you'll have to get used to the strange ways of my body – I won't go into that now – and what happened just happened. It was so lovely, and the result might not be what we would have chosen or planned but it is what it is. If you're sure you want to share it with me, that's fine.'

'And you?' he asked. 'Do you want to share it with *me*?'

'Oh, yes, Mr Gabriel. I can think of nobody I would rather have by my side, or anywhere else I'd rather be. I'm quite sure people will think we're very young and very irresponsible and—'

'They already think I'm bonkers.'

'Well, they've got somebody else they can look sideways at now, haven't they? The girl who got herself in the family way by that weird shepherd boy.'

'Are you sure you can cope with that?' he asked.

'I don't know,' she answered honestly. 'But I'll give it a try if you will.'

37

KEEPING MUM

If there is one thing I have learned in life it is this:
just let go.

Carla Carlisle, *Country Life*, 14 April 2021

Of all the uncomfortable conversations Adam had endured over
the past year, explaining the situation to his mother came pretty
high up in terms of difficulty. There was a deafening silence,
then an absence, then a time of consideration, followed by
rationalising – mainly to herself but eventually to and with
Adam. He could not recall ever feeling so apologetic or, it had
to be admitted, foolish.

But Bethany Gabriel was nothing if not practical. The situation might have taken her by surprise, but it was what it was
and must be faced up to – from her own point of view as well
as Adam's.

The two Yorkshire mothers met to discuss the situation at a
café in Skipton – neutral territory. The atmosphere was tense
at first, each standing in the corner of their own offspring.
Nothing too judgemental was said – both women were polite

enough to ensure that the meeting did not directly apportion blame to either party – though lack of common sense in both of their children was alluded to.

Their respective stance having been established, the atmosphere began to thaw, and over the second cup of coffee, pragmatism became the order of the day.

Adam and Jess had established between themselves that they were determined to bring up the child together, and neither mother was prepared or willing to go against a decision made, in the eyes of the law, by two people who had reached the age of consent. Even if Sarah Hartley and Bethany Gabriel decided to forbid their children to cohabit they had no legal right to do so. It would be futile to stand in their way. What would be would be, and the two mothers must make the best of it.

When it came to deciding where Adam and Jess would live, the obvious choice was the farmhouse. Neither mother objected to that. In fact, when push came to shove, there was little they did not see eye to eye on, and Bethany Gabriel thanked her lucky stars that, although her son had let his usual common-sense and considered approach to life slip away on some fateful evening, at least he had had the good sense to choose a girl whose family had similar values to her own. It could have been so much worse.

Three weeks later Jess moved in. Langstroth Farmhouse, while not being the height of luxury, at least had three bedrooms and two bathrooms – Bethany had insisted on the latter when Adam had reached his teens and sharing meant that, for all his relative tidiness around the house, one woman and two men could not possibly co-exist with a single facility for their collective ablutions. Luke knew when he was beaten and a small bedroom, connecting directly with their own, was swiftly converted.

The only fly in the current ointment was when Bethany insisted that Adam and Jess should have her bedroom and en-suite and she would move into Adam's old room. It made sense, she said, especially bearing in mind Jess's current condition, which might necessitate her getting up in the middle of the night. And, anyway, she had never liked sleeping in that room on her own when for the previous umpteen years she had shared it with Luke. The move would give her a new start, she said. It would suit her frame of mind, rather than being an imposition.

The pair knew when an argument was lost, and on their first night together as a couple in their own room, Adam felt a kind of completeness, a sense of security and happiness he could not recall having experienced before. He could have been nervous. He could have been fearful. Instead, an all-enveloping feeling of love and contentment overwhelmed him.

It was impossible not to think of his father as he lay in the room his parents had shared. Talking about love was not something that would ever have occurred to Luke Gabriel, whether that love were for his son or his wife, but Luke had had his own way of demonstrating his affections: a ruffling of his son's hair as the boy sat at his father's feet in front of the television; a single lingering kiss for Bethany when he left the house each morning, and another on his return. Adam remembered that the door between the small sitting room and the kitchen would be closed while his mother and father discussed the events of the day out of hearing of their young son.

And now he had taken his father's place – unwillingly, but out of necessity. It was the strangest of feelings, a kind of moving on – unexpected and unfortunate in its timing, but a sign of life moving forward, often in an unexpected direction. He sighed heavily and the body beside him stirred.

'Are you happy?' asked Jess, as she lay with her head on his chest.

'It's not enough,' replied Adam.

She raised her head and looked him in the eye. 'What do you mean?'

'"Happy" isn't enough.' He tried to explain further, but the words wouldn't come. Instead, his eyes filled with tears. Wrapping his arms around her, he repeated, 'Not enough.'

Jess smiled and ever so gently wiped away the tears with her fingers.

Adam had assumed that Jess would stop work immediately, but she was having none of it. 'I'm carrying on as long as I can.'

'And how long will that be?' he asked.

Jess shrugged. 'At least another three or four months.'

'Don't be daft!'

Jess raised her eyebrows. 'It's not daft. It's practical. I know a Swaledale shepherdess who carried on until the day she was due.'

'Well, that's ridiculous. She might have done it once but I bet she didn't do it again.'

'She did it nine times.'

Adam stood still. Speechless. Young he might have been, but he knew when it was futile to argue. He also knew the woman to whom she referred. He had always had a sneaking admiration for her – and the amenable attitude of her husband. There was much to be learnt from them both.

'Shall we just take it a week at a time, then?' asked Jess.

Adam nodded. 'If we must. But no heavy lifting.'

'Oh, I'll get you to do that. Or Jack.'

Jack Knaggs had smiled to himself when he heard the news. He was secretly delighted that this young girl, in his eyes, was destined to become a part of the family. He had seldom encountered any female so capable, so receptive to learning and so easy to get on with. 'Yon Kiwi', as he called Isla, had been a dab hand at shearing, but something about her had unsettled him, a kind of knowingness that had made her difficult to assess. Jess, on the other hand, was bright, cheerful – female, yes, but straightforward. She let him know when she was happy or unhappy with a particular set of circumstances and he could relate to that. The situation the young pair had got themselves into might have happened sooner than anyone would have predicted, sooner than they would have wanted, but they were neither flighty nor impetuous. Maybe this state of affairs would give them longer together than would otherwise have been the case, and as someone who had lost his spouse too early in life he had learnt to look on the positive side.

He was also pleased that Adam seemed to have regained something of his old spirit. He was different, yes, but there was a new glint in his eye. For the first time in the young lad's life he seemed to have an intimation of his own worth.

It had been painful for Jack to witness the diminution in Adam's confidence where both animals and people were concerned. Once he had exhibited a naturalness around livestock that was reminiscent of Dr Dolittle, but Jack had seen that easy familiarity suddenly evaporate. Adam would still treat them kindly – it was not in his nature to do otherwise – but the close bond he had had with the animals became more impersonal. Only with Nip did he seem to evince that magical relationship, but no outside agency could possibly diminish the closeness of this man and his dog. Theirs was a friendship immune to change: each had known the other too long – shared too many mutual confidences – for that to happen.

Jack had worried that Adam would withdraw into himself, that the encounter with the local doctors had pulled the rug of life from beneath his feet and left him rudderless. Having watched the boy grow up and held his hand – both literally in the early years and metaphorically in later life – Jack felt a mixture of anger and sorrow that the boy's innocence, along with his undoubted gift, should be wrenched from him in such an unfeeling and unceremonious way. The ingratitude made his blood boil but, aside from the odd remark that refused to remain unspoken, he kept his counsel and watched as the weeks and months went by, hoping for an improvement in Adam's demeanour and general outlook. He was not disappointed. It took time, but as a man of the land since birth, Jack knew the value of that commodity, now seemingly in short supply in the fast-moving world of town and city.

Jack, more than most, was painfully aware of the weight of Adam's burden. A gift it might be, but it came with its own baggage. Yet it seemed that a corner had been turned. Adam had lost his father, but now there was someone else who would look out for him.

After years of being pointed out as different from the norm, this girl's love had given Adam the kind of reassurance that had hitherto been lacking. At last, thought Jack, after so many months of tragedy and upheaval, life on the farm could take on some semblance of normality.

That normality was to be short-lived, and the reason for its interruption came from a completely unexpected quarter.

38

A ROCK AND A HARD PLACE

Desperate diseases must have desperate remedies.

Sixteenth-century proverb

Despite the fickle April weather, Jess had been true to her word and pulled if not all her weight on the farm then as much of it as could be useful. She and Adam had settled into a way of life that gave them both pleasure. They had converted the third bedroom in the farmhouse into a sitting room so that they were not constantly under Bethany's feet and she under theirs. 'Good fences make for good neighbours' had been one of Luke Gabriel's dictums, and as such it translated to the inside of the house as well as the fields beyond. (The other he quoted most frequently related to his marriage and his willingness to go up the fells in the morning with a packet of sandwiches and a flask of tea: 'For better for worse, but not for lunch.')

Thus the three residents of Langstroth Farmhouse could be together when they wished, but apart when it suited them, with the odd incursion from Jack when circumstances dictated.

That day the four of them were sitting round a newly

purchased but ancient wooden table that had been set up in the farmyard to allow for alfresco lunches when the weather permitted. The warm sunshine had conspired to give them all a feeling akin to that of the Mole in *The Wind in the Willows*, and while no one actually said, 'Hang spring cleaning,' there was among the party a feeling that winter had sloughed from their shoulders and a new year – soon to be confirmed by the imminent commencement of lambing – was upon them.

They did not expect to be interrupted by the arrival of a car. All four turned in time to see Dr Blackstone step from his battered Volvo estate and walk towards them as they paused in their repast.

'I'm sorry to arrive unannounced.' His expression was apologetic in the extreme, as if he were the bearer of tragic news. The four glanced at one another, then back at the doctor, awaiting information.

'I wonder if I might trouble Adam for a moment?'

Bethany, aware of her own shortcomings the last time she had committed her son to the care of Dr Blackstone, was determined that this time she would not be found wanting.

'I'm sure you can say what you want to us all, Dr Blackstone.'

The doctor glanced at Jack, as though he questioned the wisdom of saying what he wanted in the presence of someone who was not a member of the family.

Bethany put him right. 'We have no secrets from one another. Jack has been a part of this family longer than most of us. You can speak freely.'

Dr Blackstone looked uncomfortable. Bethany was determined to do nothing to ease that discomfort. It was unlike her, under normal circumstances, not to lighten the atmosphere, but Dr Blackstone had forgone the normal courtesies when he had exposed her son to what she considered a mischievous, if not downright brutal, encounter with his colleagues. For that she could not and would not forgive him. And so, the doctor shifted his weight from one foot to another and endeavoured to articulate the reason for his visit.

'If you're sure?' he offered, by way of one more attempt at a private conversation.

'I'm sure,' countered Bethany. Her eyes were unusually piercing and her gaze unflinching.

'It's Dr Cruickshank.'

'My doctor?' Jess heard herself say. She regretted it the moment she had spoken: she had let Bethany down by appearing to be friendly.

'Just so,' replied Dr Blackstone, his voice containing a note of gratitude for the slender olive branch. 'I'm afraid she's not very well.'

'I'm sorry to hear that,' said Bethany.

'She's been unwell for some time. You've probably noticed, Miss Hartley, that Dr Scarlett has been covering for her.'

Jess smiled understandingly but declined to offer any further encouragement.

Aware that he would have to continue the conversation by way of a monologue the doctor began to explain. 'Dorothea – Dr Cruickshank – has been diagnosed with a brain tumour. It is serious, as I'm sure you can understand, and, while she has been seen by the finest surgeons in the country, I'm afraid there is nothing they can do. The tumour is inoperable and Dorothea has had to come to terms with that.'

Bethany might have been cool towards Dr Blackstone, but she was not heartless when it came to the plight of a fellow human being, especially one whose life had been devoted to healing the sick. 'I'm sorry to hear that,' she said, with feeling. 'How dreadful. But I don't see . . .'

'Dr Cruickshank realises that when she met Adam, over a year ago now, she was less than understanding of his gift.'

Adam lowered his eyes, reluctant to resurrect the feelings of antipathy and disappointment that had overwhelmed him when faced with the intimidating panel of four sceptical medics.

'She has charged me with offering an apology.'

Bethany glanced at Adam, who was showing an extraordinary fascination with the slices of apple on his plate. 'That's good of her,' was all she could bring herself to say.

'Rather more than that,' the doctor continued. 'She has asked if Adam would visit her.'

At this, four pairs of eyes looked up to meet Dr Blackstone's.

'She understands that Adam will have every reason to refuse her request, but she would be more than grateful if he would agree to do so.'

'To apologise?' asked Bethany.

'Not simply, no. She wonders if Adam would . . . see if he could do anything for her. All other avenues having failed.'

Adam was moved to respond. 'But I explained at the time. I stopped doing what I have done all my life on that day. I said I would not treat people any more and I've been true to my word. It's been over a year now since you all made it clear that you did not believe I had any right to interfere with people's lives or to involve myself in curing people when I lacked any kind of training. That's what you accused me of.'

The doctor's face reddened. 'I'm aware of that, Adam. And I apologise. We were, I admit, sceptical . . .'

Adam corrected him. 'You were more than that. You were scathing. Particularly Dr Cruickshank. She likened me to those tele-evangelists in America. A phoney. Meddling in people's lives. She said I was lucky; that my ability to effect a cure was down to nothing more than spontaneous regression.'

'Yes. I know . . .'

'And now, when everything else has failed, she wants to use me as a last resort?'

'I suppose that's how it must seem.'

'It must seem that way because it *is* that way. But I can't help, I'm afraid. To be able to heal people you have to *feel* you can heal. I no longer have that ability. To *feel*, I mean. It left me that day. The day you all told me I had no gift, no talent, just a misguided notion that I had some power, which did not conform to what you called "orthodox medicine". I'm sorry, Dr Blackstone, but I'll be of no use to Dr Cruickshank.'

'And you won't even try?' Dr Blackstone took a deep breath and made one final attempt to change Adam's mind. 'What have you got to lose, Adam? Dorothea has everything to lose. You are the one person who might just be able to make a difference. You really are her last hope.'

Adam looked around the assembled company for some kind of support, but no one felt able to disagree with the doctor's diagnosis. Dorothea Cruickshank was going to die, unless some kind of miracle happened. In this part of the dale, miracles occasionally happened. Often when they were least expected.

39

BEST ENDEAVOURS

Women can't forgive failure.

Anton Chekhov, *The Seagull*, 1896

Dorothea Cruickshank's house was everything Adam had expected it to be: detached, stone-built and embraced by a garden that showed every sign of loving care and attention. As a physician, Dr Cruickshank might have been sceptical of any form of faith healing, but she knew the value of being surrounded by plants and flowers. The positive benefits to mental health provided by a garden were to her as clear as crystal.

She was sitting in a small conservatory at the back of her house. A plaid rug was draped over her legs. Orchids and scented-leaf pelargoniums were arranged about her on tiered wooden shelves; she sat among them like a coloratura soprano, centre stage at the opera, about to deliver the telling aria.

Adam was shown in by a small bird-like housekeeper, who hopped from one leg to another after the fashion of a nervous sparrow, a trait last seen in Dr Blackstone when he visited the farmhouse. There was no Mr Cruickshank. There never had been. Dorothea had had little time for affairs of the heart, having grown up and graduated in a man's world when for a woman to do so was, if no longer a rarity, then still something to be admired and remarked upon.

And admired she was, locally, if not for the warmest of bedside manners, then certainly for her no-nonsense approach to medicine. She could spot a malingerer at fifty paces and kept what sympathy she did possess cloaked in matter-of-factness and practicality. Her purpose in life was to cure the sick and see off time-wasters, and for that she was well respected.

The Dr Cruickshank that Adam stood in front of now was a pale shadow of the one who had addressed him so witheringly all those months ago. There was about her an air of resignation rather than ferocity, as though she were a spent force: a lost soul desperate for some kind of lifeline. A tortoiseshell comb slithered from its anchorage on the thinning grey hair as she looked up to greet him.

'Hello,' offered Adam, as the housekeeper scuttled from their presence.

'It's good of you to come,' said the doctor.

Her voice had none of the stentorian resonance he remembered. It seemed that every sentence represented a supreme effort of articulation.

'Especially when I was rather harsh on you when we last met,' she added.

'Yes,' agreed Adam.

'Sit down. Please.' She indicated a wicker chair opposite her own.

Adam did so.

'I don't very often eat humble pie,' confessed his interlocutor. 'Never had much appetite for it. But needs must . . .'

'When the devil drives?' offered Adam.

Dr Cruickshank smiled weakly. 'Just so.'

Adam tried to speak kindly. 'The thing is, I really don't think I can help. I'd like to but . . .'

The doctor held up her hand, and as she did so, the little housekeeper reappeared with a small tray containing a pot of coffee, a cup and saucer, a small milk jug and a plate of digestive biscuits, which she put down on the woven wicker table next to Adam's chair, then left as surreptitiously as she had arrived.

'I quite understand how you must feel.' The doctor motioned him to help himself to the coffee and biscuits. 'I don't expect you came here willingly. I was hardly encouraging of your efforts when we last met.'

'No,' confirmed Adam, and took a sip of coffee. He was anxious for the doctor to do most of the talking, rather than being forced into making a fool of himself, which, he felt, was more than likely.

'You are, as you have no doubt guessed, my last hope. My fellow doctors – and the surgeons – have given up on me. There is nothing more they can do, nothing that conventional medicine can contribute to my declining state of health. It set me thinking of the alternatives, of which there are few. Palliative measures are helpful. They ease the pain. My garden is a great solace – more people should recognise the therapeutic qualities of growing things, the stewardship of the land that sustains us, but you know that. Your life as a shepherd connects you to the landscape in a way that few others experience.'

She paused and breathed heavily, reaching for the leaf of a lemon-scented pelargonium, which she rubbed gently between her fingers to release its perfume. Lost for a moment in reverie, she smiled at the freshness of the aroma. Her explanation was clearly taking considerable effort as, no doubt, did that diet of humble pie she had confessed to eating before asking to see someone whose ability was, at the very least, unproven and, at worst, ridiculously optimistic.

Adam felt moved to speak again. 'The thing is, I believed in myself when we met. Since then I've found it difficult to do so. I wouldn't want to . . .' He hesitated.

'Build up my hopes?'

'No.'

She smiled at him. A kindly smile. 'I have no hopes left, but it seemed that I should at least give you the benefit of the doubt.'

It was a compliment, he supposed. A backhanded one but a compliment nevertheless.

He tried to explain: 'I used to do what I did without thinking. It came naturally. If I saw an animal in distress it seemed only right to try to help it. It didn't occur to me when I was very young that my . . .' He was reluctant to name his gift. 'It seemed the most natural thing to do. Then, when my school friends discovered I could make aches and pains feel better, and they couldn't, I began to realise it wasn't . . . normal.'

'And did you feel uncomfortable with it? With being different?'

'Of course. But I knew I couldn't change myself, so I just had to learn to live with it.'

'Until you were rounded on by four doctors who should have seen beyond their professional prejudices and realised that someone with a feel for nature and the countryside had more to offer humanity than would at first seem to be the case.' Dorothea Cruickshank murmured something to herself that Adam couldn't quite catch, then asked, 'And have you done nothing since, by way of healing the sick – animals or humans?'

Adam shook his head.

'I see. Were we so discouraging?'

Adam was surprised at her inability to grasp the devastating effects of his interrogation that day by four disbelieving doctors of medicine. 'You destroyed me. It sounds dramatic, I know, but any feeling of self-worth in what I had been able to do left me that afternoon. It wasn't just anger. It was an entire break-down of confidence. Any ability I had was founded on some kind of subconscious . . . well . . . power. You forced me to stare it in the face, to confront it with your established logic. I suppose it might have been partly a conscious choice, but my talent was something I had come to rely on without questioning it. When you told me it didn't exist – that it couldn't exist – something just snapped. You might not have taken away my ability to heal – who knows? – but you took away my will to use it. And when you stop using something you forget how it works. The machinery gets rusty. Eventually it crumbles and disappears until you forget what it was in the first place. Some time ago I was faced with a ewe having a difficult birth. Once I could probably have saved both the ewe and the lamb. I would certainly have tried. Now, all I could do was stare at it and feel sorry for it. I had to call the vet, but it was too late. Both the ewe and the lamb died. It wasn't that I didn't *want* to help, it was that I *couldn't*. The gift I once had has disappeared. It's as simple as that.'

'And if one of those who was so discouraging to you admits that she was misguided, cruel even, do you think that such a confession might unlock those powers and allow them full rein once more?'

Adam sighed. 'I don't know. I don't think so. Not now.'

Dr Cruickshank pushed herself upright in her chair and fixed him with her still beady eye. 'The fact that you heal – or healed – gives us something in common, Adam. Once you're committed to it you're committed for life. The enthusiasm for it may ebb and flow, but deep down it's innate. It's a part of our being. It might become rusty, as you put it, but it never completely disappears. To elaborate on your analogy, it may just need a little oiling to get it back in working order.'

'But really I—'

Dorothea Cruickshank raised her hand again. After a life of taking charge, it was a gesture that brooked no contradiction. 'Do what you have to do. That's all. Whatever the outcome I shall not reproach you. I shall always be grateful to you.'

'Why?'

'Because whatever gift you do or do not possess, you are without pride.'

'But I *am* proud!'

'Of your life as a shepherd?'

'Yes,' he confirmed.

'That is a different kind of pride. I am proud of being a doctor. I am not proud of being unable to believe in things I do not comprehend. That is a weakness. A closed mind does not lead to advancement in either science or human relations. We have seen too much of that lately – an inability to respect ideas and beliefs that do not conform to our own. How else are we to move forward if we do not question our own mores, our own opinions, our own entrenched ideals?' She paused, as if processing her thoughts. 'I should have known better. I should have been more sympathetic to a belief at variance with my own.'

Adam did not answer, but smiled at what amounted to a confession of the doctor's own failure to believe that there was any possible way he could help the sick.

'And then, above all, there is kindness, and in your case, the most valuable attribute available to humanity. An attribute all too frequently underused.'

Adam looked at her enquiringly.

Dorothea Cruickshank smiled at him, then said softly, 'Generosity of spirit.'

Adam smiled back at her, grateful for the compliment, before the doctor posed her final question: 'Will you do me the honour of at least trying? Please?'

40

O YE OF LITTLE FAITH

Success has many fathers, while failure is an orphan.

Mid-twentieth-century proverb

Dorothea Cruickshank died three weeks later. The *Craven Courier* made much of her lifetime of devotion to the folk of the dale and the high regard in which she was held by her patients and members of the local community. They reported the cause of her death and, as a footnote, remarked that in spite of being attended by the finest in the land, nothing could be done to treat her condition.

And there it would have rested, had not the friendly postman who knew everybody's business alerted the *Courier*'s terrier of a reporter to the visit of one Adam Gabriel in the weeks before her death.

The arrival of Belle Barclay in the middle of lambing was as welcome as a thunderstorm at harvest time.

'Could I have a word?'

'What now?' asked Adam, the desperation in his voice as

clear as could be as he struggled to ease into the world the second of the twin lambs the ewe was struggling to deliver.

'It won't take long. Simple question. Did you attend Dorothea Cruickshank before she died?'

'Why do you want to know?'

'Oh, come on, Adam!'

The desperate ovine situation over which he was currently presiding, and the need to get Belle Barclay off his back once and for all, led to an untypically brusque reply: 'Yes, I did. And she died. Are you happy now?'

Belle Barclay looked taken aback. 'Happy? No. Content with your answer? Well, I suppose I'll have to be, won't I?'

'I'm sorry. It's just that this is not a good time. I was asked to see Dr Cruickshank and I agreed. I don't do that sort of thing any more. Not since . . .'

'Since?'

Adam thought better of opening the old wound. At least Belle Barclay had not got wind of the doctors' inquisition, and there was no reason why she should.

'I just don't get involved, OK? I'm sorry. That's all I have to say.'

She nodded in the direction of the struggling ewe. 'I can see you're busy. I won't detain you any more.' With that, she snapped her notebook shut and tottered off in the direction of her car.

As she wended her way down the track, Adam stood up and looked after her, wondering if it would have been a good idea to explain things more fully. The musing did not last for long. There were lambs to deliver, more pressing things on his mind for now.

The death of Dorothea Cruickshank had come as no surprise to him. He had returned from her house in low spirits. Try as he might to recall the familiar feeling of empowerment that would almost consume him in days gone by his heart was simply not in it. He was aware of going through the motions, but the fire did not burn within him. Standing over her, willing himself to make a difference, he was overtaken by an all-consuming feeling of futility. He was a fraud. There was no other word for it. For all the good he would be doing he might as well have been waving a magic wand from a children's box of conjuring tricks. It was hopeless. Power? What power? Had it ever been there, or was his so-called 'gift' nothing more than the product of an overactive imagination? He would never know. But what he did know was that there was no way he could make a difference to the suffering of Dorothea Cruickshank. She was going to die. The doctors and surgeons had said so and it was laughable to pretend that a simple shepherd, whose modus operandi was 'the laying on of hands', could affect her future wellbeing.

As he made to leave the house she thanked him, but he detected in her voice a despair that matched his own. She knew that his intervention would make no difference to her prognosis. Perhaps it was enough that she had given him the benefit of the doubt and salved her own conscience by allowing him to attempt some kind of cure. Her cynicism, like as not, was as entrenched as it had ever been but she had, in her last few weeks of life, revealed the quality she so revered: generosity of spirit. At least he had in some small way allowed her to feel better about herself. Perhaps that was enough.

Thursday's edition of the *Craven Courier* settled, once and for all in Adam's eyes, the question of whether or not he had the ability to heal the sick:

Good Shepherd Fails to Save Local Doctor
by Belle Barclay

Every community has its heroes and heroines. Some conventional, others less so.

Dr Dorothea Cruickshank (64), who died last week, was a respected local physician who had practised in the dale for more than forty years.

Her untimely death comes as a blow to her many patients who will recall her no-nonsense attitude and her personal dedication to the health of the local population.

Known for her brusque manner and distrust of what she referred to as 'quackery' – her all-encompassing term for alternative medicines, from acupuncture to homeopathy – it is surprising to discover that Dr Cruickshank was attended in the final weeks of her illness by local shepherd Adam Gabriel (18), known for many years as 'The Boy with the Gift'.

Stories of Adam's ability to heal animals and humans are well known in the dale, so it will come as a sadness to many to discover that he failed to save Dr Cruickshank, who was diagnosed with a brain tumour some months ago.

Perhaps Adam's intervention came too late. Perhaps Dr Cruickshank's illness was too far advanced even for someone with Adam's gift to make a difference. Or perhaps, as Dr Cruickshank herself would have insisted, there is no proof that such forms of 'faith healing' have any basis in fact.

Whatever the reality behind such presumptions, Adam Gabriel continues his day-job as a shepherd on the fells above Yockenthwaite and has explained to this newspaper that as far as he is concerned his days of healing are over.

One can only speculate as to why this situation has arisen. Has his failure to cure Dr Cruickshank caused Adam to doubt his own ability? Have others intervened to discourage him? Whatever the case, we wish him and his family (soon to be added to, we understand) a bright and fulfilling future among the rolling dale that remains his home.

41

RETURN OF THE NATIVE

Why do people so love to wander? I think the civilised
parts of the world will suffice for me in the future.

Mary Cassat, Letter to Louisine Havemeyer, 1911

In the days that followed, Jess and Bethany did their best to lift
Adam's spirits. At first it seemed to him that the very core of
his being was being harpooned by public opinion, or the opinion
of Belle Barclay, which purported to represent it. It was quite
clear to him now that the world would regard him as a charlatan
and a fraudster, when all he had set out to do was follow his
instincts and help his fellow man. 'Too pure a motive for the
cynics,' remarked Jack Knaggs, giving voice to a rare philosophical nugget.

It was Jack who first took Adam on one side and attempted
to console him. 'It's time you knew the facts of life, lad.' It then
occurred to Jack that such a statement might be misconstrued.
'Not the ones tha's known since tha was a nipper. I know there's
no mystery there by t' state o' yon lass.' He cleared his throat
to cover what he hoped would not be taken as a criticism of

Adam's current situation. 'No, I dun't mean that sort o' fact. Just that folk is too ready to think t' worst of thee. Come on. Buck up. Tha's a grand lad wi' good intentions. Don't let the buggers grind yer down.'

And there the lecture ended, brief but to the point.

Adam was staring into the middle distance. 'No,' he said, getting up off the stone bench on which the two of them were sitting for their morning tea. 'Not really worth it, is it? And, anyway, I've other people to think of now. People who care for me whatever I might do or have done. It's time I started concentrating on them.'

'That's reet.'

The great advantage was that there was little time for brooding, with lambs being born at every hour. All four of them were working flat out all day and much of the night, Bethany and Adam taking care to ensure that Jess rested as much as possible. To her were given the responsibilities near to home, looking after those ewes confined to the barn, thanks to complications of one sort or another.

'Is this to test my maternal instincts?' she teased Adam, who just smiled and kissed her cheek before heading up the fellside to check on the rest of the flock.

It was, as usual, towards the end of the lambing season when the familiar baritone echoed across the fells, heralding the arrival of Brother Wilfrid. As he had failed to materialise the previous year, Bethany and Adam wondered if they would ever see him again. But they had not given up hope. There had been times in the past when he had skipped a year, then magically reappeared as if nothing untoward had happened. The song this time had a particularly joyous ring to it: 'Guide me,

O thou great Redeemer, Pilgrim through this barren land; I am weak, but thou art mighty. Hold me with thy powerful hand.'

Jess ventured out of the barn with a bucket in her hand, thinking that Bethany must have turned up the volume on the radio. She stared open-mouthed at the sight of a man in a monk's habit, loping down the grassy moorland above the farm, thinking perhaps that some inmate from the local psychiatric hospital had succeeded in making a bid for freedom.

'Hello, young lady!' he hailed her heartily, disappearing down a dip in the land, then rising again, like some supernatural creature of the moors, a smile on his face and a spring in his step.

He walked towards her with his free hand – the one not grasping his shepherd's crook – outstretched. 'Brother Wilfrid. I'm afraid I don't know your name.'

'Jess. Jess Hartley.'

Her confused expression prompted Brother Wilfrid to explain: 'I drop in on my annual sojourn to see Mr and Mrs Gabriel and their son. To pass the time of day, catch up on events and . . . er . . . sometimes I partake of refreshment or even stay the night. It's a yearly catch-up, which we've done for, oh, a long time now. Except that last year I was unavoidably detained. Are any of them about? I try to arrive at the end of lambing time so as not to cause too much inconvenience, but I fear I'm slightly earlier this year due to an adjustment in my plans.'

Jess looked not a little embarrassed, which was thankfully alleviated by the appearance of Bethany at the door of the farmhouse. 'I thought I heard you, Brother Wilfrid. Come in.'

'Praise the Lord, Mrs Gabriel, you look no different from

when I saw you two years ago. And how is young Adam? And Mr Gabriel?'

Over tea and biscuits, Bethany explained the ins and outs of their current situation to the attentive pilgrim. He avoided the customary verbal expressions of sympathy, but sat quietly and listened, clearly affected by what he heard. Bethany explained about Luke's sudden death, about the arrival of Jess and the consequences of her son's new-found affections. There was no sign of admonishment on the face of the monk, no judgement of Adam's actions and the circumstances they had brought about. Bethany explained about the meeting with the doctors, Adam's subsequent visit to Dorothea Cruickshank and the report in the *Craven Courier*. Through all this, Brother Wilfrid remained silent, occasionally nodding gently to signal that the information was being taken on board.

'And so,' said Bethany, with a degree of finality, 'here they both are, living under my roof. "Living in sin", as some might say. I will quite understand if you disapprove, Brother Wilfrid. The events of the last year or two are rather a lot to take on board in one go. They have been for me but—'

For the first time during the long conversation the monk interrupted. 'It is not my place to approve or disapprove, Bethany. You have done what you consider to be right by your son – and by his new-found love. What good mother would not have done the same?'

'Oh, quite a few, I can tell you. I notice the looks when I go to the shops. I haven't been to church since Luke died. My heart hasn't been in it and now, to be honest, I don't think I would feel comfortable.'

Brother Wilfrid leant forward and took her hand in his. She

could not recall him having done so ever before. 'The trials of life are never easy, Bethany. And I'm not going to fob you off with a lot of platitudes after the fashion of "The things that don't break you make you." Such aphorisms are of little consolation when you are journeying through the Slough of Despond. All I can say is that you have been the most wonderful help to me over the years.'

'But you only—'

'I know I'm here for barely a day each year, and sometimes not even that. But when I return I've been constantly renewed and refreshed by the attitude of you and your family, and for that I shall always be grateful. I seem to offer little practical help, I know, but I do keep you all in my heart and my prayers, if that is of the slightest consolation.'

Bethany squeezed his hand and smiled. 'It is. And it's always good to see you.' She stood up. 'Now, you'll stay for supper? And spend the night with us?'

'Well,' Brother Wilfrid looked about him, 'only if there's room, bearing in mind your current situation.'

Bethany laughed softly. 'They don't sleep in the barn, and I know that's where you prefer to be.'

'Among the sweet-smelling hay!' he responded. 'It was good enough for the Baby Jesus and it will be good enough for me!'

'I don't recall him having much of a choice,' retorted Bethany, with a smile.

'Ah, but he grew up with the scent of the countryside in his nostrils – granted, it was the scent of sandy earth in a far-off land, but I'll settle for the sweet, fine fescue of moorland pasture. Whenever I feel it beneath my feet and its scent assails my nostrils I know I'm on home ground. Well, my adopted home anyway.'

With that he rose from his chair, winked at Bethany, grasped his crook and went out through the open door humming softly the tune of some vaguely familiar Handel oratorio.

42

WHO CAN TELL YOU WHY?

We live and learn, but not the wiser grow.

John Pomfret, *Reason*, 1700

Jess had never met anyone quite like Brother Wilfrid, but who had? She had expected a man of the cloth to be disapproving of her over dinner, perhaps even refusing to acknowledge her presence, but he had treated her with the same courtesy he showed to Bethany and to Adam. He made no mention of the circumstances leading up to their current situation; neither did he refer directly to her condition, though the omission did not appear to be a reflection of his opinion, rather that he seemed to have taken the entire state of affairs in his stride. His manner was sunny and optimistic, and aside from raising his glass of wine and toasting 'Absent friends' he seemed keen to talk of the future rather than the more recent past.

Adam explained his and Jess's intentions – that they would continue with the farm, under Bethany's guidance, and beyond that they were happy to take things as they came.

It was early the following morning, when Brother Wilfrid

took his leave that he and Adam had their most intimate conversation, as if the monk had been biding his time, waiting for the right moment to say things that he clearly felt a need to share. He had asked Adam to walk him to the edge of the Gabriels' land and wave him off, as usual. But as they reached a familiar rocky outcrop, with Nip at Adam's heel, he motioned Adam to sit, positioning himself slightly above and looking out across the valley. The dog lay beside his master, head on paws, as if settling down for the duration.

'You've had quite a time,' said Brother Wilfrid.

'You could say that,' agreed Adam.

'A lot of growing up.'

'Well, in some ways. But perhaps I should have been *more* grown up in others.'

'Oh, we all have little lapses. Who's to say they cannot lead us to a better place?'

'You think?'

They were looking in different directions; the younger man out across the valley; the monk upwards towards the crest of the moor, as if seeking divine inspiration. After a few moments of silence, with the bleating of lambs the only audible contribution to the atmosphere, Brother Wilfrid turned and looked across the line of rolling turf, studded with outcrops of limestone, for all the world like currants protruding from a rock bun. Quite close to them was a shake hole – a rounded aperture in the ground. 'They always make me think,' said the monk, almost to himself.

'Sorry?'

'The shake holes. They always make me think of what's below and why they are there.'

'It's where the boulder clay has eroded over time. Been washed away. They're the gaps between outcrops of limestone. We get lots of potholers exploring the deeper ones that turn into underground caves.'

'Yes. I know the scientific explanation. But don't you ever wonder if they might just be something else? Secret pathways to places we know nothing about? A real underworld rather than that imagined by storytellers? What if they're like C. S. Lewis's wardrobe and lead us to Narnia?'

Adam frowned. Brother Wilfrid was not normally one for wandering off into the realms of fantasy. 'All I know is that when cavers get stuck down there the local rescue teams have to risk their lives in getting them out.'

'Oh dear! Where is the boy with the imagination now? Where has he gone?'

Adam felt embarrassed at his perceived lack of empathy. 'Sorry, I didn't mean . . .'

'I just don't want you to lose that special magic you had simply because others failed to recognise it as something special.'

Adam looked his interlocutor in the eye. 'And you think it *was* special?'

'I *know* it was special.'

'How?'

'Because of life's experiences and what they have taught me.'

'But I don't know anything about your life. We only meet once a year, for a day or so, and then you're gone. And last year . . . We like you very much, Brother Wilfrid, but we know nothing about you.' Adam smiled, to reflect his fondness for a man who had always been something of a mystery.

'Indeed. It suits me to remain . . . shall we say a little mysterious? Not for any selfish reason, you understand. Well, maybe a *little* selfish, but mainly to avoid muddying the waters. It's all too easy to construct an inaccurate picture of someone when they appear in your life with a history compounded of the gossip and hearsay of others. Better – purer – if they come to know you for what you are to *them*, rather than how you are regarded by other people.'

Adam looked confused. 'You mean some people think you're not what you are to us?'

'Maybe.'

'You've not really answered my question.'

'No. I've not. And you deserve an answer. There comes a moment when mystery is not always helpful.' Brother Wilfrid got up from the rock on which he had been sitting and followed Adam's gaze out across the velvet green of the valley. 'This landscape is such a special place, don't you think? A place that helps a man to know himself. There are none of the sophistications of metropolitan life to get in the way. Here Nature confronts you and lets you know when you're found wanting.' He turned to Adam and was unsurprised at the baffled look on the young man's face. He came and sat nearer to him on the huge limestone outcrop, stroked the dog's head and continued in his rather old-fashioned way of speaking to which Adam had become accustomed.

'When I was a young man I was ordained. I became a Catholic priest. It was what I had always felt I was meant to be. I served in quite a wealthy community in a Surrey town. I remained there for many years, ministering to the sick, the bereaved, the young and the old. It was a comfortable living in an appreciative community. The Easter collection was always generous. But over time something happened to me. My outlook changed. My reason for living changed. Each Sunday, in particular, I became aware that I was simply going through the motions. My faith had somehow, very slowly and imperceptibly, faded away. There was no single event that caused me to lose my way. The Church has its flaws but many of those in the ministry have good intentions. I had no reverse Road to Damascus experience, just a gradual diminution of belief until the great realisation came that not only was my heart not in my ministry but, it seemed, God was no longer in me. He had abandoned me. I had become a hollow instrument making all the right noises but empty of conviction.'

He stopped and sat silently, gazing out across the valley, but his face displayed a warm smile. The contrast between his words and his expression struck Adam as odd. 'So what did you do?' he asked.

'I gave up my calling. My living. My life as it was. I moved away. I changed my name and I went to work with my hands rather than my heart as a labourer on building sites, moving from town to town. Nobody really bothered about who I was. I had no real responsibility other than turning up for work on time and collecting my pay packet at the end of the week – when we had such things. I did this for several years. I had a good living. I enjoyed myself. I had no responsibilities and spent my money as I wished with little thought as to the consequences. I became, if you like, a latter-day Prodigal Son – except that both my parents died when I was young so I had no home to return to, just an empty room in whatever digs I happened to occupy at the time. And then one day I gave it all up. Just like that.'

'But why? If you were happy in your work and had a decent living and no responsibilities, why not carry on as you were?'

'Because it was not really what I was meant to be, meant to do. Not that I realised it at the time. My mind was full of all kinds of things that I could not reconcile. I thought that as God seemed to have forgotten about me then it wouldn't matter if I forgot about Him. But, as you will discover, Adam, life finds you out. If you let it.'

'I don't understand.'

'Sorry. I'm not making myself very clear, am I? The problem I had – both as a priest and as a builder's labourer – was that in both occupations I was simply thinking about myself, about what I was getting out of it – a comfortable living. For many people – and I do not judge them for it – that is enough. And yet I knew, in my heart of hearts, that it was not enough for me. I sought a purer life, independent of materialism and – more than anything – predicated not on what I could get out of the world but what I could put into it, even if that conviction was neither appreciated nor acknowledged by anyone else. I came to understand that introspection is the most counter-productive of all mental states. It does not make for peace of mind. Neither does it improve us as a society. So many of those personal goals we aim for seldom match up to our expectations once we have achieved them, and the result is a life of dissatisfaction. And so I changed.'

'How? What did you do?'

'I did what I am doing now. I went out into the wilderness. I left behind my dog collar, donned my old black cassock and I walked.'

'So you are not really a monk?'

'No. But I am a brother, a brother traveller on the journey of life.'

'And you found your faith again?'

'Not straight away. But I felt a need to go looking for it.'

'And you found it?'

Brother Wilfrid smiled. 'Eventually I realised it had been there the whole time. Just covered up by my own devices and desires. When I had the courage to strip them all away – fearing I would find nothing beneath them – I came face to face with the real me.'

'Who is?' Adam shook his head, still not grasping his companion's meaning.

'Someone who realises that the greatest gift in life is to work towards easing the burden of others rather than looking inwards and seeking personal and material gain. Contentment and real fulfilment can only come if we look outwards rather than inwards.'

'So what do you do? I know you come and see us once a year but . . .'

The cleric sighed heavily. 'I spend my time doing what most people think is pointless, Adam. I pray. I pray for the people I meet – for their wellbeing and their continued health and happiness. I do it every day as I walk the land. Today I am in Langstrothdale as Brother Wilfrid. Tomorrow I shall be . . . well, who knows where, as Brother Jerome, then another twenty miles away as Brother Anselm. Not for any sinister reason, you understand, but simply to retain some kind of anonymity, an absence of self in a way, and to avoid unnecessary complications. I am all these people and I am no one. But I am *their* brother. My prayers for those I meet are deeply felt and sincere. My life is devoted to thinking of them, rather than of myself, and it is the one I was meant to lead. I know that.'

'And you are happy?'

'I am . . . content. There will be those who think my life is pointless. What good can be achieved simply by thinking about people and praying for them? But in some strange way I have never felt more useful. It is certainly exhausting – both physically and mentally – which is why I occasionally have to take time off, why I'm sometimes absent from your company, though I confess that I do miss it.'

'And where do you go then?'

'Oh, here and there. I can generally find a monastery that will take me in and allow me to live in solitude and silence for a few weeks or months. To recharge my batteries and clear my head. Of course, you could argue that there is selfishness even in that, that I do what I do for my own satisfaction and peace of mind. But it is the purest approach to life that I have been able to find, and that is what I want you to remember. Not about me, but about yourself.'

'What do you mean?'

'Your healing. You must not give up your calling because of the cynicism of others.'

'That's what Jack said,' murmured Adam.

'And he's quite right.'

'But just as you lost *your* faith,' said Adam, defensively, 'so I seem to have lost *mine*.'

'Then you must be patient and wait for it to return.'

'If it ever does. I can't think it will. I had it and it slipped away. It's simply not there now.'

'And yet, given time and the right frame of mind, it may return.'

'Maybe.'

Brother Wilfrid rose to his feet. 'I must be away. Places to go, people to see – as they say. But think on what I've said, Adam. And, if it's not too much to ask, I'd rather you kept our conversation to yourself. Is that selfish of me?'

Adam smiled. 'No. It's not selfish. Thank you for sharing it with me. I feel very . . . honoured.'

The cleric shook his head. 'It is I who am honoured as I have been these last years, watching you grow and seeing you exercising a far greater and more tangible gift than mine, which few can comprehend. Because it is not understood doesn't mean it doesn't exist, and you just hang on to that thought. Remember, Adam, "There are none so blind as those who will not see." Sometimes if our faith is strong enough it can move mountains, but what it sometimes needs is a little belief in its capacity to exist from those who benefit from it. Do you understand?'

'I'm not sure.'

'Perhaps you'll find out what I mean. One day. I do hope so. In the meantime, look after that wonderful girl. I can see she's special. There is between you a rare chemistry, in spite of your tender years. That, in itself, is a gift. Cherish it.'

He grasped Adam's hands firmly and added, 'You know, now, that I shall be praying for you. All of you.'

And with that he picked up his shepherd's crook, turned and clambered northwards over the limestone outcrops. As he disappeared down a dip in the land, Adam could hear the strains of some medieval canticle drifting over the moorland turf.

43

FOR EVERYTHING THERE IS A TIME

Reclothe us in our rightful mind . . .

John Greenleaf Whittier, 'Dear Lord
and Father of Mankind', 1872

Life in Langstrothdale settled into its early summer routine – grass
was growing, lambs were fattening, and Jess, too, between visits
to Dr Scarlett, became larger and more immobile, yet still refused
to relinquish walking the fells, crook in hand, keeping an eye on
the various flocks. Adam reconciled himself to the fact that before
very long his life would change for ever. He would become a
father. The whole prospect seemed unreal, and although he was
nervous it surprised him that he was not more apprehensive.

The arrival of the letter, though, made his heart beat faster.
It bore a New Zealand stamp, which meant it could have come
from only one person.

It was lying on the kitchen table when he returned after a
day on the moors. Jess was up in their room lying down before
supper. Bethany was at the kitchen stove. She saw him out of
the corner of her eye. 'You've seen the letter?'

'Yes.'

'Perhaps you ought to open it when you're on your own.' And then, as though to reassure her son, 'Jess hasn't seen it. I kept it safe until you came in. That is, I don't mean . . .'

'No. Fine.' He could feel his mother's discomfort.

'Why don't you have a glass of beer outside? It's a lovely evening. Quite warm. Only a day away from the summer solstice. I'll come and join you in a bit.'

Tactful as ever, thought Adam. He took a bottle of Black Sheep ale from the fridge and carried it, and the letter, to the old pine table in the farmyard. He laid the envelope on the scrubbed wooden boards, poured the beer into a half-pint mug and took a large gulp. Then he picked up the letter and stared at it, turning it over in his hand as if to divine the contents. What could it contain? He had not seen Isla for two years. Was she about to return? Noah had mentioned some kind of family crisis, which had kept them away for last year's shearing ritual, but what now? The butterflies in his stomach reminded him that his feelings for Isla, though neatly compartmentalised in his mind, would still be far from dormant if she were actually here. He felt the texture of the envelope between his thumb and forefinger. Acknowledging that such tactility, however sensitive, was unlikely to reveal anything, he slipped his finger under the flap, removed and unfolded the letter. The handwriting was neat, stylish.

Dear Adam,

I am writing this letter rather than sending an email for various reasons, not least because I know your internet coverage is crap and because I know you hate all this modern technology and I bet you wouldn't have read it anyway. Also because it seemed just too convenient to tap out things on a keyboard rather than to set them down on paper with a pen. So, having found one that works, here goes. I know that Noah will be with you next month for shearing, and I imagine you may be thinking that I'll be coming over with him. I know, also, that we have not had any communication since that meeting outside the farmhouse two years ago. This does not mean that I have forgotten about you. Far from it. I have often thought what it would be like when we met again, and if anything might happen between us. I'm sure (well, I hope) that you felt the spark I felt. You are so special and I can't believe that we will not meet again one day, though I'm afraid it will not be this year. Last year family problems kept us away and, yet again, I am to be deprived of your company. Such a shame.

The thing is, I thought about you so much but knew that, thanks to visas and suchlike, I would not be allowed to stay in the UK for very long. I also knew that being young it would be a good idea to 'live a bit' before settling down.

The thing is, Adam, I did 'live a bit' and as a result I am due to give birth any time now. I know this will come as a bit of a surprise to you and I will quite understand if you want nothing more to do with me. I mean, it's not as if anything was said, and I don't want to presume that I have any claim on your affections. It's just that I wanted you to know the situation and to understand that in spite of the fact that we only know each other for a week or so you will always be special to me.

The father of my child is long gone – someone I was

drawn to in the heat of the moment, but not that I want to spend the rest of my life with. He knows about the baby and is cool with me bringing it up on my own. I am asking nothing of him in the way of obligations – financial or otherwise.

The thing is – and I really don't want you to take this the wrong way – but when my son is born (and I know it's a boy – the world has given me enough surprises for a while) I wondered if you would mind if I called him Adam? You will probably say that I can call him what I want, and I know I don't <u>have</u> to ask you but, well, it would mean a lot to me if you said yes.

The chances are that you might now think I'm some kind of nutcase who is going to descend on Langstrothdale one day and wish myself upon you. Nothing could be further from the truth. I just feel that my own little lamb would benefit from having someone like you in a far-off land thinking about their namesake from time to time. I know our encounter was brief but I like to think that I'm a good judge of character (with one notable exception, clearly) and I have always felt that in some way we were soul-mates. (God! I do hope that doesn't sound too heavy.)

I wanted to write and tell you all this myself before Noah arrives in July and offers you some garbled version of this story. He means well, but sometimes the facts don't come out quite right.

I wouldn't want you to think I was just sleeping around. I made an honest mistake in terms of my last – brief – relationship. The truth is that, in my limited experience, we don't often meet someone with whom we have an instant rapport. In our case the stars did not really align for us – different people from different lands and all that – but I don't want to forget you, that's all. I hope you won't want to forget me, though after reading this that would be quite understandable.

Anyway, let me know what you think. I promise not to be a pain in the arse and bother you much. My address is at the top of the letter. I have chuntered on about me but asked nothing of you. Do let me know how you are and what is happening there, if you can be bothered.

I the meantime I send lots of love and so many thoughts,

Isla xxx

Adam folded the letter and slipped it back into the envelope, took another gulp of beer and stared, as he did so often, at so many times of the day, out across the valley at the sheep-speckled moorland.

'Anything interesting?' asked Bethany, nodding towards the letter as she came out to join him with a glass of beer in her hand.

'It's from Isla.'

'I guessed that,' said Bethany, sitting down opposite him. 'I saw the stamp.'

Adam thought for a moment, then slid the envelope across the table. 'Are you sure?' asked Bethany.

Adam nodded.

His mother put down her glass, carefully took out the letter, read the contents in silence, put it back and laid the envelope on the table between them.

'Will you show it to Jess?' she asked.

Adam looked surprised. 'Do you think I should?'

Bethany shrugged. 'It's not up to me, but it might reassure her. Clarify a few things.' She smiled. 'Not least that she is unlikely to have competition in the near future.'

'It's not like that, Mum.'

'Isn't it? I remember your dad telling me you were quite smitten.'

'Dad said that?'

'Only because he rather admired her. Thought she was good for you. Up until then you'd not really shown an interest in girls. Isla was your dad's kind of girl – beautiful and practical. Just like Jess. I think he'd have liked her, too. I know he would.'

'But if I show Jess the letter . . .'

'It will prove to her that you are open and honest about your relationship, that you have no secrets from each other. She might be a bit upset at first but she's a bright girl, and when she realises that the reason you've shown it to her is because you've moved on and have nothing to hide . . .' Bethany paused. 'You have moved on, haven't you?'

'Of course. Jess is the one, the only one now.'

'Then take the risk, Adam. Show her the letter.'

44

WORTHY IS THE LAMB

Learn well how to think right and then be
your own shepherd.

Mehmet Murat ildan

The summer solstice dawned bright and early. Adam and Bethany took their breakfast outdoors at the table in the farmyard, he returning from scooting up the moorside on the quad bike to repair a broken gate, she having prepared scrambled egg and bacon for his return.

The birdsong was almost deafening: everything from blackbird and woodlark to plover and curlew, the midsummer orchestra of the moors in full and glorious voice.

Bethany put down her cup of coffee and listened, entranced. 'Wouldn't your dad have loved this?' she murmured.

Adam nodded, his mouth full.

His mother turned her head towards him. 'And I think he'd have been very proud of you.'

Adam swallowed hard and coughed. 'Really? I think he'd have given me what-for.'

339

His mother shook her head. 'He might have been a bit quiet to begin with, but he'd have come round when he saw how thoughtful you've been. He was a quiet man, your dad, but he knew the importance of looking after his family, just like you're doing.'

'Why wouldn't I?'

'Oh, there are plenty of lads your age who don't take their responsibilities seriously – who don't have any responsibilities at all. You might not have planned to be in this situation but I reckon you've made the best of it.'

Adam took a sip of coffee and lowered his cup. 'Do you think he'd have liked Jess?'

'I know he would have. I told you, she's his sort of girl. Good-looking and practical.'

'Just like you?'

Bethany smiled. 'I've made your breakfast, you don't have to flatter me.'

'I'm not. You're practical and . . . well, not bad-looking.'

'Do you want a clip round the ear?'

'Mmm. I think I'd probably have got one of those from Dad. For getting myself into this situation.'

'Unlikely. And, anyway, parents are not allowed to hit their children nowadays. I can count on one hand the number of times your father smacked the back of your legs.'

'There was the time I played with a box of matches when I was sitting on a hay bale.'

'Yes, well, let's not go there. And you only did it the once. And you were just five . . .' Bethany's eyes became misty. 'I do miss him,' she whispered.

Adam reached across the table and squeezed her hand. 'You don't talk about him much.'

'Maybe not. But I think about him every minute of every day.'

'Me too. Well, every day, anyway. I wish he'd met Jess.'

'Oh, I think he's looking down, you know. I'm sure he approves.'

'You don't . . .' Adam hesitated '. . . you don't mind us living here together?'

Bethany answered swiftly, 'That's up to you. You were adamant that's what you wanted. Have you changed your mind?'

'No. Not at all. I just wanted to check that you were still OK with it.'

The smile he received in answer was genuine. 'I can't think what life would be like without her now. She's good company for me as well as you, and nobody could argue that she doesn't pull her weight. I just wish she'd stop now that she's so near term. How far gone is she?'

'Thirty-six weeks. Another month to go.'

'Has she said when she's going to take things easy? I know she's slowed down but . . .'

'I've tried to get her to stay here but . . .'

'And have you shown her Isla's letter?'

Adam nodded.

'And?'

'Just as you said, she was a bit miffed at first, but then when I explained things, when I managed to convince her that it was all in the past, just as her previous relationships were in the past' – and here there was the slightest twinkle in his eye – 'I think she understood.'

'So all's well between you.'

'All's well. I've promised to take her—'

Their conversation was interrupted by Jess who came out of

the farmhouse and walked across to the table where they sat. She was carrying a mug of tea and a plate bearing a slice of dry toast. 'You talking about me?'

'Only in a concerned sort of way,' teased Bethany. 'I was wondering when you were going to stop wandering off up the moorside and stay nearer to home.'

'Oh, in a week or so. I'm fine at the moment. And there are those ewes over the top that need to be checked for fly-strike. I'll tidy up the barn this morning, then do that after lunch. I can walk slowly. It's so glorious and it's not a strenuous job.'

'But I can do that,' offered Adam.

'You've got that wall to repair up at the top of the stream, remember?' countered Jess. 'And you wouldn't want me to have to do that, would you?'

Adam glanced across at his mum. 'You see? What can I do? She has an answer for everything.'

Jess grinned. 'Just because I stand up to you . . .'

Adam pushed his breakfast plate away, drained his mug of coffee and rose from the table. 'All right. I'm off. I'll be back for lunch, just to check up on you. I've got a mobile phone with me.'

Bethany turned to Jess. 'That's more than he'd ever do for me.'

'I only hope I can get a signal when I need to, that's all,' replied Adam.

They parted again after lunch. Adam, reassured that all was fine on the maternity front, returned with Nip to the repair of his broken dry-stone wall. Some little time later Jess wandered off on her own up the side of the moor in search of the flock of ewes, the pleadings of Bethany and Adam ringing in her ears that she should return home the moment she felt slightly tired.

'At least it will be downhill all the way,' she reassured them.

The day wore on. Adam finished his repair work, instructed Nip to leap aboard the quad bike and made his way back down the track towards the farmhouse. He was surprised to find Bethany alone when he went indoors. 'Where's Jess?' he asked.

'Not back yet,' confessed Bethany, the concern evident in her tone.

'What time is it?'

Bethany hesitated. 'Half past seven.'

'What? I thought it was about half five.'

'It's because it's so light,' explained Bethany. 'I saw you'd gone without your watch but did you not think to check your phone? It does tell you the time, you know.'

Not for the first time Adam felt ashamed of himself. He had been so busy with his precious wall that, even though his thoughts had frequently turned to Jess and how she would be managing, the fact that he had lost all sense of time, and his phone had not rung, meant he had carried on regardless.

A rising sense of panic began to engulf him. 'I'll go out and look for her.'

'She's probably done the same thing,' Bethany reassured him. 'She didn't leave until well after two and she'll be walking slowly so she's probably not noticed how late it is. I'm sure she'll be fine.'

He talked to Nip all the while as he scoured the moorland searching for her, the dog sitting in front of him on the scarlet quad bike, looking out as avidly as did Adam. To left and right their eyes scanned the rugged moor, Adam calling her name, and listening for a response amid the breeze that fanned the cotton grass and the bracken.

343

Right and left he went, feeling an increased sense of panic as the sun sank towards the horizon and the full moon, perfectly timed by Nature for the summer solstice, began to rise above the moorland fell.

'Jess! Je-e-e-ess!' he called across peat bog and heather knoll, the urgency in his voice clearly audible to the surrounding wildlife. A chorus of grouse lifted from the rough heather in front of him: 'Get-back, get-back.' Their alarm call fell on deaf ears.

Still the man and his dog motored on, shouting, calling, hoping for the sight of her waving from a rocky outcrop or walking down a rough stone-strewn path towards them.

They came to a scattered row of shake holes that peppered the surface of a patch of high moorland. Adam stopped the bike and turned off the engine before setting out on foot over the now treacherous terrain . They were half a mile from the farmhouse now, and the light was fading, though Adam knew it would be another two hours before it was completely dark. That, at least, was a comfort.

Man and dog skirted the first two shake holes – dark and gloomy passages that led down towards the centre of the earth. Surely she could not have fallen into one of these. God! If that were the case they might never find her. He had warned her about the treachery of such a landscape and she was sensible, not foolhardy, especially in her current condition.

Reaching the last of the darkened openings in the earth, Adam turned and looked upwards towards the horizon. His eyes followed the line of a dry-stone wall as it snaked sinuously upwards until it eventually crested the hill. And then he saw her. Sitting with her back to the wall – a small speck but clearly visible against the moss-covered stones.

'Jess!' he yelled. 'I'm coming! Are you all right?'

She made no reply. Adam and Nip scrambled recklessly over tussocks of unyielding moorland grass and through waist-high swathes of bracken, like a man and dog demented. While Nip ran on ahead, nimbly skirting rock and stream, Adam stumbled over the uneven ground, losing his footing and falling headlong into rocky gully and boggy channel until his legs were like jelly and his jeans drenched with peaty water.

When he finally reached her side he could see she was in pain, her face contorted in agony.

He cradled her shoulders with his arm. 'We're here now. It's all right. Tell me what I can do. Can you stand up?'

Perspiration bedewed her brow. She smiled weakly and shook her head. 'It's coming. Well . . . it's trying to, but it won't . . .' She looked at him pleadingly. 'Help me, Adam! Help me!' Then came a groan so deep-seated and plaintive that it tore at his heart.

'But I've never . . .'

Jess shook her head in desperation. 'It doesn't matter. Just try.' She fixed him with a penetrating gaze and spoke in a matter-of-fact tone that brooked no contradiction: 'You *can* help me. You *know* you can. We need to get our baby out of here.' Her face contorted once more as the contractions came ever more rapidly.

A feeling of desperation began to well inside him; fuelled by anger and frustration at his apparent inability to do anything constructive. Here was the woman he loved most in the world, lying in front of him, trying to give birth to his child, and all he could do was stare at her, bewildered and hopeless. Where was the Adam he had known, the Adam he had been, the Adam he surely still was, somewhere deep down? His father had died at his feet; Dr Cruickshank had died in spite of his ministrations, though on that day he knew that the power had left him and there seemed no way to retrieve it. Kind-hearted as he was, he did not love Dorothea Cruickshank and – more to the point – she did not believe, in her heart of hearts, that he could help her. He had been a last resort and, in her eyes, a futile one at that. He had gone through the motions, knowing that no good would come of the encounter.

But Jess loved him and he loved her. How could he do nothing to relieve her agony? How could he stand by and see her, and their unborn child, suffer? How could he watch them die? The image of the ewe and her unborn lamb rose in his mind and he could remember the sense of emptiness, powerlessness, futility. But this was no ewe and lamb. This was Jess. This was his first-born child. No one could save them out here on the moor. No one but him. He could kneel beside her, stroke her hand and make soothing sounds. Or he could actually *do* something.

And then the fear subsided and the old familiar feeling began to rise within him. There was no panic now, just a powerful sense of calm, of a need to help, to make a difference, to heal the girl he loved, if delivering a baby could be regarded in some way as healing.

He seemed to her to be functioning on autopilot, his conscious fears, if such there were, being overtaken by some kind of instinctive know-how that inspired in her a state of calm, despite the pain and the critical nature of her situation. He eased her forward on to the bed of soft grass in front of the wall, slipped off her boots, trousers and underwear and laid his own jacket on the ground. 'Turn over,' he murmured, almost as though he were in a trance. She did as he said without demur and found herself on all fours. There was no embarrassment between them, only a quiet matter-of-factness as he examined her almost as he would a Swaledale ewe about to give birth to a lamb. But this particular lamb was a human being, his own child, and he could tell that it was in the breech position.

How he accomplished the feat neither he nor Jess would ever know, but Adam Gabriel righted the position of his own child in her mother's belly just as he had righted the position of many a lamb. He delivered his daughter safely on to the dew-laden grass of the Yorkshire moors by the light of a full moon on the eve of the summer solstice, lifting her up and presenting her to her mother under the roof of stars, wrapped in the shirt from his own back. Her first cries joined those of the barn owl that heralded her birth and Adam Gabriel could hardly see her for the tears that were coursing down his cheeks.

45

NEW LIFE

See how the Fates their gifts allot.

W. S. Gilbert, *The Mikado*, 1885

It was a story for which Belle Barclay would have walked bare-foot over hot coals. But it was a story she never got to hear. Jess and the baby were brought down from the moors through the combined efforts of Adam and Bethany, ably assisted by Jack Knaggs, Nip, a mobile phone, which magically received a signal, an ancient little grey Fergie (in working order at last) and a flat-bed trailer generously carpeted with straw. It was not until mother and baby were tucked up in bed that Dr Emma Scarlett arrived to see that all was well.

'I'm afraid I don't understand,' she confessed, after examining Jess and the baby. 'First, why on earth were you out on the moor in your condition?'

Jess apologised for her bloody-mindedness and explained that she had taken her mobile phone with her but it had run out of charge, and as she was a month off her due date she'd thought she would still be fairly safe doing light duties.

'Well, we know all about your inner workings, don't we, and the fact that they're a law unto themselves? That much has been confirmed.' She turned to Adam. 'Tell me about the delivery. As you're a shepherd I know it won't have been your first, but it probably was your first *human* delivery. Was it straightforward?'

Adam looked uneasy. 'Not exactly.'

The quizzical look on Emma Scarlett's face encouraged him to continue. 'It was a breech birth.'

'So the baby came out feet first.'

'Er . . . no.'

'I'm sorry. If it was a breech birth . . .'

'I managed to get the baby into the correct position.'

The doctor looked at him suspiciously, then at Jess.

'The baby came out head first,' confirmed Jess. 'I was on all fours. I could see . . .'

Emma Scarlett found herself struggling for words. 'You mean, the baby was in the breech position but you managed to turn it?'

'Yes.'

'Well, I've heard some things in my time but . . . and yet . . . as the baby was only thirty-six weeks – four weeks short of term – it is possible, if someone knows what they're doing. If Jess had gone full term and the baby had engaged that would have been a different story. But even so I have to say I honestly cannot understand how somebody without proper medical training could bring about . . .' The doctor paused. Her face broke into a bemused smile. 'And yet, the proof is here – in your baby daughter.' Then she murmured under her breath, '"There are more things in Heaven and earth, Horatio, than are dreamt of in your philosophy." Even Dorothea Cruickshank had to acknowledge that.' Then, coming back into the moment, 'I take my hat off to you, Adam. I will never completely understand how you achieved what you did. There is no rational explanation for it but, then, I suppose I should have been open-minded enough to expect the unexpected where Adam Gabriel is concerned. Well done, is all I can say. Very well done.'

With her verdict given and her examination of mother and baby complete, she stood up and made to leave. 'The midwife will be up tomorrow to see that everything is in place, and you've at least done me the service of vindicating something that for the last couple of years I've always insisted upon.'

'What's that?' asked Bethany, who had been looking on with interest and no small amount of pride in her son, his partner and her first grandchild.

The doctor addressed Adam: 'You remember the degree of incredulity that you met when you came to talk to me and the other doctors?'

'How could I forget it?' muttered Adam.

'Well, I perhaps should have admitted at the time that, apart from spontaneous regression, there are certain other things in the medical world that defy what we would consider to be a logical or rational explanation. One of them is this. Every year at the summer solstice, and also at other times whenever there is a full moon, expectant mothers frequently give birth before their due date. Our local birth rates spike. I always ask my midwives to avoid taking time off when the calendar indicates either of those occurrences. Last night was, in common parlance, a double-whammy – the summer solstice *and* a full moon. So there you are. I think it's rather appropriate that your daughter was one of those born on that particular night, don't you?'

*

351

It might not have been a complete vindication, or the acknowledgement of what the medical world as a whole would have
called 'a gift for healing' but, as far as Dr Emma Scarlett was
concerned, Adam's ability quite clearly defied any rational
explanation, and that – for him – was acknowledgement enough.

Adam Gabriel knew that when push had come to shove (a
pertinent phrase, bearing in mind the circumstances), he had
managed to bring his own daughter into the world in spite of
events conspiring to make her delivery at the very least chal-
lenging and, in the given circumstances, extraordinarily perilous.
As she lay in her mother's arms, gurgling happily, there came
over him a feeling of completeness the like of which he had
never experienced before. He gazed into the pale blue eyes of
his new-born and, like many a father of daughters, his eyes
filled with tears of joy.

Her name? Well, there was really only one that fitted the bill:

Summer Gabriel. She's five now, a fair-haired, blue-eyed child
just like both of her parents, and she's a dab hand with Nip at
rounding up sheep.

As for Adam, his powers of healing have returned. It was, as
Dorothea Cruickshank pointed out, just a matter of oiling the
machinery (even though this piece of machinery was alien to
her). They are brought to bear when needed just as they always
were, without fanfare or ceremony, but those who know and
believe in them are grateful for their existence.

Bethany presides over her brood like a mother hen, proud of
their achievements and forever wishing that Luke could see his
son and grandchild, believing in her heart that somehow, somewhere, he is watching over them and the family farm he loved
so dearly.

Jack has retired but comes to see them every week. He has

given Summer his crook. It is too large for her at the moment, but it leans by the front door in readiness for the day when she has grown into it.

And Brother Wilfrid? Oh, he's out there somewhere, walking the moors and singing as lustily as ever, though his stride is shorter now and his vocal pitch a little less reliable. His visits are more sporadic, and when he does arrive the extra bedroom they have built on to the farmhouse is rather more conducive to the comfort of old bones than a barn full of hay.

The Gabriels know they cannot predict when or if he will turn up at all, but they have become accustomed to the fact that life is full of surprises and, as he himself would say, there are things in this world that many of us do not understand. What is important is that we do not make the mistake of thinking that, just because they are beyond our comprehension, they do not exist.

On that point he is quite adamant.

ACKNOWLEDGEMENTS

Writing about my home turf – the Yorkshire Moors – and the people who live there has been a delight, but I owe a huge debt of gratitude to all those who have guided and advised me along the way about everything from sheep farming to medicine in its various branches. Thank you to Rowena Webb, Olivia Barber and Hazel Orme, my editors, for their assiduity and keen eyes; to Amanda Owen 'The Yorkshire Shepherdess' for her willingness to answer questions about livestock even while out on the moors in a howling gale; to Mary Flower for sharing a lifetime of experience as a midwife; to Luigi Bonomi my encouraging and inspiring literary agent, and to my wife Alison for her patience, especially on those days when my self-criticism is particularly acute. This book is dedicated to my much loved daughters, Polly and Camilla. It is a dedication which should really be shared with all those people like Brother Wilfrid who believe that faith and generosity of spirit can sometimes achieve remarkable things, even if we do not quite understand how or why.